A Thriller

PROTECTIVE INSTINCT

JOY YORK

This is a work of fiction. Names, characters, places, and incidents are products of the author's imagination or are used fictitiously and are not to be construed as real. Any resemblance to actual events, locations, organizations, or persons, living or dead, is entirely coincidental.

World Castle Publishing, LLC
Pensacola, Florida
Copyright © 2024 Joy York
Hardback ISBN: 9798891261174
Paperback ISBN: 9798891261181
eBook ISBN: 9798891261198
First Edition World Castle Publishing, LLC, January 16, 2024
http://www.worldcastlepublishing.com

Cover: Cover Designs by Karen
https://www.cover-designs-by-karen.com
Editor: Karen Fuller

For my husband Terry for all the love, support, and encouragement he has given me in my writing journey. He is my rock.

CHAPTER ONE

"The calls are escalating. That's the fifth one today. A record so far. We have told them for the past two weeks that you are unavailable, but it doesn't seem to dissuade them one bit. His people aren't buying it. Look, Bash, you need to start taking this seriously. I'm worried about your safety. A man with that kind of reputation has plenty of resources to learn everything he needs to know about you. He could have someone tailing you right now," Gray said, as he crossed the room and loomed over Bash's desk with his tree trunk-sized arms across his muscular chest. It was not the first time Gray had tried to use his post-college linebacker body to intimidate him. It never worked, and they both knew it.

"What exactly do you suggest I do? Write the book and end up a food source for the lamprey in Lake Michigan?" Bash said, slamming his laptop closed in defiance.

A couple of weeks ago, Bash received a letter from Maximilian Fontana, a notorious billionaire from New York City. Fontana Property and Development Corporation was a conglomerate of international companies reputed to be deep-rooted in white-collar organized crime. Although their illegal activities were hidden in legitimate businesses and political influence, it did not make Bash feel any better. How he showed up on Fontana's radar was a mystery, but he was hellbent on Bash writing his memoirs. Aside from the obvious fear factor, he was a crime fiction writer, not a biographer.

Sebastian Bartoli, nicknamed "Bash" to his close friends, had written eleven books, all of which had reached number one on the bestseller lists. He wasn't an eloquent writer, only a good storyteller, and somehow, it worked for him. When his first book took off, he figured it was a fluke. After the success of his second book, he realized there was something about his straight-forward, down-and-dirty style that appealed to many readers.

"Drop the sarcasm, Bash. You know there is no way I want you anywhere near that man, but we think we have a solution to put a stop to it," Gray offered.

"Let's hear it," Bash said, rolling his chair back from his desk and putting his hands behind his head. *This should be good.*

"Hide," Gray said with a straight face.

Bash burst out laughing. "You're joking."

"I'm not."

"That's your plan? Jesus, Gray. How do you think I can hide from one of the most well-connected men in the country in today's technology environment?"

Grayson Lewis was Bash's best friend, agent, and overall handler. One of the few people he trusted with his life. They had both grown up in a small rural town in southern Illinois, population 3210. On their first day of kindergarten, Gray offered to swap his uncooked hot dog and cold baked beans for Bash's fried Spam sandwich. It struck Bash as a good deal. Gray was a naturally good-natured kid, while Bash had a quick wit and snarky attitude. With both being the "only child" of single mothers with no other family in their lives, the boys developed a close bond and became inseparable. Eventually, their mothers became best friends, too, and the four of them became adoptive relatives of sorts.

"Hear me out before you trash my idea." Gray pulled a chair in front of his desk close enough to rest his elbows on the top. "Bryan will ask someone in his office to lease a car and a vacation rental for a couple of months and put it in their name. We'll give them the parameters of what you're looking for (lake, mountains, beach, whatever) but no specific location. They'll pick that out themselves. The car will be at a predetermined location with the lease contracts and keys in the glove compartment.

"You will have several burner phones, and only Alex and I will have the numbers. Credit cards can be traced, so we will load bank gift cards with as much money as you think you'll need. Thankfully, you aren't dating anyone of consequence, so we won't have to fabricate anything elaborate to explain your absence. The message will be simple: You're taking a writing sabbatical. No one will know exactly where you are, which will make you safer if anyone tries to strong-arm one of us into divulging your location."

Bash scrutinized Gray's face long enough to determine that he was serious about the insane plan Alex, Bryan, and Gray had come up with.

Bryan Stillman, Bash's editor for the past ten years, had always been reliable, and he made too much money from Bash's books to want anything bad to happen to him. Alex Herrera was Bash's attorney. Gray, Alex, and Bash had been fraternity brothers at the University of Illinois. Although their fields of study were different, they remained tight throughout college. When they graduated, Gray and Bash followed Alex to Chicago, where he was attending Loyola University School of Law. As soon as Bash's first book became a hit, Gray left his marketing job to become his agent. Bash was on his second bestseller when Alex passed the bar and became his attorney. The three friends worked together to build the Sebastian Bartoli Brand, and they all received success and financial rewards from their collaborations.

The plan they devised for him to avoid Maximilian Fontana seemed extreme. Bash had never written about organized crime, so his knowledge of the methods they used to coerce people into doing their bidding was limited to things he had seen in the movies: broken kneecaps, plucked teeth, cement shoes, and the like. He was sure there were also plenty of career-ending things they could threaten that he couldn't begin to comprehend.

"Why a couple of months? Is that the prescribed time you think it will take for a mob boss to lose interest?" Bash's voice was laced with sarcasm.

Gray let out a heavy sigh. "You can't help yourself,

can you? Fontana is not a traditional mobster. He is a highly connected businessman. If you become his enemy, I doubt you would ever see it coming. This little getaway is precautionary. It might not even take a couple of months. After you leave town, I'll send Fontana a list of the top biographers in the country. He's going to realize that trying to find you isn't worth the effort."

"How am I going to get any work done without my assistant? Can I take her with me?" He knew it was a ridiculous suggestion as soon as it left his mouth.

"What part of 'nobody knowing your location' did you miss? She can set up a dummy email for you to send her your drafts, research requests, or whatever you need. It won't even be necessary for her to be in the office more than a couple days a week. Working from home is her favorite thing. You know, if anyone calls looking for you, she's a vault."

It was a lot to take in, but he needed to give it some thought. "It might work."

"Any ideas about where you would like to go? It's the beginning of autumn, so maybe you could be a leaf peeper," Gray joked.

The suggestion was not worth a response. "Find me a house on a nice calm lake. Preferably somewhere south where it's warm. An isolated cove would be good. See if they can arrange to have it fully stocked with groceries before I arrive. And a boat with a cuddy cabin in case I want to spend a few days on the water."

Gray pushed his chair back and stood up. "All doable."

"And what are you going to do while I'm gone?"

"As hard as it is for you to admit, you are not my only client. My most demanding? Yes. Most irritating? Certainly. But not the only one." Gray shook his head.

"But the one who makes you the most money."

"Maybe not for long...those hot contemporary romances are racking in the cash," he sing-songed.

Just like Gray to put me in my place.

"Now grab your laptop and anything else you'll need for

the next two months."

Bash was stunned. "Why? We've got plenty of time to decide."

Gray ignored him, grabbed Bash's soft-sided leather satchel off the sofa, and set it on the desk in front of him. "Quite the contrary. We are out of time. Fontana sent me an email a couple of hours ago notifying me that he will be flying here to meet with you at 9 a.m. tomorrow morning. Didn't seem to care what prior engagements you might have. You and I have a meeting with Bryan and Alex in thirty minutes at an undisclosed location to get this all moving."

"Holy shit," Bash breathed, throwing anything he might need into his briefcase. As they walked out the door, he turned to Gray and asked, "Why do you think he has singled me out?"

Gray shook his head. "I honestly have no idea. Maybe he likes your books. Could be an ego thing to have a bestselling author write his life's story. Or he has a hidden agenda. That's why we are taking it seriously, Bash. It doesn't make sense."

Bash felt a chill run up his spine. "Why didn't you just tell me about Fontana's plan to show up here tomorrow when you first walked in?"

"Yeah." Gray snickered. "Like that would have worked."

CHAPTER TWO

Morgan Skylar breathed a sigh of relief when she read the sign announcing her arrival in Guntersville, Alabama. Although she had visited multiple times during summer vacations with her best friend, Beth Worthington, and her family, who owned the property, this was the first time she had driven by herself. The pouring rain made it difficult to find familiar landmarks, and the fact that her GPS did not recognize the roads only compounded her frustration. Her attempts to reach Beth for the past three hours had gone to voicemail. With non-stop thunderstorms, she was also running late. Beth, whose drive from Nashville was much shorter, should already be safely tucked in the cabin with plenty of food and wine for their week-long vacation. It took two stops to find someone who could give her directions to the Worthington's lake house.

The magazine cover-worthy home sat in a secluded cove on a hill overlooking the shimmering water. Being included in the Worthington's vacations over the years had been some of the best times of her sheltered life. As she pulled up to the main driveway, her cell phone rang. Beth's face popped up on her screen. Morgan knew it would take all her concentration to maneuver down the steep driveway in the torrential rain, so she pulled over to the side of the road and stopped.

"Hi! I've been trying to get you for hours. I was about to pull in the driveway." She was met with silence. "Beth? Are you there? Did I lose you?" More silence. "Doggone, I lost her," she muttered to herself and was about to end the call when she heard a heavy sigh.

"I'm here," Beth said, sounding hesitant.

"What's wrong? Are you okay? Did you have an accident? Do you need me to come get you?" As a kindergarten teacher, she could not help when her worst-case scenario instincts kicked in, mostly because with small children, it often was.

"I'm fine, Chip. No accidents. No skinned knees, runny noses, or lost erasers." Chip was her nickname, and Beth was always playfully poking fun at her job.

"Whew. You had me worried. That's great! We're going to have the best week ever! I'm so excited!" Not even a little rain was going to dampen her spirits.

"I don't know how to tell you this, so I'm just going to say it. Chin and I got married! We were so sick of our parents trying to hijack our wedding plans that we decided to mutiny. The only people who really matter in the wedding drama are Chin and me. When he suggested we hop a plane to Las Vegas, we jumped in the car with no luggage and caught the first flight!" She finally took a breath.

"That's wonderful! I'm thrilled!" Morgan said with exaggerated enthusiasm, trying not to reveal her disappointment over their lost time together. Beth had been her best friend since her freshman year of high school. They were both in their second year at Emory when Beth met Chin and fell in love. There was no way she was going to allow herself to feel let down. There was so much to celebrate. "Have you told your parents?"

"Not yet. You're the first person we've called.

"Hi Chip," came a male voice.

"Congratulations, Chin. I love y'all, and I'm so happy."

"Thanks. Don't be mad at Beth. She feels terrible. I made her do it," he laughed.

"Go order us some more champagne, and let me talk to my BFF," Beth scolded him good-naturedly.

"I really am sorry I didn't call you last night. We got so caught up in the craziness of the whole thing I totally forgot about our week together. Now you're stuck there by yourself, and I feel awful. Especially after you lost Pops. He was everything to you. Your only relative, and now I've abandoned you." She began to cry.

Morgan felt tears seeping from the corner of her eyes and shook her head to force them always. "Please don't be upset, Beth. Even if you had called me last night, I would have come anyway," she lied. "It's so beautiful up here, and it'll give me plenty of time to destress for the week in your family's beautiful home."

"Well...there is another thing," she choked out. Morgan held her breath, unable to think of what could be worse than spending a week alone. "Dad forgot we were staying in the lake house this week. Or at least that's what he told me yesterday. He doesn't usually start the winter rentals until next month, but somebody paid him an ungodly amount of money to stay there for the next two months, so he couldn't say no. I figured we would stay in the old caretaker's cottage my brothers use. It's much closer to the water. Even has its own pier. I know it's not as fancy, but it does have a kitchen, two bedrooms, and a decent bathroom. Dad says it's still in good shape. What do you think? If you want to turn around and go home, I'll pay for you to stay in a motel tonight and for the gas you wasted. I feel horrible that I've done this to you."

Morgan was familiar with the cottage. It was built by the previous owners so their caretakers could live on the property. The Worthington's never saw the need, and over the years, it became a party shack for Beth's brothers. She remembered sneaking over at night to a few of those parties.

Morgan inwardly sighed but reached for her perky, glass half-full voice. "I remember it. It's precious. Yellow with white shutters. It'll be great, and I don't need much room." She hoped her voice was full of the sunshine she did not feel.

"When I looked on the weather radar before I called, I saw you are under a severe thunderstorm warning for the next five hours with an expected three inches of rain. The driveway to the cottage isn't paved. It can be a mess when it gets soaked, and I was supposed to bring the groceries. Do you think you can find the grocery store? If it rains for too long, you might not be able to get your car back up the hill from the cabin," her voice broke.

The more Beth thought about missing their vacation trip, the guiltier she felt, and Morgan wasn't going to let her ruin the happiest day of her life fretting.

"I know exactly where the grocery store is. I had to stop for directions, so I picked up a few things. No worries. I've got enough to last me until the roads dry out."

The only edible things she had in her car were a large bag of BBQ potato chips, two bottles of chardonnay, and a package of Skittles that she confiscated from 5-year-old Benny Stewart. Her intention had been to return them to his mother, but she was now kind of glad she had forgotten. No nutrition but a few calories. It would have to do because the road was too narrow for her to turn around and head back to the store.

By the time they hung up, she had fully reassured Beth that a crisp mid-October week at the lake with access to one of the boats was going to be blissful.

The cottage was the very next driveway from the main house. It was not as steep as the driveway to the main house, but unfortunately, it was covered with loose gravel. Her nails dug into the leather steering wheel as her compact car literally slid down the rain-saturated driveway until the front tires stopped on a log with a jolt, keeping her from rolling into the lake. *See, there is a silver lining. Yeah, log.*

By the time she dragged her luggage through every mudpuddle between the car and the front door, she was soaked to her underwear. The key was thankfully under the stone turtle by the welcome mat, as Beth had instructed. As she inserted the key in the lock, she had an eerie feeling she was being watched. She turned her gaze up the hill toward the main house and could barely make out the form of a man. He was standing on the main deck, his face obscured by dark-colored rainwear. Wiping the rain from her eyes, she took another look to make sure it had not been her imagination. He was leaning over the handrail of the deck, watching her. Not wanting to appear rude, she waved. He pulled his hood back to get a better look. Their eyes locked for an instant before he turned and walked into the house without acknowledgement. *Maybe he couldn't see me*, she reasoned, not wanting to believe she had been ignored.

Pushing the door open, the stale smell of beer, marijuana, and sweaty gym shoes crinkled her nose. The rain was still too heavy to open the windows, so she was forced to wait to air the place out. She found the light switch on the wall inside the door, but when she flipped it, nothing happened. Not to be discouraged, she tried the switch in the kitchen. Nothing. Inwardly sighing, she peeked in the cabinets to see if the guys had left anything worth eating. The only things she found were a 48 oz. jar of muscle-building powder and a half-used bag of toasted wheat germ. *Yummy.*

"Water it is," she said, grabbing a glass from the cabinet. She turned on the cold-water faucet, but nothing came out. Forcing down a groan, she walked back to her dirty, rain-soaked luggage, zipped it open, fished out a warm bottle of wine, screwed off the top, and took a long gulp.

Despite the faint vomit smell emanating from the couch, she plopped down and put her feet on the cigarette-burned coffee table. All her attempts to get the utilities turned on had failed. She thought about the man on the deck, who she preferred to believe had not intentionally snubbed her. It wasn't in her nature to think the worst of people. She hoped he would be the kind of neighborly guy who would help her get the water and electricity in working order.

A half bottle of wine, coupled with the stress of her long drive, was making her drowsy, so she decided to take a short nap. Hopefully, when she woke up, the rain would be gone. Then she would swallow her pride and ask the man renting the lake house for assistance.

CHAPTER THREE

Despite Sebastian's objections, Gray, Bryan, and Alex had insisted he leave town as soon as their clandestine meeting was over. Apparently, the three of them had cooked up the emergency escape plan within days of the first call Gray received from Maximillian Fontana's assistant. He felt he had no choice because their escalating concerns were contagious.

Alex handed him four burner phones, all purchased at different locations, and Bryan gave him $5000 in cash and $20,000 applied to various bank gift cards. Gray confiscated his cell phone, then handed it off to a woman who took out the battery and sealed it in a metal box probably lined with kryptonite. After they laid out the strict rules for his communication and movements, Bash was driven by a detective friend of Alex's to a parking lot in Naperville, IL. The detective handed him the keys to a blue sedan with instructions not to speed. It was no surprise when he recognized his overnight bag in the backseat. The detective assured him the rest of his luggage was in the trunk. He was to drive to Indianapolis, stay overnight in a pre-arranged Airbnb, then pick up a black Highlander the following evening at 7 p.m. in the parking lot of a local movie theater. Inside the glove compartment would be the contract, keys, and location of his temporary hideout. By that point, Bash was beginning to feel as though he was going into witness protection.

The drive from Indianapolis to Guntersville, Alabama, took most of the night. With all the cloak and dagger stuff, he almost jumped out of his skin every time a car got too close.

Once he reached Guntersville, he had to pull over to read a hand-drawn map with instructions to the cabin. When he turned onto the driveway at the designated address, the car tilted downward at an almost 90-degree angle, giving him the illusion that he was barreling into the depths of the lake sparkling in the headlights. Luckily, the lighting along the steep driveway led him around a curve and to the three-car garage of the two-story house. He quickly entered the code provided and pulled the car inside. Once in the house, he threw his luggage on the floor and stumbled into the first bedroom he found and face-planted on the bed, fully clothed.

Bash woke up later in the afternoon, totally disoriented. Once he remembered where he was, he glanced down at his wrinkled, sweaty clothes and moaned. After taking a long leisurely shower, he grabbed a ham sandwich from the fully stocked kitchen. He moved his luggage into the master bedroom and explored the house. In the light of day, he found it was a beautiful, rustic house made of dark wood. It had a glass front with floor-to-ceiling windows that provided a magnificent view of the lake, with each floor having its own spacious deck. The rental contract guaranteed that all sides of the private cove were part of the homeowner's property, and it was posted with no-trespassing signs to prevent unwanted visitors.

Bash was just about to go down the long stone stairway to the water to check out the dock and boathouse when the sky opened its wrath. The main deck was covered by the deck above, so he found a comfy padded lounger and read through the brochures and maps to familiarize himself with the area.

He didn't realize he had nodded off until he was startled awake by the whine of a car engine. The house was too far from the road to hear the infrequent passing cars, so it had to be close. As the sound got louder, it seemed to be coming from the left side of the house, which made no sense because the driveway was on the right side. Dreading the idea of confronting an intruder in the pouring rain, he went back into the house to find an umbrella.

Pulling the black rain slicker he found in the entry closet

over his head, he walked to the edge of the deck and leaned over the rail. Annoyance gripped him as he watched a small car skidding and sliding its way down a narrow drive on the left side of the house. *So much for privacy*, he thought. His pulse quickened as it appeared the car wasn't going to be able to stop its current trajectory toward the lake. He was going to be doubly aggravated if he had to go for a swim to rescue the trespasser. Before he had time to react, the car came to an abrupt stop. *Thank God for small favors.*

A few minutes later, someone got out of the car carrying a plastic bag. The driver, who he assumed by the smaller statue was a woman, was drenched within seconds with her shoulder-length hair plastered to her face and neck. She wore a dress that clung to her slim frame like lycra. Watching her splash through puddles, lose a shoe in the mud, and hang on to the car as she maneuvered around to pull a huge piece of luggage from the trunk was worthy of a slap-stick comedy skit. If he had not been so upset about being lied to about the privacy and the cottage, he would've enjoyed the show. Now, his only concern was how to get rid of her.

The woman barely made it to the door without landing on her ass. Then it occurred to him that she might be his housekeeper or perhaps a cook, which would be a good thing. As if she sensed him watching her, she stopped outside the door and glanced up at the house until she spotted him. She waved a hand in greeting, appearing polite despite her uncomfortable circumstances. Being the arrogant asshole he was, he turned and walked away.

He immediately texted Gray to find out who the hell the woman was and why she showed up unannounced on his rental property.

Bash: *A woman just pulled into a small cabin next door. Do I need to explain to someone what privacy means?*

Gray: *What the fuck are you talking about? Are you messing with me? Stay inside until I can make some calls.*

Obviously, no cook or cleaning fairy as he had hoped. He decided to explore the kitchen to see what he could cook for dinner.

An hour later, he received a text from Gray.

Gray: *The owner's daughter made plans to use the lake house with a friend, not realizing he had already rented it. The owner didn't think it would be a problem if they stayed in the old caretaker's cottage. It has a separate driveway and dock. The daughter ended up eloping to Las Vegas with her fiancé without telling him or her friend, so the woman is alone for the week.*

Bash: *Shit. Now, what am I going to do? Is she a college kid?*

Gray: *Her name is Morgan Skylar. She's 25, not an irresponsible kid. A kindergarten teacher. How much trouble can she be? Do what you do best. Growl and send her packing, but she sounds harmless. Before you go all apeshit on her, you should know she just lost her only relative. Your call. To be a dick or not to be a dick, that is the question.*

He didn't respond. "Fucking great," he muttered.

The chicken picante, fettuccini with olio, and Caesar salad were on the table. He was about to open a bottle of Sauvignon Blanc when he heard a knock at the door. Either his friends had done a shit job of hiding him, or it was the woman he had seen earlier. Taking a swig from the bottle of wine and gritting his teeth, he walked to the door. A look through the peephole confirmed it was his neighbor, a little drier than she had been earlier. He opened the door, forcing himself to keep his aggravation in check.

"Hi! I'm Morgan!" she said, with a bright smile and cheery southern drawl. She stuck out her delicate hand to shake. Suppressing a groan at the intrusion, he reluctantly took it and was surprised by her firm grip. Her demeanor was expectant. "Sorry to disturb you, but I just moved into the cottage next door and ran into a few little quirks. Do you mind if I impose upon you to give me a little assistance? I'm kind of in a jam."

He stared at her for a few moments, debating a response as she patiently waited, her cornflower-blue eyes opened wide. She was a slim young woman, around 5' 7". Ginger-red hair hung in loose natural waves from her bangs, brushing her eyebrows to her shoulders. Her facial features were delicate, with a small, slightly turned-up nose. Light freckles covered her face. An adorably cute "girl next door" type. Thankfully, Gray had mentioned she was 25, or Bash would never have let her in the house, assuming she was closer to sixteen.

"What kind of little quirks," he asked cautiously.

She held up her hands and began to count the "quirks" off on her fingers. "The electricity is turned off. I think I found the electrical box in a closet, but I'm afraid to touch it because the roof leaked and left a huge puddle on the floor. I've got candles but no lighter. The water is shut off, and I haven't been able to locate the on/off valves. I know there is a huge lake out there, and it may be okay for a bath, but soap wouldn't be environmentally friendly to the fish, and it's not drinkable. Oh, and my best friend Beth was supposed to bring the groceries, but she got married instead." She stopped and rolled her eyes in mock exaggeration. "That's a long story. Anyway, my car is kind of stuck in the mud, so I won't be going anywhere until the driveway dries or I get a tow up the hill. My on-hand food sources consist of a bag of BBQ potato chips and a few Skittles. That should last me for a day or so. And if you have any rice I could borrow, that would be great."

The whole damn cottage sounds like a disaster. "How can you cook rice without electricity?" he said, stating the obvious.

"It's not to eat. I need to dry out my cell phone. Must have gotten wet when I was moving into the cabin," she said, twisting her naturally pouty lips. Considering the unfortunate calamities, he felt the asshole persona he was all geared up for beginning to dissipate. He must have taken too long to respond because he caught her smile falter for an instant, then reappear even wider.

"Well, I can see this is not a good time. I hope you enjoy your stay," she said quickly, then turned to leave.

"Wait!" he barked. She froze at his harsh command. He caught her sharp intake of breath and remembered Gray telling him that she had just lost her only relative. Sending her away felt like pulling the wings off a fairy. When she turned back to face him, her sweet smile waned. *Christ. If I say the wrong thing, I might break her.*

"It's okay, really. Not your problem. I'll work it out," she said.

Shit, I hate that I'm going to say this. "I was just sitting down to dinner, and there's plenty of food. I'm not a bad cook if you compare it to a bag of chips."

A wry grin spread across her lips. "I don't know. Potato chips are on the top of my food list. That's a challenge you might lose," she said wistfully.

He shook his head. "I'll risk it. Why don't you join me, and then we'll go over and see if we can get your utilities turned on."

"Are you sure?" she asked wearily.

He half-forced and half-meant the reassuring smile he gave her.

CHAPTER FOUR

Bash added another place setting across from his in the window-framed breakfast nook and filled their plates. She nodded to the glass of wine he offered. He suddenly remembered he had just taken a swig out of the bottle and shrugged. *What the hell.*

The rain finally stopped, and dusk had turned into a moonless night, filtering out all traces of light except for the path lamps lining the stairs leading down the hill to the lake. As Morgan got settled, he struggled to come up with a conversation that would help alleviate the awkwardness. She beat him to it before he took his first bite.

"Well, here we are. Two complete strangers sharing a meal together. Pops was wrong. There *are* still good people in the world," she said, flashing a disarming smile.

It made him feel like a fraud knowing he had begrudgingly asked her to stay.

"Is Pops your father?" he asked. Although he already knew from his conversation with Gray that it referred to her grandfather, he didn't want to give away his prior knowledge.

She politely finished chewing her bite before her face lit up. "My grandfather. He raised me. Most people would call him a suspicious, old grump, but I knew he would do anything for me. Or at least try."

Her forthrightness caught him off guard. "What do you mean?" he asked, not sure he was interested, but conversation was better than silence. She was chatty, so he decided to let her do most of the work.

"When I was in grammar school, the girls at school were always making fun of me. I didn't have any women in my life, so I never understood all the girl stuff they liked to talk about. One day, I came home crying to Pops about how dumb those girls made me feel because I didn't know how to fix my hair. The next day after school, I found two books from the library on hair styles. Then, every week after, there were more books on fashions, cooking, etiquette, and girls' bodies. Whenever I had questions he couldn't answer, I'd get a book. Pops told me to never let anyone know they hurt me, or they would use it against me. That was one of his first Popsisms.

"He was afraid of being a bad parent. He said he got into lots of trouble when he was young. His mom and dad weren't good people. The library ended up being his answer to good parenting. Smoking, drinking, drugs, sex, gambling … you name it, and I read about the dangers and how excess could ruin my life. Every time he found something in the newspapers or on television that he hadn't warned me about, a book would appear. He started paying me $2 for the medium-sized books and $5 for the thick ones. Didn't take me long to figure out I had a moneymaker on my hands. It helped that I loved to read." Her laughter made him smile despite himself.

"Where did you grow up?" he asked, genuinely curious.

"In a rural town not far from Gainesville, Georgia. It was too small for a school district, so Pops drove me 25 miles to and from school every day. What about you? Where did you grow up?" she asked, backing up in her chair. Her hands suddenly flew to her mouth. "Oh, my goodness. I just realized I don't even know your name!"

He had to chuckle. It had occurred to him she might know who he was and was playing dumb, but this young woman was so guileless it didn't seem to fit. He hated deceiving people, so he didn't.

"Bash Bartoli. I grew up in a little town in southern Illinois." He felt a morsel of guilt for not giving her his full name.

"Big family?" she asked, before she expertly wrapped her

fettuccine around her fork with her spoon and took a bite, the etiquette books appearing to have paid off.

"Not really. Just me and my mom," he said without elaborating.

A cloud passed over Morgan's face as she laid her fork down and swallowed hard, then met his eyes. Bash could almost feel the pain on her face. "Pops was my only family, too, but we did okay. He passed a couple of weeks ago. He was everything to me. I do have Beth, my best friend. Her family owns this house. This trip was her attempt to cheer me up. I've come here with her family for the past ten years. They are nice folks who have always accepted me as one of them. Didn't matter that I was from a hick town in North Georgia." She took a long drink of water, seeming to calm her emotions. When she glanced back at him, that unpretentious sparkle was back in her eyes. "I can't tell you how much I appreciate you inviting me for dinner tonight. Even if nothing gets fixed in the cottage and I turn around and go home tomorrow, I will remember your kindness and this lovely dinner."

"You're welcome," he said, clearing his throat and feeling guilty it hadn't been his intent. "Do you work in Gainesville?"

"Dunwoody, Georgia. Just north of Atlanta. I teach preschool and kindergarten. After I graduated from Emory and got my teaching certificate, I stayed in the area. What about you?"

"Chicago. I'm a writer." He closely watched her face to see if there were any flickers of recognition but saw none. *Maybe she's not a crime fan.*

"That's so exciting. Obviously, you're not a starving one, or you wouldn't be staying here," she laughed, waving her hand at the surroundings. "But doing what you love is its own reward. I'm sure somebody famous said that, but it's so true. I don't make a lot of money, but teaching kids is my passion. Especially the little ones. They are so brutally honest and appreciative of what you do for them ... well, most of the time. Little kids are like vacuum cleaners ... they suck up everything whether you want them to or not. Many parents would die of embarrassment if they had any idea what their five-year-olds have shared with the class."

"I bet," he said, unable to help being charmed by her zealousness for teaching.

When they finished dinner, she insisted on helping him load the dishwasher and clean up. Bash found himself enjoying her completely unfiltered manner. Her stories about her four and five-year-olds as a kindergarten and preschool teacher kept him entertained over brandy, two for him, one for her. When she subtly reminded him that she needed to get back to the cottage to find the water valves, he realized it was almost 10 p.m. He had been so relaxed in their easy rapport he hadn't noticed the time.

Armed with two flashlights and a small toolbox he found in the garage, they made their way to the caretaker's cottage.

CHAPTER FIVE

The walk back to the cottage was dark and uncomfortably silent. Morgan's flashlight stayed trained on the ground, making sure she didn't accidentally step on a snake. When they reached the cottage, she stopped to pull the key out of her pocket. Bash tripped over the doormat and stumbled into the already-opened door. If he hadn't caught the doorframe, he would have tumbled to his knees.

"Fuck," he yelled, straightening back up.

"Are you okay?"

"Just peachy," he mocked testily. "I know this place is secluded, but it's not safe for you to leave the door open. You have no idea who might be wandering through these woods, private property or not, and a bear could have easily gotten inside."

She knew she hadn't left the door open and figured the latch might be broken. When she turned to apologize, the beam of her flashlight hit him square in the eyes, which didn't help his mood. He swiped it away with his hand.

"Jesus!" he snapped.

His change of attitude stung, but she held a smile on her face even though he couldn't see it in the dark. When she showed up at his door earlier, she could tell he wasn't happy about her intrusion. She hated to impose on people, but desperation had driven her there. If she hadn't felt the squish of water in her shoes right before she grabbed the main switch of the electrical panel, she would be dead. Sheer panic sent her scurrying to the main house for help. Of course, she didn't tell him that, wanting to win him over by being herself. It seemed to have worked until now. Apparently, it didn't take much to set him off. There was no point defending herself.

"I'm sorry," she said contritely.

They cleaned their shoes of mud and pine straw on the outdoor mat before entering.

"Where's the electrical box?" he asked, not acknowledging her apology.

The cottage opened into one large room that contained a small sitting area, a kitchen, and a dining room table for two. The room connected to a short hall with a bedroom on each side, one smaller to accommodate the tiny bathroom at the end of the hall.

"In the closet of the bedroom on the left. Be careful. There is water on the floor," she reminded him.

Bash slowly flashed his beam on the furnishings in the room. "The poor caretaker got the short end of the stick with this dump, didn't he?" he commented dryly.

She couldn't help feeling defensive for the Worthingtons. "The cottage was here when the Worthingtons bought the property. Beth's teenage brothers use it to party with their friends." Again, no response. He disappeared into the bedroom.

"I saw a rubber mat in front of the kitchen sink. If you'll grab that and something to clean up the water, I'll see if I can get the lights on for you," he hollered from the closet.

She met him at the closet door with the mat, a mop, and a bucket. The water had leaked from a pipe instead of the roof. Although it was only a drip, it had grown over time. After Bash dried the area and put down the mat, he checked the electrical box to make sure no water had penetrated the equipment. He used an insulated tool to flip the power on.

"Let there be light! Yea!" she whooped as the lights came on in the bedroom. He snickered at her excitement.

"I'll check for a water valve if you'll make sure all the lights came on."

Rushing to the main room, she basked in the glow of the lights for about two seconds before she noticed muddy tracks all over the scarred wood floors. They began at the front door and made trails in every direction, which made no sense because neither of them had opened the cabinet doors in the kitchen. She looked at the bottom of her shoes. No mud. *Where did the mud come from?*

"*Bam!*" A shriek escaped her throat when the front door slammed closed.

"Well, hockey sticks!" she mumbled. *Didn't Bash secure that door when we got here?*

"Everything okay out there," he called.

"Dandy!" she hollered back.

When the door banged again, she inspected the locking mechanism. The latch was broken, as she suspected, but the freshly splintered area around it was concerning. The door continued to bounce open and closed from the wind.

"Hey, Morgan!" Bash called. "Can you come here? I think I've got the water in the bathroom working."

"Coming," she called, but stopped short when she noticed two sets of footprints leading into the bedroom where she had put her luggage.

"Bash!" she screamed. Her clothes and toiletries were strewn all over the floor, luggage upside-down.

He came running down the hall and stopped, eyes following her gaze. "Well, shit. I don't suppose you had a hard time finding something to wear tonight?"

She stared at him. Horrified.

"Sorry. Bad joke. Is anything missing?"

Morgan walked over to her carry-on and found the zip compartment where she kept her cash. Then she searched under the bed but found nothing amiss. "The $500 I withdrew from the bank before I left home is still here, and my phone is on the nightstand. Neither were hard to miss."

"What about your laptop and handbag? I'm assuming you have those."

She pulled a mini leather credit card holder out of her pocket and held it up with her electronic car key. "I had my credit card, driver's license, insurance card, and keys with me. Pops taught me a long time ago to never leave any identification, luggage tags, or car keys in my room when I was out of town. My laptop is in the trunk of my car."

"Your grandfather was a cautious man."

"You don't know the half of it," she said, blowing out an exaggerated breath.

"Give me your keys. I'll be right back," he said, holding out his hand. Then he noticed the floors. "Guess it was too dark to see all these tracks when we came in."

He stopped to inspect the lock on the front door that was still bouncing from the wind. Slowly shaking his head, he stepped out into the night. A few minutes later, Morgan heard the car door close, and then the trunk slam shut. When Bash came back inside, he was carrying her blue flowered backpack that held her laptop. She sighed with relief.

"The passenger window is busted, but the glove compartment is still locked. So was the trunk. Maybe they heard us coming and fled."

"By the look of these tracks, there were two of them," she said. "What could they possibly want with me? If it was burglary, why didn't they take my money and cell phone?"

"I don't know. The television isn't too bad either," he said, motioning to the 54" flat screen.

He rubbed his chin for a couple of seconds and turned to look at her. "Did you have a fight with your boyfriend? An ugly break-up? An angry parent whose kid didn't get an A in finger painting?" he suggested flippantly.

Just when she thought her day had taken a turn for the better, it had all gone to poop, and she didn't need Mr. Moody insulting her or her profession. She would find a way to deal with it. She always did.

Glancing up at him, she plastered on her warmest smile. "You know what, Mr. Bartoli? You have done more than enough tonight. I can't impose upon you any further. I've got it from here. Thank you for getting my utilities on. And for that delicious meal. If you don't mind, tomorrow morning, I would like to use the landline phone in the house to call for a tow. This trip just wasn't meant to be." She wondered if he noticed the more formal usage of his name. It didn't matter. His irritation with her was clear.

Bash furrowed his brow as he scrutinized her. "You don't even have a lock on the door. It won't even fuckin' close," he said with annoyance.

"If you leave that little tool kit, I'll fix it right up. And I can always put a chair under the handle. Have a good evening," she tried to hint, but he didn't move.

"They already broke the door. It sure as hell wouldn't be hard to break in a window."

"This is my problem, Mr. Bartoli. You wanted a nice private vacation, and all I've done is disrupt it by inviting myself into your home-away-from-home. As soon as the morning rolls around, I'll be a distant memory."

She wished he would just go before her disappointment got the better of her, but it wasn't hard to read the indecision on his face. She was offering him a graceful way out. Then she recognized it. Observed it on her kindergartener's faces every day when they realized they had hurt someone's feelings. He was feeling guilty about walking away and washing his hands of the whole matter, even though that was exactly what he wanted to do. At least he had a conscience. That was good to know. Maybe he wasn't so bad after all.

His eyes flipped back and forth between Morgan and the busted door a few times before he walked back into her bedroom. She followed. He turned her luggage right-side up and set it on the bed.

"What are you doing?"

"Either you repack your bag, or I will. I'm not leaving you here unprotected after a break-in. If you want to leave in the morning after you get your car towed out of the mud, that's fine. There is plenty of room in the house, as I'm sure you are aware. Please get your shit in the bag, and let's get out of here. For all we know, whoever broke in is watching us right now. It's a good thing I locked and set the alarm on the house before we left."

"I didn't leave the door unlocked," she said with a touch of defensiveness.

"I know."

"And I don't have a boyfriend, nor did I just break up with one," she said, not sure why she felt the need to explain.

"Girlfriend?" he asked without judgement in his tone.

"No one. I haven't cared that much about dating since college. No helicopter moms with a grudge. Nothing going on in my life that would have provoked a break-in. No one is looking for me, I assure you." *No one left to care*, she thought, feeling a touch sorry for herself. Pops would be scolding her about now.

A shadow passed over Bash's face for a brief moment. Had he remembered something?

"I'll wait by the door," he said and walked out.

CHAPTER SIX

It was almost midnight, and Morgan was wide awake. For the past 45 minutes, she had been watching fragments of a spider web bouncing in the air blowing from the vent. The room she chose to sleep in was Beth's. They shared it on previous visits, and there was something comforting about the familiarity of it. Plus, it was on the second floor, giving her a clear view of the cottage through the trees. She had left the lights on in the cabin, hoping to dissuade another break-in. Also, whenever possible, she picked a room with an easy escape route. That was another important Popsism. After all, she was staying overnight with a perfect stranger, and heaven only knew who had rummaged around in her luggage.

When Mr. Worthington first bought the house, Beth selected her room because it had access to the roof to sunbathe, and the drop from the roof on the back of the house to the ground was only six feet due to the house being built on an incline. It was ideal for sneaking out at night to meet her brothers and their friends, sometimes taking the boat out to drink beer and cheap wine under the cover of darkness. Pops' rules were strict. No partying and no dating until she was eighteen. Her vacations to the lake house were the only time she got to be around boys. Beth promised that even if her parents caught them, they would never tell Pops. They didn't agree with his obsessive need to keep Morgan isolated.

When they got back to the house, Morgan and Bash said goodnight and went their separate ways. Now, not only did she have insomnia, but she was starving. Since Bash was probably asleep, she decided to tiptoe down to the kitchen to see what was in the refrigerator. What difference would it make if he found her eating his food? After tomorrow, he would never see her again anyway. *It's not like he could feel any worse about me.*

The refrigerator was loaded with lunch meats, containers of salads, cheeses, and dips. There was a healthy veggie tray that wasn't of interest to her. If she was going to eat a rich guy's food, she was going for the good stuff. And there it was ... a small 5 oz. tin of Beluga Sturgeon Caviar. Since she had never eaten fish eggs before, it seemed like an opportunity she couldn't pass up.

Morgan placed the tin on the breakfast table. Assuming fancy crackers were the appropriate complement to caviar, she began her search in the pantry. She spotted a package of rice crackers, or what she called rice paper because that's what they tasted like, but right next to them was her all-time favorite food — potato chips. Not a classy appetizer by most people's standards, but she had eaten chips with just about every other type of food, so why not caviar? She found chilled sparking water and loaded a plate with grapes, a few squirts of cheese whiz, hot okra peppers, and a handful of potato chips. Her eyes widened when she spotted the condiment no self-respecting southerner could live without...Louisiana Hot Sauce.

"Obviously, Mr. Moody didn't do the grocery shopping," she muttered to herself.

The caviar turned out to be too salty with the chips and not exactly to her uncultured taste. The best combination was the Cheese Whiz with hot sauce on chips, which was no surprise. She was just about to clean up when her phone chimed a few times, notifying her of incoming text messages. Before she had gone to bed, she left her cell in a plastic container of rice on the counter, hoping it would dry out.

"Who is Chip?" came a male voice behind her.

Startled, she jerked around to find Bash holding her cell phone in his hand. Jumping out of her chair, she tried to grab it from him, but he held it out of her reach, reading the partial messages displayed on the screen.

"Hey! That's personal!"

Bash turned the phone so she could see it, a suspicious frown on his face. "All these notifications, Messenger, Facebook, Text Messages, are for Chip? Not Morgan. Whose phone is this?"

She jumped up and yanked it out of his hand. "It's mine. I'm Chip. Or it's my nickname."

He furrows his brow. "Chip? How do you get Chip out of Morgan?"

She could tell he didn't believe her, but she went for it anyway. "Pops called me 'Chip' when I was a kid. The only way he could get me to eat my vegetables was to sprinkle them with potato chips. I was skinny and extremely picky. Potato chips were my favorite snack, so that's how he got me to eat things I hated. Only Pops and Beth call me that. Those messages are from her."

He walked up to the table, his eyes scanning over the jar of peppers, canned cheese, and a partial chip sticking out of the mostly empty caviar tin.

"If I didn't see it with my own eyes, I never would have believed it," he said, shaking his head.

She tried to read his expression. "Sorry, I ate your caviar. It was a new experience I couldn't resist. I'll replace it for you."

He nodded his head. "It's $175 an oz., and that's 5 ozs., so…you do the math," he said, crossing his arms, waiting for her reaction.

She took in a deep breath and choked on her saliva. When she stopped coughing, she cleared her throat. "Are you on Venmo?" It would put a crimp in her budget, but she had it in savings. Also, Pops' lawyer was supposed to be transferring money from his bank accounts to hers within a few days. She wasn't sure how much it would be, but surely it would cover the cost of some stinky fish eggs her inexperienced palette had not appreciated. *How do those guys seduce beautiful girls on their fancy yachts with fish breath?*

Bash burst out laughing and couldn't seem to stop.

"What's so funny?"

"You're going to transfer $875 from your bank account to mine?" he asked, wiping the tears from his eyes.

"It's not like I get any of your personal information," she said defensively and a bit insulted that he didn't think she was good for the money. "If you prefer, I'll get a cashier's check when I get to town."

He sat down in a chair across from her and gave her a broad smile. "I don't give a flying fuck about the caviar. Can't stand it. It's a running joke with my agent and administrative assistant. They love it and don't understand why I hate it. Whenever I go on vacation, they have it stocked in my refrigerator. If you hadn't eaten it, I would have left it. Combining it with chips is certainly a new twist."

"Well, let me tell you, it wasn't that hot," she said, squinching her face up.

Curiosity must have gotten the better of him because he picked up a broken chip from her plate and dipped it in the Bugula tin, popping it in his mouth. He forced it down with a sip from her sparkling water. "Mild improvement," he said, smacking his lips. "Even creative."

She snickered. "It's better with the hot sauce."

"I guess I didn't feed you enough."

"Couldn't sleep…"

They were interrupted by a loud knock on the front door.

His eyes flew to hers. "Did you use the landline phone to call anyone?" he asked nervously.

She slowly shook her head. "I'm assuming you aren't expecting anyone. Maybe we should turn off the lights," she suggested, waving to the clear glass windows on the front of the house that made them highly visible.

"They've probably already seen us, don't you think?"

"Not if they came from the driveway. There aren't any windows on the first floor on that side of the house."

He twisted his lips. "Would it worry me to know how you know that?"

"Naw. Sneaking out of the house stuff when we were

teenagers. Got to know where the blind spots are." She got up and flipped off the kitchen and hall lights, leaving them in darkness. The knocks came again. "I'm going to look through the peephole and see who it is."

"They could be watching through the windows," he whispered.

"I'll stay low." Morgan stepped into the great room, crouched, and duck-walked toward the door, staying behind chairs and the long sectional sofa for cover. When she reached the foyer, where she was no longer visible from the windows, she made her way to the peephole. Standing at the front door under the porch light were two hulky men in black suits. They looked like they could flip over a tire from a transfer truck with their pinky fingers and did it quite regularly.

"Who is it?" Bash whispered in her ear, nearly giving her a heart attack.

She swatted him in the chest. "Don't sneak up on me!" she shout-whispered. "You almost scared the poop out of me."

"Poop? Didn't anyone teach you how to cuss?" he grinned.

She rolled my eyes. "Story for another time. There are two goony guys out there that could crush us with their big toes." Bash wasn't a large guy. About 5'10", and even though he was well-toned for his size, he was no match for the dudes at the door.

His face fell, all humor evaporating.

She lifted an eyebrow and cocked her thumb to the door. "Those guys aren't here to sell you a lawn maintenance contract. They're more like the 'help you meet your maker' kind of guys."

He leaned into the door for a glance and turned back quickly. "Oh fuck!"

"Would you please stop using that word? For a writer, your descriptive use of the English language seems to be a bit limited. You have used that word as an adjective, adverb, and subject. Luckily, I haven't heard you use it as a verb yet."

"I'll take that into consideration. In the meantime, we've got to get out of here," he said, rubbing his hands through his hair.

"If one of us doesn't answer the door, they'll think no one is home, and it's okay to break in," she whispered. "We have to let them know people are home."

Three loud knocks again.

He walked in a circle, wringing his hands, then stopped, looking her straight in the eyes. "They can't see me. Or know I'm here."

That statement prompted a million questions, but there wasn't time. She threw up her arms, flailing her hands in frustration. "My Pops spent his whole paranoid life preparing me for this very scenario, and it never happened...until now. And it isn't even about me. Grrrrr!" She poked him in the chest. "Get in the closet." He looked at her like she had lost my mind. "Or you can open the door and let them in."

"I'm not a coward, and I'm certainly not leaving you to face them alone," he said sternly.

"I promise. I've got this. Please trust me."

His eyebrows knitted together. "Are you sure you know what you're doing?"

No, not really. "I guess we'll find out," she said, pushing him into the coat closet. She looked down at her short-sleeve jersey and sleep shorts, then pulled her hair up into a high ponytail using the elastic band around her wrist to tie it up. *Yeah, I can sell this.* Opening the door, she looked up at the two burly men towering over her and yawned.

CHAPTER SEVEN

"Are y'all back for another warrant?" she said, wiping her eyes with her fists, appearing so unaffected you would have thought she answered the door to strangers every night.

The men looked at each other in surprise, then back to her.

Before they could answer, she threw another question at them. "You want me to wake up the judge or not? This is the second time tonight, so if you didn't get it right the first time, Daddy's going to be mad as a hornet."

They still had not found their tongues. Too baffled.

She reached up and snapped her fingers in front of their faces a few times. "What's it going to be, boys? I want to get back to bed. Got a tennis date at the country club tomorrow morning bright and early."

The guy with a shaved head spoke. "We don't know anything about a warrant. We're here to see Sebastian Bartoli."

Sebastian Bartoli? Sebastian Bartoli? Holy cow poop! Nickname, Bash. Well, fiddle sticks. She wanted to swat herself in the head.

"You mean that famous writer?" she said excitedly, bouncing on the balls of her feet. "Does he have a lake house out here, too? Wait until I tell my friends. Which one is it? The A-frame on the next cove?"

The other guy with a blond buzzcut held up his hand. "No! He's supposed to be here," he grunted.

She took a controlled breath to keep her nerves in check. "I wish he was staying here, but he isn't. My daddy's a federal judge, and he gets all kinds of interruptions when we're on vacation.

That's what happens when you're the kind of judge who issues a warrant at the drop of a hat. The detectives love him. Now. Like I said, this is the second one tonight, but I'll go wake him up, and maybe he can help you." As she turned to leave, the blond guy put his hand on her shoulder, sending chills down her back, and then he quickly withdrew it.

"Wait! Maybe we've got the address wrong," he said, handing her a piece of paper.

It read *12 Redbud Drive, Guntersville, Alabama.* This address. *Think! Think! Think!* She could tell by the northeastern accents they weren't local, so she reasoned they probably didn't know anything about the area. She took a big chance.

"That's our address for sure, but Daddy has owned this cabin for years." She paused for effect and tapped her chin with her pointer finger. "Oh, I get it. I bet you are looking for Redbud North. This is Redbud South. You need to be on the other side of the lake. If you go back to the main highway, it's the first turn to the left on the other side of the bridge."

They look at her blankly for a few beats, then back at each other. The bald guy nodded to the blond guy, and they turned to leave. Before she could shut the door, one of them called back in a threatening tone. "If this is bullshit, we'll be back." She swallowed hard, closed the door, and leaned against it, waiting for them to drive away.

Bash came bursting out of the closet and stood in front of her. She couldn't tell by the expression on his face if it was gratitude or shame. For the moment, she didn't care. Getting her heart rate back in line was more important.

"Fuck. I guess I owe you a thank you," he said with sincerity.

She pushed away from the door and began walking away. "You owe me an explanation, Mr. Sebastian Bartoli, famous author and major grumpster, but right now, we need to get dressed, pack whatever stuff we need, and leave. Either those guys took the bait and left on the merry-go-round I sent them on, or they are still outside watching the house. Meet me at the top of the stairs in five minutes," she said, rushing for the stairs.

"Hold up," he called after her.

She turned to face him.

"Who the hell put you in charge, and why should I..." he stopped, trying to determine how to phrase what she knew would be an insult, so she said it for him.

"Why should you listen to a little redneck kindergarten teacher from the sticks who uses caviar as chip dip? I wasn't trying to give you orders, Mr. Bartoli. I was trying to help save your life. I thought I just proved that, but I guess whatever you would have done when you answered the door to those two no-necks would have netted a better outcome. I don't know what issue those men have with you, but by virtue of our brief association, I am now in their sights, too. We can part ways right now if you want. I'm sure you have plenty of agents and lawyers and assistants who are much smarter than me to get everything all fixed up for you. You might want to get them on the phone because I'm thinking you've got about 20 minutes max before they come back. I'd appreciate it if you would give me the keys to one of those boats down there because I want to live to see tomorrow. You can think my request over while I get dressed and pack, but Beth already told me I could use the smaller boat. You do what you feel is right for you. My survival instincts are apparently geared up a few more notches than yours." Then she ran up the stairs.

CHAPTER EIGHT

The burglary at the cabin should have been his first clue, but he was irritated and in too much denial to acknowledge it. He had blamed Morgan for everything that went wrong. For inconveniencing him. He was so wrapped up in begrudging an innocent woman from sharing a plot of land with him that he didn't even consider he was the one who brought the danger to her. And how could Gray and Alex allow this to happen? They had promised he would be alone and safe, neither of which was the case.

When it became clear that it was about him, she still stepped up and lied for him while he cowered in the closet. Everyone had taken care of his needs for so long that he couldn't even think for himself. He let a 110 lb. kindergarten teacher save his ass, then challenged her for continuing to do so. When had he become such a self-centered, egotistical prick? *So, this is what humble pie tastes like.*

Bash found a waterproof backpack in the closet of the master bedroom and packed as many clothes and toiletries as he could fit. Then he grabbed his leather shoulder bag that held his laptop, burner phones, money cards, and other essentials. Before he walked out the door, he looked around. Taking a lesson from one of Morgan's Popsisms, he ripped off the luggage tags, then grabbed the rental contracts and stashed them in his leather case. There was nothing in the car that would identify him.

When he got to the stairs, Morgan was five steps ahead of him. She stopped and looked at him questioningly.

"I'm an asshole. I'll try to do better."

She gave him an accepting nod. *What a forgiving soul.* As they started back down the stairs, they heard a car approaching the house.

"Shit!" Bash breathed.

Morgan shook her head. "We've got to work on your vocabulary. This way," she said, running back up the stairs.

Bash followed her into a low-lit bedroom where her muddy luggage and clothes lay on the bed. She walked to the window, unlocked it, and pushed it open.

"Where are the keys to the boats?" she asked.

He fished a set of keys out of his pocket and held them up. "Only one set. I ordered a larger boat with sleeping quarters so I could stay on the lake."

"Good. Hang on to them. Shut the window behind you and keep up," she said before she climbed out on the roof.

The roof was flat, so it wasn't difficult to track her movements in the dark. When they got to the back of the house, they heard pounding on the front door. He watched as Morgan threw her backpack down first, scooted to the edge on her butt and jumped. A short grunt followed.

"You okay?" he whispered.

"Yeah. It's not that far a drop. Just remember to bend your legs and fall forward. It's an incline. Beth and I did it all the time when we were in high school. If you have a laptop, toss me that bag first, and I'll try to catch it. Wouldn't want to lose any literary artistry," she snorted.

He didn't comment that he was a 34-year-old man long past the flexibility of his teens. Instead, he used the light on his cell phone to show her where the leather bag was located before tossing it down.

"Got it," she said.

After dropping the backpack, he sat on the edge and pushed off as she had done. He fell forward and was met with a sudden jolt, the mud instantly seeping through the knees of his jeans. The drop was much shorter than he had anticipated.

Picking up the backpack, he threw it over his shoulder. Morgan handed him the leather bag. Between the moonless night and the cover of pine trees, he could barely make out her silhouette in front of him.

She explained there were only two constructed paths down to the water, one from the house and one from the cottage. The first was the winding stone stairs lined with path lights that began at the house and ended at a dock that surrounded three sides of the boathouse. The second was a cruder slate-stone path that led from the caretaker's cottage to a 20-foot pier. A gravel sidewalk along the water led from the pier to the only boathouse. The walkway from the house to the cottage met in the lower part of the stairway. The rest of the property was natural woods with underbrush and pine needles covering most of the ground. Considering the house was about to be invaded by hostile intruders, none of the obvious options were open to them.

"How can we find our way down to the water if we can't see shit in the dark?" Bash asked.

"The security lights on the side of the house should provide some light, but we will have to stay in the trees to keep from being seen. There is an unofficial trail that cuts through the woods. It was part of our escape route when we wanted to be undetected by Beth's parents. We memorized the way during the day because we couldn't use flashlights. Take my hand," she said, reaching for him.

He wrapped his hand around her warm, slender fingers and felt her pull him toward the corner of the house. After making sure they wouldn't be seen, she led them through the pine trees for a good fifteen paces. She stopped at what he thought was an oak tree that seemed out of place among the evergreens. They could still see the house, but it was dark enough that no one could see them.

She let go of his hand. "This is where we start down the hill. Pine needles are pretty slick when wet, so be careful. And stay right behind me."

Morgan was right. They slipped and slid down the hill,

grabbing onto small trees and branches to hold themselves upright. It was impossible to see all the bushes and limbs before they smacked them in their faces. If they hadn't both worn sweatshirts, they would have been covered in scratches. Bash tried to imagine a 17-year-old Morgan sneaking out of the house with her friend to meet boys and drink beer. For some reason, he couldn't get that visual in his head. There was a big difference between having the wits to protect herself and drinking beer with a bunch of horny teenagers. The innocent vibe he got from her didn't fit that persona. He suspected she was more of an observer than a participator.

They were forced to stop when they reached the gravel path that ran between the pier and the boathouse because it was bathed in floodlights. They were about 30 feet from the boathouse.

"Do you think they're inside the boathouse?" he whispered.

She pointed up toward the house that was visible through the trees. The house was lit up like a Christmas tree. The bald guy stood in front of the window of the great room, talking animatedly on his cell phone. The other guy was not visible.

"The switch for the light in the boathouse is inside the house by the door to the deck. That guy is probably keeping an eye on the boats while the other one searches the house."

"You're right. They don't have to be rocket scientists to know both of our cars haven't moved. Looks like the boats are out," he said with disappointment.

"Maybe not," Morgan said, handing him her backpack. She twisted her mouth around as if she was turning something over in her mind. Then, without explanation, she grabbed the hem of her sweatshirt, yanked it over her head, and tossed it at him. His mouth fell open when she slipped off her shoes and socks, shimmied out of her jeans, and shoved her clothes into his arms. It might have been dark outside, but he couldn't help but stare at her standing before him in her practical white bra and panties. *Nothing screams innocence like 100% cotton. At least they aren't labeled with the days of the week.*

"W...What are you doing?" he asked dumbfounded.

"If we want a boat, I've got to get wet. I'll swim around to the lakeside of the boathouse and go under the door to get inside. After I unlock the padlock from the inside, it should be easy to push the boat out. Once I'm clear of the doors, I'll turn on the engines. They're going to make some noise, so we need to move fast. As soon as you see the boat, run back down the gravel path and wait for me at the end of the small pier. If those guys hear us, I'm not going to be able to stop to let you on. You'll have to jump on board as I idle by. The cove isn't very deep, which requires a slower speed. We must stay between the buoys until we get out on the lake."

It seemed like an absurd plan, but he didn't have a better idea. She wrapped her arms around herself, shivering in the cool evening, probably in the lower 50s. He could only imagine what temperature the water must be.

"I'm a strong swimmer. Why don't you let me get the boat?" he offered.

"Appreciate that, but I have the advantage of knowing the lay of the land. It would cost us too much time for you to figure out where everything is located."

"You act like you've done this before."

"A few times with Beth and her brothers," she chuckled, "but it was in July, not October. Keys, please." She held out her hand.

"I'm assuming you know how to drive a boat?" he asked, dropping the keys in her hand.

She grinned wryly. "I don't, but when I get inside, I'll pull the instructions manual out of the console." And with that, she slipped into the water and disappeared.

Surely, she's kidding.

Bash briefly glanced at the still brightly lit house. The man who had been on his cell phone was no longer visible. He checked his watch. Time seemed to drag. It had been eight minutes since Morgan entered the water, but it felt like hours. He nervously paced back and forth, praying the water was too cold for water moccasins. The muffled sound of a motor whining drew his attention back to the boathouse. Unless the intruders were standing on the outside deck, he doubted it could be heard from the house. The noise had to be the motorized door opener.

A couple of minutes later, he made out the outline of a boat, much larger than he had expected, silently gliding backwards out of the boathouse. Morgan's silhouette, crawling across the bow toward the cockpit, was barely visible. Tightening his grip on their bags, Bash made a break for the pier.

The boathouse spotlights provided just enough light for him to see the boat drift to the middle of the cove. Morgan sat at the helm, waving at him.

"Bash," her voice carried softly across the water.

"Yeah. I'm on the pier," he called, wincing as their voices magnified.

"This sucker isn't a boat, Bash. It's a yacht. They are going to hear it the minute I fire up the engine."

"I'll be ready."

"It's got a high deck. Be careful."

"Got it."

Seconds later, he heard the thunder of the engines roar to life, and the running lights appeared. She was correct. It was huge. He watched her maneuver the boat his way. Hopefully, the pier extended out far enough that she wouldn't scrap the bottom.

"Stop!" he heard someone scream. When he glanced toward the house, he saw the two men running across the deck toward the stairs.

"Get ready," Morgan yelled.

He focused his attention back to the boat, the bow just beginning to pass the end of the pier. As Morgan warned, it sat high in the water. The height and the railing on the foredeck made it impossible to leap on, especially with the three bags he was carrying. He waited until the bow had passed, then leaped onto the double rear seat at the stern, grabbing the overhead bikini cover to keep from falling in the water. He padded all his important parts to make sure everything was still in tack, counted three bags still hanging on his shoulder, and made his way to the cockpit.

"You good?" Morgan asked.

"Just peachy, Chip. Get us the fuck out of here!"

"I'm the captain of this vessel, Matie. Sit your patootie down! And don't call me 'Chip!'"

He launched in the seat. "Right now, you're my hero, so I'll call you whatever the hell you want."

She maneuvered the boat toward the middle of the inlet and headed out of the cove. There was nothing she could do about speed until they cleared the warning buoys.

Bam! Bam! Bam! Gunfire erupted, echoing through the night.

"Turkey feathers! They're shooting at us," she cried. Without warning, she gunned the engine, throwing him back against the seat.

"Who taught you to pilot a boat?" he shouted.

"Pops!"

Figures.

CHAPTER NINE

"You have got to be freezing!" Bash shouted in Morgan's ear over the roar of the engines. They had reached open water and could no longer hear gunfire.

She glanced down at her almost naked goosebump-covered body and sighed. In her rush to get out of firing range, she totally forgot she was in her bra and panties, and not attractive ones either. Bash's comment brought her back to reality. Mere moments before, she was feeling the thrill of escape. A rush of adrenaline she hadn't felt since her teenage years sneaking boats and beer with Beth. Pops had prepared her for the worst, but Beth pushed her out of her rule-abiding comfort zone. As scary as it was taking the boat from underneath the noses of the goony guys, she had found it exhilarating. But the second Bash reminded her that she was almost naked, her teeth began to chatter, and her body shivered uncontrollably.

Bash rubbed her upper arm. "You're crashing. Let me take over for you. Go below and change," he said, reaching for the steering wheel while she slid off the seat.

Grabbing her backpack, she opened the hatch to descend to the lower deck. Her fingers shook so badly she could barely get the zipper open. The sweatshirt and jeans were crammed on the top with her shoes. After removing her wet underclothes, she quickly redressed and then sat down on a cushioned bench to catch her breath.

The cabin was luxurious. Everything was lacquered white ash, baby blue, butter-soft leather, and stainless steel. The kitchen had every appliance you would need, and the cabinets were fully stocked with food. She chuckled to herself when she found a tin of caviar in the small refrigerator. To her dismay, there were no bags of potato chips. If Bash required future rescue missions, she was going to insist on a full supply.

The instructions to convert the table into a double bed lay on the counter, along with a map of where the blankets, linens, and towels were stored.

As Morgan explored the wine rack, the sudden jolt from a drastic reduction in speed had her clutching the sink to keep from flying across the galley. It occurred to her that Bash might not be experienced at piloting a boat this size. That thought sent her scurrying back up the stairs.

"There you are," he said, when she poked her head out. "I was worried I was going to end up in Tennessee before you came back up. Thinking about tooling along out here in the dark without being able to see shit didn't seem like the safest plan. If you know a place we can pull over and not get run over by a barge, that would be awesome. We can regroup in the morning."

"Did you think to grab those maps you told me about earlier?" she asked.

"I was planning to pick them up on our way out, but under the circumstances, it didn't seem prudent. They are sitting on a lounger on the back deck. If our new friends find them, they will have a guide to navigating the waters and a better chance of finding us. They might also have found the keys to that second boat you told me about."

"We're all good on that front. There was no second boat. Seems this baby barely fit in the boathouse by itself," she said, patting the dashboard. "The other boat must be docked at one of the marinas."

With the cruiser on idle, he stood up and surveyed their surroundings. "I can see the lights on a bridge up ahead, and I'm assuming the massive glow to the left is the city of Guntersville. With that in mind, any ideas of where we might anchor for the night?"

She extended her hand. "That must be Highway 431, and Marshal County Park is on the right. Go under the bridge, and we'll look for a place to drop anchor. Watch out for buoys. We don't want to tear a hole in the bottom. If we're lucky, the water patrol won't make us move, but it's probably too late for anyone to bother with us."

With the boat secure, they moved below deck. Morgan gave him a mini tour. It didn't take long for Bash to assemble the bed. She mentally fretted over sharing the bed, but they were both exhausted, so she didn't have the heart to insist he sleep in a chair. It was resolved without issue when Bash found a blow-up mattress with a battery pump. It fit comfortably on the floor, and Bash chivalrously settled in.

She had barely gotten under the covers when she heard his soft breathing. For some reason, the steady rhythm of his breath gave her a sense of comfort, and before she knew it, she was out.

The next morning, Morgan awoke to a gentle rocking and steady hum of an engine. Her head was in a fog, and she couldn't immediately decipher where she was. Her eyelids were so heavy she thought she might need a crowbar to pry them open, but the smell of coffee wafting through the cabin perked her right up.

"Good morning," she yawned.

"I sure hope so. Though I do have some news you might find disappointing," he said.

She swung her head in the direction of his voice, expecting the worst. He stood over the stove with a spatula in his hand.

His face mocked regret. "Alas, there are no potato chips of any kind in the pantry, so you're going to have to make do with plain eggs, turkey bacon, and toast this morning. On the upside, there is caviar."

She burst out laughing. "Oh, my Goodness! I don't eat potato chips for breakfast. And I already discovered the no potato chip thing last night."

"Good to know. Just trying to be a good host," he said lightheartedly.

She wiped her eyes. "What time is it?"

"7:30. Coffee? Tea? We have both."

"Coffee," she said, savoring the smell. He handed her a mug. "May I have some cream and sugar?"

"Already in it. Took a wild guess. Well, not so wild. Few women I know drink their coffee black."

She decided to overlook the sexist remark.

"I've been up since 6 a.m. I wanted to scope out our surroundings in the daylight. My paranoia of being in the path of a barge got the better of me. According to the internet, thousands of barges send millions of tons of cargo down the Tennessee River. I didn't want us to end up kicking our feet behind one."

She giggled. "We usually stay on the lake and out of the commercial traffic lanes on the river."

"If you can muster enough energy to get out of bed, I'll put the table back together so we can eat breakfast and figure out where to go from here."

CHAPTER TEN

The sunshine and bright azure sky were a welcome sight that helped wash away some of the anxiety from the previous evening. So much had happened in less than 24 hours. There was no way they could go back to the lake house. Her vacation certainly hadn't turned out as she had expected.

Bash swiveled his chair toward hers and reached for her hand. The sincerity of the gesture stunned her.

"I'm truly sorry I ruined your vacation with my drama. It hasn't helped the situation that I've been a complete ass. You could have walked away and left me to fend for myself last night, but instead, your quick thinking saved our lives. I'm not making excuses for my behavior, but you've seen firsthand why I was hesitant to reveal my identity. Bash is the nickname my close friends call me, and I *am* a writer. In my defense, I didn't lie about any of that. Since you obviously didn't recognize me, it didn't seem important to elaborate. It never occurred to me the cottage break-in could be linked to me. I shudder to think what might have happened had you been there alone."

She shrugged her shoulders and flashed a mischievous smile. "It wasn't a complete disaster. I had a delicious dinner with a bestselling author. Took a little midnight swim. Got to spend the night on a luxury boat. All in all, not a terrible 16 hours."

He shook his head. "Only you would see it that way."

"I'm a glass half-full kind of girl."

"I see you are."

"So, why don't you tell me what's going on. Why are those

men after you?" she asked, hoping she had earned his trust.

Bash ran his hands over his face, scratching his unshaven beard, trying to figure out how much he wanted to reveal. For some reason, he looked younger in the sunlight despite the fine lines on his forehead and around his eyes. Maybe it was his unguarded smile that brightened his handsome features, making his rainforest-green eyes gleam. His wavy, sun-streaked caramel hair curled just under his ears with a light sprinkle of premature gray woven around his temples. She hadn't noticed any of those things last night, perhaps because he seemed so unapproachable, merely tolerating her presence. Maybe he still was, but she hoped not.

Bash took a deep breath. "An extremely powerful man, Maximillian Fontana, who is rumored to have ties to organized crime, has asked me to write his memoirs. Or maybe it's a complete biography. I'm not sure of the details. He's been extremely persistent about it and doesn't seem to want to accept my refusal. I don't want to be privy to the man's secrets, nor does it make sense that he would come to a fiction writer. My friends, who also manage my business, cooked up this elaborate plan for me to disappear. No one, including them, is supposed to know exactly where I am. Imagine my surprise when, less than 36 hours later, you showed up at my door."

"Wow. Sounds like your friends need to stick to what they're good at and engage a high-risk security company to handle your safety. I promise you I had no idea that you would be in the house. Beth called me literally minutes before I turned into the driveway to tell me she wasn't coming and that her dad had rented the house to someone else. Then, she offered me the cottage as an alternative. Everything went downhill from there. I'm not handy with household repairs, so the man I saw standing on the deck next door..." With her free hand, she flipped her pointer finger at him and cocked her head "...looked like my only option. And that's the honest to God's truth."

He released her hand and sat back in his seat. "I believe you. I'm just not sure what to do at this point. We can't go back to the lake house, and I've got to get as far away from those guys as soon as possible. Somehow, in this elaborate plan, someone was compromised. Now I don't know who I can trust."

"Pops told me when I was faced with a problem without all the facts, I had to rely on the things I was 100% sure of. You don't know who you can't trust, but do you know one person who you can trust? Someone you would stake your life on?"

"Another Popsism?" he asked. She nodded.

"Gray, for sure. He's a lifelong friend and my agent," he said without hesitation.

"Good. Then that's your only contact for now," she suggested.

He rubbed his chin and met her eyes. "You have this way of simplifying things."

She gave him a wide grin and stuck out her hand. He cautiously took it. "Hi! I'm Morgan Skylar, kindergarten teacher. Breaking complex things into simple terms is my specialty!"

He chuckled. "I guess it is. Keeping all my communication with Gray sounds like a smart idea. One of many you seem to be good at coming up with. Let me ask you something. You've made a few offhanded comments about your grandfather being suspicious and overprotective. When those men showed up, you muttered about preparing for something like that all your life. What exactly did you mean by that?"

If he could open up to her, she figured she should do the same for him.

"I've never told anyone this. Not even Beth. I mean, she knew Pops was crazy paranoid, but she never knew why. Just thought he was over the top. In all the years we've known each other, she's never once been to my house. Or even met Pops."

Bash's eyes narrowed. "How is that even possible?"

"He's talked to Beth and her parents on the phone, but it took years for him to develop that trust. They've never met face-to-face. I usually went home with her after school. If Pops dropped me off at her house, he never got out of the car. She was my only friend, and her house was the only place I could go. Pops even paid to have a background check done on Mr. Worthington before he allowed me to play with her."

He looked confused. "That's extreme. I don't understand. They didn't see each other at school events? You know…plays, school picnics, football games?"

"The only time Pops went to my school was to enroll me in kindergarten. After that, his communications were either through mail, online, or a phone call. He never attended any of my school activities. I didn't either unless it was required. Thanks to Beth, some of that changed when I was fifteen." Saying it out loud brought back the pain she had felt being alone among the families of her schoolmates. The looks of pity. Feelings of being an outsider.

"What did Beth do to change his mind?"

"Found out where Pops' bike repair shop was and called him. She told him he was ruining my life. I was lonely, and he only had himself to blame when I ran away from home. Not if but when. She said she would help me, too. Either he loosened his grip on me, or she was going to the school counselor. And she wanted me to spend my vacations at the lake with her family. Beth can drive a hard bargain. Of course, she made up the running away part, but it worked. He admired her moxie. I could go to school activities, but only if I went with her. And he begrudgingly agreed to the vacations after he talked to Mr. Worthington. I didn't have any real freedom until I went away to college. That's where I had my first date."

"Did he have a valid reason? Or was he just overprotective?"

She took a deep breath and blew it out. No one knew about her family. "A bit of both, I think. My mother died of a drug overdose, and my father was in prison. Still is, as far as I know. Pops wouldn't tell me why he went to prison but said it would be for a long time. His biggest fear was if my father got out early, he would come looking for me.

"Pops got in trouble a lot when he was young, and he wasn't married. He knew the courts would never let him have guardianship of me. He didn't want me to go into foster care, and he never wanted me to be in my father's custody, so he took me away. He changed our names, bought a house in a rural area, and he opened a bike repair shop twenty miles from where we lived. It was a cash only business. We didn't live off the grid, but Pops went to great lengths to stay off the public radar. I don't even know my real name."

She could read it on his face. It was too unbelievable. Or perhaps he suspected the same thing Beth had feared. Had Pops kidnapped her from her real family?

"Haven't you ever wondered…" he didn't finish.

"If it was all a lie? Beth suggested it all the time. How did I know I wasn't kidnapped from my real family? One day, she brought me two DNA kits from one of those places that trace your ancestry. If I was so sure I was really Pops' granddaughter, I shouldn't be afraid to prove it. I had a heck of a time getting his saliva, but I did. When the results came online, it confirmed we were related. There were enough DNA markers for him to be my grandfather. And no. Pops has never hurt me in any way.

"Pops wasn't a touchy-feely guy, but I was everything to him. He gave up his whole life to protect me and give me a good start in life. Never once did he let me go anywhere unless I was with him or Beth. He didn't have guy friends or girlfriends that I knew of. The only place we went on vacation together was our cabin in the Appalachian Mountains. It sits right on top of a mountain in the Nantahala Forest, not far from Cherokee, North Carolina. He paid cash for all four years of my college in advance and insisted I never come home again. I spent my summer vacations working in Atlanta. Either Pops came to visit me, or we met at the cabin for a week during breaks and holidays. No one knows the location of the cabin but Pops and me. Now…just me."

"How did he die?"

"The sheriff's report said he had a heart attack while he was stopped at a traffic light. I never got to…say goodbye. When I got a call from his lawyer, he had already been cremated."

Bash appeared baffled by the whole story. "Where will

you go from here? Home? I think you're safe. Unless you left something in your car, those guys don't know your name."

"I don't leave paperwork in my car."

"Popsism?"

"Yeah. After my vacation with Beth, I planned to drive to the mountain cabin. I didn't know Pops had a will until I got the call from his attorney. Apparently, there were a few things he kept from me. I found out he sold our house and his repair shop a couple of years ago. He moved into an apartment, but I'm not sure where. The lawyer is supposed to transfer some money into my account, but I haven't checked to see if I have received it yet. It would make it too real. Mr. Watson told me Pops left me something important in the cabin. It was his safe place. His sanctuary."

"Was it your sanctuary too?"

"As I got older, it got a bit boring. We hiked. Fished. Played board games. I read. He worked on the cabin. That was the only place he wasn't constantly looking over his shoulder, so I guess it was."

"Sounds isolated."

Her face brightened. "Exactly the kind of place you need. Would you like to come with me? There's plenty of room, and it's a safe place to stay until your friend finds you something more to your liking. It's not fancy, but it has all the basics. Running water. An electric generator. K rations. No neighbors for miles."

"K rations? You're kidding, right?" he asked with disbelief.

"We can stop at a grocery store on the way, but yes, there are K rations. The cabin has everything you'd need to survive a world crisis. It's just a suggestion. I can't imagine those guys finding it."

Morgan hadn't intended to invite him, but as she began talking, it seemed to be the ideal place for him to temporarily hide.

"I appreciate the offer but let me give Gray a call first. He may already have a backup plan.

CHAPTER ELEVEN

Bash excused himself and relocated below deck to make a private call. He needed to talk to Gray and figure out what the hell to do next. Pulling out one of the burner phones, he made the call.

"Bash! I've been going out of my fucking mind. I haven't heard from you in two days! Did it not occur to you to check in? Someone broke into Bryan's office. We know for sure they got into his assistant's desk, but we don't think she had anything relevant to you. They must have gotten spooked by something. Never made it into Bryan's personal office."

"What do you mean she wouldn't have anything relevant to me? Bryan's my editor, for fuck sake!"

"Calm down, Bash. All the client files are secured in Bryan's office."

The whole incident soured Bash's mood. Too many things were happening at once. "You could have called me if you were so worried."

"That's not what we agreed. You were to make first contact, so I would know you were free to talk. I'm assuming you are at the lake house."

"Your assumption would be incorrect. Your safety plan lasted less than 36 hours. I'm on the boat you rented, sitting in the middle of the lake, and it isn't by choice. Who made the reservation for the lake house, anyway?" Bash huffed.

"What do you mean my safety plan didn't last? I have no clue where you are, so how could anyone else?"

"Answer my damn question, Gray. Who made this

reservation?" he bellowed.

"Christ, Bash. Bryan asked someone in his art department, but they had no idea who it was for. Bryan gave the guy a $5000 bonus to keep quiet and implied it was a love nest for a married writer and his mistress. What makes you think someone knows where you are?"

"Because two muscled men showed up last night at my door!" Bash proceeded to tell him the entire story.

"I don't even know what to say, Bash. I honestly don't think it was leaked from Bryan's office."

Bash could picture him walking around in circles, rubbing the back of his neck. Gray was a planner, and he hated when things fell apart. Whoa, be to the person who screwed it up.

"Well, you need to figure out who sold me out. If I'd been alone, I guarantee they would have either taken me or killed me. In the meantime, I speak only to you. Not even Alex until you figure out what happened. It's not that I don't trust Alex. It just limits my communication. Your main job right now is to find out where the leak came from."

"God. I'm so sorry. What are you going to do? You can't stay on that lake. They will eventually find you."

"I'm assuming you guys didn't make a plan B?"

"Even if we did, I wouldn't want to use it. Not until I figure out who can be trusted. Maybe you should go to the mountains with the Skylar woman. At least until I get a handle on things. I'll start with Bryan. Tell him what happened and that you're in the wind. Get a read on him. Go from there." He released a long sigh. "Fuck! Just fuck!"

"What happened when Fontana found out I was gone?" Bash asked.

"I sent him an email telling him you wouldn't be available for a couple of months. You left on a sabbatical to catch up on your writing. A list of award-winning authors you recommended was attached. The only response I got came in a text directly from him to me. Not sure how he got my private cell."

"What did it say?"

"It said, 'That's not going to work for me.'"

"That sucks."

"That about says it. After last night, we got the message loud and clear. We screwed up. I should have gotten a security specialist involved."

"Don't beat yourself up. It seemed like a good plan. I should have taken it more seriously, but yeah, we need a security company to consult on this. For now, it's probably best if we talk as little as possible. Do me a favor. Get your family out of town. It's no secret we're best friends. You need to warn Alex, too," Bash said.

"I'll send the family on vacation without me and join them later. If you're going to the mountains, you may not be able to get reception. Call me before you get out of range. We'll find a way to fix this, buddy. I swear. Stay safe."

"You too. Thanks."

In the light of day, Morgan was able to get her bearing on the lake, making it easier for them to plan their next steps. There was a large marina close by, but they decided it would be the first place their pursuers would look. Morgan remembered a grocery and bait shop in a more obscure location that the Worthington teens frequented. A kid who worked there would sell them beer for the right price. It wasn't located on the map, which was to their advantage. Since it was dangerous to go back to the cabin to get either of their cars, they had to find transportation and a place to dock the boat until it could be picked up.

CHAPTER TWELVE

As Bash idled toward Ray's General Store, he gritted his teeth, praying a ripple from the cruiser's wake wouldn't send them crashing into the small pier where two fishing boats were docked. Morgan jumped onto the wood planking just in time to maneuver one of the boats out of the way and place the fenders to prevent a collision. Crisis averted. Morgan to the rescue again. With a deep sigh, he jumped off the boat and stood beside her.

"She's all tied up. I don't think the owner's going to like that we've taken up one whole side of his dock space, especially when he finds out we want to leave her here," Morgan said, nodding over his shoulder.

Bash turned to see a slim man in his 60s heading their way. He was scruffy-looking with stained denim jeans and a faded Grateful Dead t-shirt. The scowl he wore was probably a result of witnessing the close encounter on his dock.

Bash gasped in surprise as Morgan hip-bumped him out of the way and, through the corner of her mouth, said, "I've got this."

"How y'all doing today?" she asked, in her perky southern accent. "Beautiful day to be on the lake, isn't it? And you get to enjoy this sight all the time!"

Bash watched the man's hardened expression soften in the presence of Morgan's sunny disposition.

"Yes, ma'am. Been lookin' at it for the last 36 years." He turned to Bash. "That's an expensive sucker you got there," he said, waving up at the cruiser. "What you folks be needin' this mornin'? We got bait. Basic groceries. Beer. Nothin' fancy." There was a trace of aggravation in his tone. The man had already pegged him for a rich asshole. Not wrong.

Morgan laid on her sweet charm. "I'm Chip, and this is my boyfriend, Bash. We came down a couple of days ago to meet some friends. Unfortunately, they had to rush home for a medical emergency, so we're stuck here with the boat we rented and no transportation home. We need a place to temporarily dock the boat. The rental company can pick it up this afternoon. We would pay you $500."

"It's fully stocked with food and liquor. You're welcome to help yourself," Bash added.

"Is that $500 cash?" he asked. Bash nodded. "How are you two gonna get out of here? Where you headed?"

"Birmingham," Morgan said. "We were hoping to find someone we could pay to drive us."

"I'm willing to pay $1500 cash plus gas if we can leave within the hour," Bash said, pulling out his wallet.

"Upfront?" the owner asked.

"That will be $1000 now and $500 when we arrive," Bash countered.

"Looks like we've got ourselves a deal," he said, sticking out his hand to shake. Then, he gave Bash the address to text the rental company. "I'll call my grandson. He just graduated from the University of Tennessee this past spring. Nice kid. Still lookin' for a job. Y'all mind ridin' in a truck?"

"Whatever will get us there," Morgan said.

Twenty minutes later, Jonah, a blond-headed, gangly but clean-cut young man, showed up in a black Ford F-250. Bash handed Ray a $1000 in cash.

Ray did a quick introduction to Jonah, and they were on their way. It took less than fifteen minutes to get to County Road 35, and that's when Bash asked Jonah to take Highway 71.

Jonah shook his head. "No, Sir. We need to go southeast on 35 to I-59 south. That will take us straight into Birmingham. Highway 71 goes to I-59 north. We'll end up in Chattanooga."

Morgan looked at Bash and smiled. Their trip to Birmingham was a misdirection and in the opposite direction of their true destination.

"How would you like to make $500 for yourself?" Bash asked.

Jonah side-eyed him with suspicion.

"You turn on 71 instead of 35 and take us to the airport in Chattanooga. I'll give you the $500 for Ray and $500 for yourself, and no one will ever know. There aren't but twenty miles difference in the trips. What do you think, Jonah?"

"You'll still fill the tank?" he asked.

"We will," Morgan said.

"I guess this is my lucky day," he said, grinning from ear to ear.

Switching locations at the last minute had been the plan all along. Ray struck Bash as an opportunist. A man who could be bought by their stalkers. Chattanooga was also on the way to the Appalachian Mountains. His bet was on Jonah not telling his grandpa about the change of plans.

As soon as Jonah dropped them off at the departure entrance, they hurried to the car rentals. After picking up a Jeep Grand Cherokee, they stopped for a quick lunch and were on the road to the cabin.

The drive through the mountains was breathtaking, but the narrow two-lane roads made the trip slow going. It was dusk by the time they arrived at Murphy, North Carolina. Morgan wasn't comfortable locating the cabin without the familiar visual landmarks, so they decided to stay overnight and do some grocery shopping the next morning. They found a small no-name motel, checked in separately under assumed names, and paid cash. After grabbing a couple of burgers and fries, they went to their separate rooms to get some sleep.

Before Bash's head hit the pillow, his burner phone rang. Gray.

"Hey, man. I thought you were going to call me."

"It's been a shit day, and excuse me if I decided to get

some rest." He couldn't figure out why he was so annoyed. Gray had done nothing to warrant his ire. It was probably because he hadn't slept the previous night, and there was the issue of someone trying to kill him. Gray had always been his sounding board.

"I talked to Bryan. We found out what happened. Doesn't look like anyone gave up your location on purpose. Bryan's assistant, Bette, was the one who contacted a guy she knew in the art department to make the reservations. She was very clear with her instructions that he was being paid to keep his mouth shut. Even had him sign an NDA. After he e-signed the contract for the house, he forwarded it to an attorney friend of Alex's in Indianapolis, who arranged for the car you picked up, along with the contract in the glove compartment. By the way, the attorney owns the car, so I guess we'll have to have someone return it to him. Anyway, Bette didn't know the jerk in the art department had a crush on her. Thought he could leverage his little favor to his advantage. He left a note on her desk after she had left for the day that said, 'All done for the mystery man. It's 12 Redbud Drive. Now, you owe me dinner and drinks.' The day he left the note was the night of the break-in in Bryan's office. It was right on the top of the desk for Fontana's men to see. The note was still there, so they probably took a picture of it."

"The asshole was paid to keep his mouth shut!"

"The guy didn't think it applied to Bette since she was the one who paid him. Sorry, Bash. We thought we were smart enough to do this ourselves, but we weren't. I swear I won't make that mistake again. In the morning, I have a meeting with Samuel Barrett of SMB Protection Agency. Sam is former FBI. Mostly works with high-profile clients. If you call me tomorrow afternoon, we should have a plan."

"Sounds good," Bash said, trying to project optimism. He hated that Gray was blaming himself.

"Are you sure you can trust this girl? Is there any way Fontana could have gotten to her? Set a trap?" Gray sounded genuinely concerned, but Bash couldn't see a connection between them. Why would she have saved him?

"I thought you did a background check?"

"Things can be hidden. You know this," Gray said wearily.

"Trusting my gut on this. If there's anything odd that I've learned, it's about her Pops. That's the grandfather who died. Morgan told me he literally kidnapped her when she was a baby. Apparently, her parents were shit. Mother overdosed. Dad is in prison for god knows what. Her grandfather didn't want her to go into foster care and knew that with his record, he would never gain custody. She doesn't even know her real name but has always gone by Morgan Skylar."

"Well, hell. That's not suspicious at all," Gray roared.

"Yeah. She had her doubts about her grandfather, too. Even had a DNA test done without his knowledge. He had enough markers to be her grandfather, but who knows if his story was true. I'd suggest a background check on him, but I have no idea what his name is. Maybe I'll find something at the cabin. If I do, I'll text you," he said, feeling guilty after all she had done for him, but it never hurt to be thorough.

"It concerns me not knowing where you are. Can you at least give me some idea of your location?"

"These were your fuckin' rules!" he snapped.

"I know, but I feel like I've abandoned you. Please call me as soon as you get to the cabin and figure out if it's a viable option. If you don't feel comfortable there, get out!"

"Got it. Stop worrying. We'll talk after you meet with the security guy."

"Sam Barrett. Please try to remember his name in case he calls you," Gray sighed. "And don't expect me to stop worrying. You're my brother in every way that counts."

"I know. You are to me, too."

CHAPTER THIRTEEN

Grief overwhelmed Morgan as she sat in the SUV, staring at the dark wood log and rough-stone A-framed cabin. She had visited every summer since she was a child. Memories of happy times on the mountain flooded back to her. Hiking. Wading and fishing in the cool mountain streams. Exploring caves. Riding bikes through the winding roads. It was their own little piece of heaven and even felt like it too when the clouds hung so low, they covered the entire mountain-top in a billowy white she couldn't quite grasp. She remembered asking Pops why she couldn't get ahold of the clouds. He told her she couldn't catch magic. It was the only impractical thing he had ever said to her.

Turning to Bash, she found him watching her with pity in his eyes. She flushed with embarrassment at being exposed at such a vulnerable moment.

"Don't feel sorry for me. There are no bad memories here," she said proudly.

"That wasn't what I was feeling. I was wondering if I should go inside and give you some privacy."

"Just give me a moment. I'll be right back," she said, opening the car door. She walked across the yard to a cluster of huge boulders sitting on the edge of the cliff overlooking the valley. Slipping off her jogging shoes, she climbed barefoot onto the smooth rocks to her favorite thinking spot. A place she could daydream.

"What a magnificent view," Bash said, startling her out of her thoughts.

She brushed a tear from her cheek and met his eyes.

"I wanted to make sure you were okay."

"Did you think I might jump?" she asked with a trace of a smile.

He shrugged. "Not really, but now that you mention it, please don't. I'd never find my way back out of here." He playfully grabbed one of her bare feet. "Why did you take your shoes off? It's got to be in the 50s up here."

"I rarely wore shoes when I was a kid. Pops scolded me about it all the time. Said I was going to cut my foot open. It was easier to run and climb barefooted. My feet were completely calloused."

He rubbed his thumb down the center of her foot, making her jerk at the sensation. "Not anymore," he chuckled.

Shaking her head, she pulled her foot away and crawled down from the rock. It made her feel like she was 10 years old again.

"Time to unload those groceries and get the generators running."

Instead of a glass front like many A-frames, this house had a stone front with a small round window just below the center eve. The heavy wooden front door was at least 4 inches thick.

The inside was one spacious room with a seating area in the middle, a kitchen on one side, and a laundry room and bathroom in the back. A faded brown leather sofa, tan recliner, and a whiskey barrel converted into a coffee table sat in front of a large flagstone fireplace with a wood-burning stove attached. A small metal winding staircase led to a loft.

Bash raised his eyebrow. "One bedroom upstairs?" he said, motioning upward.

"That is my room. Pops slept on a twin bed in the basement. If it was too cold, I'd sleep on the sofa near the wood stove. Even in the middle of summer, the evenings can get cool. Take a closer look around if you like."

Bash climbed up the metal stairs.

"You are welcome to sleep up there." He didn't answer.

"I'll be back in a few minutes. I need to turn on the electric generator and the propane for the stove," she called, as she went outside.

When she came back in, Bash had his feet on the coffee table and a beer in his hand.

"Glad you made yourself at home."

"It felt like a beer kind of moment. Where's the basement? I want to see my alternative sleeping arrangements."

Morgan pushed his feet off the coffee table and slid the barrel over a few feet. Then she flipped up one side of the area rug, exposing a trap door. When she pulled it open, Bash stood up and peered down.

"No shit. I did not see that coming. What's down there?" he asked with wariness in his tone, then took a swig of beer as if to fortify his nerves.

"Why? You worried I'm going to trap you and make you my sex slave," she snickered.

Bash was so shocked, he literally choked on his beer so violently that it came out his nose. Morgan slapped him on the back, laughing hysterically.

"Y…you never cease to surprise me," he said, wiping his face with the back of his hand.

She grabbed a dishcloth from the kitchen and tossed it to him. "Like Pops always said, 'keep them off balance.' And just what are you more afraid of, Mr. Bartoli? Being locked in the basement or being a sex slave?" she asked wryly.

"It's just not something I would expect a kindergarten teacher to say," he said, clearing his throat. His eyes narrowed with suspicion. And it hurt. She was only attempting to lighten the mood. And it backfired. He was questioning if she was serious. Maybe not about the sex part, but about being locked in the basement.

"Pops would have called you a 'wussy city boy,'" she said playfully, attempting to defuse the tension.

"I'm not a wuss. It just occurred to me that we are in the middle of nowhere, and we would be hard-pressed to get help if we needed it. And absolutely no one knows we are here."

Masking her anger and disappointment, she walked to the kitchen and pulled a butcher knife out of the drawer and returned. He flinched and stepped back.

"Here," she said, handing him the knife handle first. "So you can protect yourself from me. I'll go down first. If I make any sudden moves, you can stab me in the back."

He held up his hand. "No, Morgan."

She ignored him. Putting the knife in his hand, she wrapped his fingers around the handle. *Pops was right. You just can't tell about people, no matter how you think you've got them figured out.*

"Take it or stay up here," she said. Turning away before he saw her watery eyes, she climbed down the ladder.

When Bash reached the bottom of the stairs, the knife was no longer in his hand. He caught her arm and turned her around to face him.

"I'm just jumpy after the last couple of days. Please forgive me. My paranoia has gotten the better of me. I've lived in my own sheltered world for too long. I trust you. Although I haven't given you a reason to believe me, I'll prove it to you, and maybe you can learn to trust me."

"I already trusted you, Bash, because *you* haven't given me a reason not to." He winced and nodded slowly. She could see the sting of her words hit their mark, but she had to shake it off. They were stuck together. Waving her hand, she said, "You can look around, but I've already decided that I'm going to sleep down here. I'll feel closer to Pops."

His eyes roamed around the room. "This isn't bad."

There was a fabric lounge chair, a tall bookcase with Pops western paperbacks and a stack of motorcycle magazines, a twin bed covered with a multi-colored homemade quilt, and an old wooden desk with a manilla envelope lying on the top. It said, 'For Chip'. The sight of it took her breath away. His presence in the room lingered so strongly that she half expected him to appear out of thin air. She reached for the envelope with shaky hands and clutched it to her chest. His final words to her. They had only ever had each other.

Bash ushered her to the chair, then sat on the bed beside her. She fought the waterworks again. Pops hated them.

"Would you open it for me?" she whispered.

He took it from her hands, opened the sealed flap, and pulled out two sheets of paper. She immediately recognized Pops chicken-scratching.

"Want me to read it?" he asked. She nodded. He cleared his throat.

Dear Chip,

You know I was never much for words, but you have talked enough for the both of us over the years, and I always assumed you knew me well enough to figure out what I was thinking. I told you a long time ago I was not a good man and did not know how to be one. The only thing I knew how to do was feed you, put a roof over your head, protect you from harm, make sure you could protect yourself, and get you educated so you would have a better life. I failed my son, and I regret that. I tried my darnedest not to fail you. Despite the mistakes I have made, you turned out better than any parent could ever hope. You were the north star in a dark man's life. As long as we had each other, I never lost my way. I didn't deserve you, Chip. If there is a man upstairs, I owe him a huge debt.

You were born with a curious streak. Had to know everything. Drove me crazy. That's why I brought you all those damn books. You always asked about your mom and dad. I knew as soon as I was gone, you would be hell-bent on finding out more about them. Your dad and your mother's people. I'm gonna tell you why you can't do that. I also want you to know, you didn't fool me none with that DNA test. I let it go because I am your grandfather. I didn't lie about that. As hard as it is, I owe you the truth.

When you were born, I was the president of the Dragon Fire Motorcycle Club in California. We were outlaw bikers. Did it all — drugs, guns, extortion, forgery. My son, your father, was an enforcer named Asa Lion Kline. My real name is Clark Wayne Kline. Patrice, your mother, was one of the ole ladies that rode with us. Don't know her last name. She and Asa got together for a while until she got pregnant. They decided to sell their baby to a rich couple. If the baby was healthy, they would get $40,000. That was enough incentive for Patrice to stay clean. She overdosed a couple of months after you were born.

At the time, I didn't think that was a bad deal for you. Better life. That was until Asa found out he could sell you to a child trafficker for $60,000. He started pushing the club members to get their foot in that business. As bad as I was, that was one line I would not cross. I found out where they were taking Patrice for her delivery and where you were being handed over to the traffickers. Couldn't let that happen. Got all my plans made. New identifications for both of us. Place to stay until you could travel. As soon as you were cleaned off and wrapped up, I came in and took you. I handed the midwife $5000 and told her you were a boy. She nodded and took the money. She said I had to make it look good, so I hit her in the face with my fist. Only woman I ever struck. Didn't feel too bad about it because she knew the life those babies were being sold into.

It didn't take long for the club to figure out it was me who took you. Probably thought I was gonna get a better deal. I burned bridges when I left, but I also got me some insurance. I made a deal with a guy I learned was undercover FBI. If he would help me disappear and keep me informed on the club's activities, I'd give him all the information they needed to bust that trafficking ring. That's how Asa ended up in prison. I put him there. I took one other insurance policy that I thought would help protect you because they have never stopped looking for us. A couple of months ago, I found out Asa got out of prison on a technicality. He wants revenge, and he wants you in the club. He can't ever find out you're a woman. With what I'm leaving you, you will have leverage, and no one can touch you. You're good at riddles. Build it in a small box, and you can never get it out. You might be able to move it around, but you'll eventually end up back in the same place.

I got things figured out with the lawyer when I found out I didn't have long. Hope it helps. I've tried to cover any trails to you and the cabin but make this your last trip. You'll find the paperwork you'll need to sell it. The club is much bigger now and has a lot more connections.

Many in law enforcement. Don't underestimate the life of revenge.

You know feelings are hard for me, and I have never said it, but you know, Chip. YOU KNOW.

Your Pops

Morgan fell on her knees and broke apart.

CHAPTER FOURTEEN

Bash was concerned. Morgan hadn't moved a muscle in the past 20 minutes. She was in shock. All he could think to do was be there. He leaned down where she sat on the floor and lightly rubbed the top of her shoulder. A single tear trailed from the corner of her right eye, down her chin, and dropped on her sweater.

As bad as he felt for Morgan, he couldn't help the anxiety rising inside of him from the implications of her Pops words. Her father was out of prison, and his old gang was still looking for her. Or her as a man. He felt like a selfish jerk for worrying about himself when her whole world had just blown up, but it appeared their trouble had just doubled.

"Morgan?" She didn't answer. He waited five full minutes before he tried again. "Morgan, talk to me, please. You're obviously overwhelmed by the bomb that just dropped in your lap, but we need to discuss this new development. Your grandfather warned you about a very real threat. Our troubles are now two-fold." No reply.

He picked up the letter. "Okay. I'll get started on this riddle because you...ugh, we...need all the insurance we can get."

After muttering to himself for a few minutes, he felt her eyes on him. "What?"

"You said we. We need insurance," she said softly.

"So?"

"The last thing you need is to be involved with me. I can take you to the nearest town, and you can call your friend

Gray. You've got enough problems without adding mine to the list. I thought this place was safe, but apparently not so much anymore."

He studied her face. She was right. He was already in the sights of one of the most powerful men in the country and didn't need an outlaw motorcycle club with leather and steel between their legs on his ass too. Then he remembered. Morgan didn't have to get involved with him, but she chose to put herself at risk to save his pompous ass. He owed her. And he wanted to help.

"There is no way I'm leaving you. Not after what you did for me and not until I know you're safe."

She gave me a weak smile. "Thank you."

"You're welcome. Now let me get back to this riddle."

"No need. I knew what he meant the moment you read it."

He crinkled his forehead. "Really?'

In four strides, she was in front of the bookcase. "The trap door was so narrow, Pops had to take everything apart and reassemble it down here except the bookcase. He built that himself. I joked that it was so big he would never be able to get it out of here without destroying it. He could move it around, but it wasn't leaving this room. It must be in the bookcase somewhere."

They spent the next fifteen minutes going through each page of every book and magazine, finding nothing. Bash reached over and grabbed the letter to read the riddle again.

"Build it in a small box, and you can never get it out. You might be able to move it around, but you'll eventually end up back in the same place," he read out loud. "Maybe it has something to do with moving it around. Something taped to the back?"

Her eyes lit up as she scrambled to her feet. "Help me move it out from the wall."

The bookcase was 4' by 6' and made of sturdy oak, so it was heavy. They slowly inched it away from the wall until they had a 6" clearance. Bash put his cell on flashlight to see the back. He was totally stunned when he saw the outline of a door.

"Morgan, you're not going to believe this shit."

She took his phone and gently nudged him out of the

way. When she turned back, her eyes were saucers. "Well, I'll be doggone." She looked up at the ceiling and said, "You sure had me fooled Pops."

They moved the bookcase far enough away from the wall to allow them to get to the door. Morgan was about to open it when Bash put his hand on her shoulder to stop her. She swung her head around in question.

"We aren't going to find any dead bodies of sex slaves in there, are we?"

That gained him a smack on his chest and an eye roll. "Of course, and you're about to be number six!"

The first thing they saw was the glow from a computer monitor with a four-way split screen. Cameras displayed four different locations around the property.

"This must be connected to a high-voltage battery. Two of the cameras are on the right and left side of the house. The other two are the front and the back. Pops must have thought a threat was imminent if he installed these."

"Wonder how long they've been here?" he asked absently. Bash noticed a flashlight sitting on the shelf beside the computer. Flipping it on, he looked over the small room. A shop light hung on a hook from the low ceiling. He hit the switch, flooding the room in light.

The room was bare except for a folding table with the computer against one wall and a 6' by 6' stainless steel safe on the opposite wall. It had an electronic lock.

"This is some serious security. Any idea of the combination?" Bash asked.

Morgan thought for a minute. "Maybe," she said, twisting her lips. "Could you give me a little more light?"

He held the flashlight beam above the keypad while she tried a few combinations. It was hit or miss, considering she had no clue how many numbers it took. Mere seconds later, there was a tone and a click.

"Yippie! Got it, Pops!" she shouted with a fist bump to the air.

"I can't even imagine how you figured that out," he mumbled under his breath.

He lit up the safe as she opened the door.

"Fuuuuuuccckkk," he said in a long sigh.

"What did I tell you about using that word, Mr. Potty Mouth?" she admonished.

"This kind of warrants it, don't you think?" When she didn't answer, he studied her expression, trying to read her reaction to the contents. "You don't seem surprised." It wasn't a question.

She bit her bottom lip. "Not really. I've seen some of these, but not all. I assure you I knew nothing about this room. I told you Pops was a paranoid man. At least now I know why."

The vault was loaded with guns and ammunition. Every shape and size. Some Bash recognized from movies and television shows, but his knowledge of weaponry was limited to research for his novels and holding a 9mm for a photo shoot. While he stared in awe, Morgan began picking them up one at a time, pulling them apart and putting them back together with an expertise that shocked him speechless.

"Wh...What..." He was having trouble forming words.

"Checking them for ammunition. Keep the light in this direction, please," she said, as casually as if she were checking for water spots on clean dishes.

"Do you know how to fire any of them?"

"I know how to load and fire most of them," she said, slamming a clip back into a handgun. "Most of these used to be in a safe in our home. Pops must have moved them here when he sold it."

His mouth dropped open. "You didn't find it a bit suspicious that your Pops had so many guns?" he said incredulously.

"This is not uncommon in parts of the rural south. And I told you Pops was overprotective. Just thought he was being cautious. It never occurred to me he had a legitimate reason. Now I know he was preparing me to take care of myself."

A single black leather-bound book sat on the top shelf. He

pointed it out to Morgan, who waved him permission to go ahead. There wasn't enough light in the room to thoroughly review it, so he tucked it under his arm for later. After Morgan carefully checked every single gun, she pulled out two boxes of ammo and grabbed a black metallic handgun, and handed it to him.

"See how it feels in your hand."

The absolute horror on his face spoke volumes.

"Are you going to be a wuss, or do you want to live? Your choice," she deadpanned.

"My knowledge of guns is from research. I write about them, but I have no practical experience. Nor do I want to gain any."

"Like I asked. Do you want to live? Stand on your anti-gun platform with someone who isn't running from the mob and an outlaw motorcycle gang."

Bash was stunned into silence. Seeing the plethora of guns brought the precariousness of their situation into stark reality. *How the hell have I gotten myself into this mess?"*

Morgan sat him down in the only chair in the small room and knelt in front of him.

"Look, Bash. This is way too much for you to have to deal with. You didn't grow up with a grandfather putting a rifle in your hands at four-years-old. This is all surreal to you. It's commonplace for me. Granted, I never had to shoot anything other than a deer or rabbit when I went hunting with Pops. Let me get a few things for my personal safety, then we'll go. You can drop me off at the nearest car rental and head to the airport to catch a flight to Chicago. Your friend Gray will get you all set up with security."

Bash wasn't planning to bail on her. He was merely trying to get his head around the situation.

"What kind is it?" he asked.

"What kind is what?"

"The gun you gave me?"

"Does it really matter? You don't know one end from the other?"

"Morgan," he warned.

"It's a 9mm Sig Sauer. Easy to load. Easy to shoot."

"What about you? Aren't you going to take one?" he asked.

"Mine is a 9mm Glock. It's been in my backpack since we left the caretaker's cottage. It was wedged under the mattress when it was burglarized."

He took a few steps back. Dumbstruck.

"See. I didn't need a knife and a basement with a trap door to make you a prisoner. I've had a gun this whole time. Get this through your thick skull—you are not that irresistible! Now get your head out of your patootie and take this sucker. The safety is on, so you won't shoot yourself. When we get settled, I'll teach you the basics of loading and firing."

He stared at it for a few seconds. When he glanced down at her, he spoke with decisiveness. "I'm not dropping you anywhere. We are in this together. Until both of our screwed-up problems are resolved."

She nodded, and he took the gun. "Slip it in the back of your pants until you can pack it in your bag."

The cold metal against his back sent goosebumps across his skin. The ring of a phone startled him.

"It's not mine," he said.

"Mine either."

They frantically searched the room until they found a satellite phone in the corner on a small pedestal table. As Morgan picked it up, he leaned in to listen.

"Hello?"

"Ms. Skylar?"

"Who is this?"

"Robert Watson, your grandfather's attorney. Mr. Skylar gave me this number for emergencies if I couldn't reach you. Something happened yesterday that has me concerned. I wanted to notify you in case you were in danger."

They exchange worried looks.

"Go on, Mr. Watson."

"Mr. Skylar was a very private man, as I'm sure you know.

He found out he was sick a couple of years ago. That's when he sold the house and his shop and moved into a small apartment. He was afraid if something happened to him, no one would know to notify you. I suggested he send a letter to the local sheriff with instructions to contact me in the event of his death. Since he lives in a small community, the county paper listed his death with the other police incidents. One of the patrons of his shop saw it and wrote a lovely obituary about his business, expertise, and his big heart. Apparently, he's been fixing cars for people who couldn't afford it for years. The man had a picture of him sitting on a big motorcycle in front of his shop. You can tell he wasn't aware it was being taken. That letter gained a lot of attention and made its way to a popular motorcycle magazine.

"Anyway, the sheriff called yesterday to tell me about a man in his early fifties who came to see him. Claimed to be Mr. Skyler's son but he had a different name. Asa Kline." They both audibly gasped. "He had seen the obituary of his father's death in the magazine and recognized his picture. Wanted to know if there was anything left of his dad's possessions. Didn't even know where his dad had lived. The sheriff was leery, but the man seemed to know a lot about him. The sheriff told him that Mr. Skyler hadn't had anything of real value on him when he passed. Thankfully, the sheriff didn't know his apartment address. He did give the man your grandfather's wallet with $50 and his driver's license with an old address. The only other thing Mr. Skylar had on him was a piece of paper with vague directions to a cabin near Topton, North Carolina. It apparently had your name on it.

"A few minutes after Mr. Kline left, another officer came in and said he saw the man get on a motorcycle and join some men at the diner. They were some sort of motorcycle gang. The sheriff ran a quick check on the man and found out he had a violent record. Was just released from prison. Anyway, he called me in case I knew if any of Mr. Skyler's family needed to be warned. I had a suspicion Topton might be where your cabin is located. You need to be careful."

"Does he know about me?" Morgan asked in a weak voice.

"The sheriff doesn't know who you are, but there is no denying this Kline fellow now has your name."

"This was yesterday?" she asked.

"Yes, ma'am. Around 4 p.m. If you're at that cabin, Ms. Skylar, I suggest you get out."

"Thank you, Mr. Watson," her voice quivered.

CHAPTER FIFTEEN

So many thoughts ran through Morgan's head that she didn't know what to do first. She desperately wanted time to absorb the letter Pops left her. Analyze every word. So many things she never understood suddenly made sense, but now wasn't the time.

Don't panic. Keep a level head. First priority: get to safety. Pops' voice spoke in her head.

"How much time do you think we have?" Bash asked.

"Let's assume none," she answered, then grabbed a .45 automatic Smith and Wesson, checked the safety, and stuck it in the back of her jeans.

The phone rang again. This room had been a complete surprise, as was the phone. Now, it had rung twice within minutes. Her heart was ready to leap from her chest. In some weird way, she felt Pops was there orchestrating things. Prompting her to action.

"Bash, would you mind straightening the books and magazines back on the shelves of the bookcase? I'll answer the call. Whoever is calling wouldn't have this number unless Pops trusted them."

"Why take the time to put the books back? Isn't there something more important we can do, like get the hell out of here?" he asked. The phone continued to ring.

"Unless you want to supply a motorcycle gang with more guns, we need to get this room covered back up," she calmly explained, then grabbed the phone.

"Hello?"

"Is this Chip?" Morgan froze. It was a woman. How could she know her nickname? Only Pops and Beth called her that.

"Yes," she said hesitantly.

"My name is Martha. I'm a friend of your Pops. I run the beer and wine store just outside of Topton. Eli and I have been friends for years. Anyway, when he was here last month, he asked me to call this number if I ever saw anyone suspicious in my store who might be trouble. Some men on motorcycles asked if I could give them directions to Eli Skylar's cabin. I told them I didn't know him. They showed me an address of sorts, but I lied and told him there wasn't anything out there. That was a couple of hours ago. They said they were going to get something to eat and find someone who knew where Eli lived. I've been calling this number every fifteen minutes ever since. Didn't know if Eli would answer the phone, but I promised so..."

"Thank you," Morgan said.

"Is...Is he gone?" she asked with a trembling voice. *She knew. She knew he was dying, and he didn't tell me. Always protecting me.* The tears threatened again, but she didn't have time to wallow in grief.

"A couple of weeks ago," Morgan choked out.

"I...I loved him...though I never told him," she whispered. "There was only room in his heart for you. But that was okay. He didn't want you to know about me. I guess it's okay now that he's gone."

Those words stabbed at Morgan's heart. What could she say?

"Chip? Are you still there?"

"Y...Yes," Morgan breathed, clearing her throat. "I'm so glad he had you. Maybe we can meet one day." Learn more about the man her Pops had been.

"I'd like that," Martha said. "Be safe." She hung up.

"Let's go, Chip!" Bash yelled in the door, startling her back to reality.

She rushed out of the hidden room and slammed the door shut. Her blood boiled. "Don't call me that!" she screamed.

His face fell. She hadn't meant to hurt him, but he had no right. She was an emotional wreck, and if she didn't get her head in the game, she was going to get them killed. It usually took 30 minutes to get from Topton to their cabin, and that was if you knew how to get there. Someone unfamiliar with the area and the landmarks would take longer, but she couldn't count on that. It had already been two hours since they showed up at Martha's store. Time had run out.

Bash had returned everything to its place on the bookcase. Together, they moved it back against the wall. Morgan searched the floor for scratches or signs it had been moved but found none. Hopefully, if Asa discovered the trap door, he would have no reason to move the heavy bookcase.

"Anything else down here we need," Bash asked. "I took a quick glance at the leather book. It's a ledger. I'm pretty sure that's what he meant by your insurance policy. The deed to this cabin was inside it, too."

Morgan didn't know what to say to that. It was all becoming white noise, and that wasn't a good sign. She still had to get them out of there in one piece.

"Let me go up first. We need to grab our bags. At least we haven't had time to unpack anything. That call was a warning from a friend of Pops. Some guys on motorcycles were asking for directions to the cabin. They are probably on their way now."

"Shit! Go!" he said, pushing her up the ladder.

They gathered their stuff and rushed out the front door. Morgan ran around the house and turned off the generator and propane. There was nothing to be done about the groceries on the counter. Not enough time.

Bash started toward the rental. She caught his arm. "We aren't taking the SUV. There is only one way in and out of here. We'd probably run right into them. If we leave it parked here, they'll think we went for a hike. I'm hoping we'll be long gone by the time they figure out we're not coming back."

His expression was incredulous. "How are we going to get out of here if we leave our only means of transportation?"

The sound of motors traveled through the air. Panic flashed across Bash's face. "Shit!"

"This way," she said, heading toward the backyard at a full run. She knew he was behind her. It was only 40 feet from the back of the house to the forest. A good tracker could find their trail, but she doubted a bunch of biker drug dealers had that particular skill set. It was harder to maneuver through the woods with their bags, but they couldn't afford to leave any personal items behind.

"Are you going to tell me your grand plan?" he huffed.

The engines were getting louder and closer to the cabin.

"Just trust me. I'll get us out of here."

"Are you sure your job as a kindergarten teacher isn't a cover for your real job with the FBI or CIA or some other alphabet acronym?"

CHAPTER SIXTEEN

They were 15 minutes away from the cabin when they heard the engines stop. Their eyes sought each other's as they strained to listen. Silence. Bash was worried they would be followed, but Morgan assured him the dried leaves and pine needles would cover their tracks enough for the average person. At her Pops' insistence, all their hiking trails led from the front of the house. Morgan's grandfather had preplanned the escape route behind the house years ago. That was why the path remained mostly untouched.

They traveled along the top of the mountain until they reached a cluster of boulders. Morgan counted off 100 paces and headed down the mountain in a zigzagged pattern.

"I still can't hear anything," Bash said.

"That's good. We need to keep moving," Morgan insisted.

"You actually know where we're going, right?"

"Of course. Pops and I have made this trip enough times that I could find my way at night without a flashlight."

"Again. That never seemed strange to you? I think if my mom had done that, I would have had her committed as soon as I turned 21."

"Maybe yes. Maybe no. Depends on how much you trusted her."

He thought about that. His mom would have done anything to protect him, so he probably would have indulged her weirdness, too. But his mom didn't have a stash of guns to rival the local police force, either. Another ten minutes, and they reached a 25' wide stream at the bottom of the mountain. Morgan grabbed a small branch and began testing the depths. Bash assumed he was going to be getting his feet wet.

After a few minutes, Morgan threw down the stick. "Guess you figured out we're going across."

"Yep."

"We got lucky. This gets deep in the rainy seasons."

"How much farther once we get to the other side?"

"We follow the stream north around this adjacent mountain for about 30 minutes. A short walk up another mountain, and we should be right below County Road 1414. Even if those guys figured out which way we went, and trust me, they won't, it would take them at least an hour to get here on their bikes. We'll be long gone."

"Are we going to hitchhike?" he asked warily.

"You'll see."

The last few days, Bash had felt he was walking blindly into every situation. It wasn't comfortable for him, but he had to trust that Morgan had her reasons.

A while later, they were trudging up another mountain, and his feet were killing him. The two bags he carried were heavy, the weapon in the back of his pants was rubbing a raw place, and the bouncing ledger against his abdomen was chafing.

"There it is!" Morgan said excitedly, speeding her pace.

Bash tried to spot what had inspired her sudden exuberance, but all he saw was a metal shed a hundred feet away. When they reached the faded-gray shed, Morgan fished in her backpack and pulled out a key. She unlocked the padlock dangling from a heavy-duty chain on the door and grabbed the handle.

"You own this property too?" Bash asked, hoping what they were about to do was legal.

"We don't. Pops rented the land and constructed the shed about five years ago."

"And the owner wasn't suspicious of why your grandfather would want to construct a shed in the middle of nowhere?"

Morgan side-eyed him. "You are in the Appalachian Mountains, city boy. People don't stick their noses in other folk's business. You take your money and keep your mouth shut. It could be full of moonshine for all they know or care. There are probably 20 more sheds out here with a lot worse."

"Drugs?" he whispered.

She lifted a shoulder. "Who knows? Could be the remains of a trespasser or a nosey federal agent. Maybe even a famous writer," she smirked.

When Bash's eyes went wide, she shook her head. "You are just too easy." She flashed him a devilish grin. "Careful, Bash. Your wussy is showing again. Don't worry. We are about to leave this place in the dust." He stepped back as she flung the door open.

It was hard to tell when she was joking or if she was serious, but he decided too many questions would only make her wuss point. He stepped beside her and peered inside. A thrill spread through him. The contents were hidden under black protective covers emblazoned with the words *Harley Davidson*. He could hardly contain his teenage boy excitement. Grabbing one of the covers, he yanked it off.

"That one's mine," she said proudly, patting the handlebars of a shiny blue 1200 Sportster.

"You know how to ride a motorcycle?" Bash asked, surprised.

"You're kidding, right? How could I possibly be raised by one of the best motorcycle mechanics in the country and not know how to ride?"

He frowned and crossed his arms over his chest. "You said your Pops ran a bike repair shop?"

"I know. A motorcycle repair shop, but I've always called them bikes. He could do anything to motorcycles. Build them. Repair them. Dress them. You name it. Fixed classic cars on occasion, too. His business was word of mouth and cash only. His shop was out in the sticks, but that didn't matter. People from coast to coast sent their bikes to his shop. They all respected his need for privacy. It was almost like an exclusive club you had to be invited to join. I guess it makes sense that when one of his customers found out he died, they didn't think the privacy mattered anymore. That tribute was the only way my father could have found him. We didn't use social media. To answer your question. Of course, I can ride. The better question is, can you, city boy? Or are you going to have to get on the back of mine?"

No way in hell I'm going to lose my balls by getting on the back of her Sportster. "Hell yeah, I ride! My friend Alex has a couple of Harley Softtails. He couldn't decide if he wanted a black or a blue, so he bought both. Gray and I take turns riding with him."

Morgan yanked the cover off the second bike in a ta-da fashion. Bash's eyes grew into saucers at the reveal of a black Harley-Davidson Ultra Classic Electra Glide touring motorcycle.

"Wow. She's beautiful," he said, running his hands over the black leather seat. "Magnificent. This is my dream bike."

"Down, boy. We've got to get moving. There should be plenty of space in the saddlebags between the two bikes to handle the stuff we've got. The only problem is the temperature. We may freeze our patooties off, so put on as many layers of clothes as you can. Then we'll decide where we're going."

"I'll trust your expertise since I have zero knowledge of this mountain range."

"I don't think it's safe to go back to Hwy 74, so we'll have to take the backroads." She pulled out a paper map from a rusted metal cabinet. It was much more detailed than the GPS maps, highlighting obscure roads, points of interest, and service areas throughout the Appalachian Mountain range.

"We're here," she pointed on the map. "At the end of this dirt road, we intersect with Wayah Road, which will take us into Nantahala. We can get something to eat and buy some decent riding gear. Then, we'll head to Franklin, North Carolina. That's probably as far as we can get today without running out of daylight. It's too cold to ride at night. I'm hoping we'll be far enough away from the cabin to feel a little safer. Maybe your friend Gray can help us figure out our next move."

Bash nodded in agreement. She knew the area. He couldn't help thinking that Morgan had been wrong about Pops' paranoia and overprotectiveness. His timing had just been off.

Morgan opened a beat-up footlocker in the corner and pulled out a stack of folded leather clothes. She handed him a pair of chaps and a leather vest. "These belonged to Pops. He was larger than you, but if you can make it work, the chaps will protect your legs."

Next, she pulled out two high-tech-looking black helmets and handed one to him. "This is a full-face helmet with a built-in Bluetooth for intercom, integrated speakers, and a microphone. We can communicate on the road."

"Of course, we can. I would expect nothing less," he said, eyeing the new toy.

She put a few more items from the footlocker in her backpack, but Bash couldn't identify them from where he was standing without appearing nosey.

When they were packed up, layered up, and chapped up, they rolled the Harleys out of the shed and secured the padlock. Bash couldn't stifle the thundering of his heart or the shit-eating grin on his face as he turned over the engine of the sexiest machine he had ever seen. Feeling all that power between his legs was intoxicating. Morgan glanced over and rolled her eyes at his glee. He could tell she was proud of herself for making his day. She flipped her hair back, slipped on her helmet, and straddled the bike. Her leather chaps fit her like a glove. Her cute little, innocent kindergarten teacher image melted away.

Damn, that's hot! Who knew Morgan would turn out to be such a badass? A mental picture of her Pops smacking him off *his* bike flashed through Bash's head, making him flinch. He could visualize the tough old dude in his mind's eye even though he had never seen a picture. *What the actual fuck was that?* "Duly noted, Pops," he muttered under his breath as he gunned the throttle. "I apologize for mentally objectifying your granddaughter."

"Did you say something," Morgan called over the roar of

the engines. You'll need to turn up the volume on your Bluetooth like I showed you." Bash bit back a sly grin and nodded.

It was only a few miles to Nantahala. Morgan found a general store where they bought emergency snacks, sandwiches, and bottled water. The clothing selection in the store was limited, so they decided to wait until they reached Franklin to look for boots and outerwear. Bash tried to call Gray but couldn't get a signal.

Riding through the mountains on the bagger FLHTCU was a dream, but it was colder than he had anticipated. The chaps helped his legs, but even with two pairs of socks, his toes were freezing. It had to be in the mid-50s, which didn't seem that cold until they had been riding for a while. The frigid wind seeped into the creases of his clothes, making him feel like he was riding nude. Morgan had to be just as cold, but she showed no visible signs of discomfort. Little Miss glass half-full was annoying sometimes.

She led most of the trip. Now and then, she would slow down and check on him. Even though the helmets were equipped with radios, neither spoke unless it was necessary. He was too busy trying to figure out how the hell he ended up in this nightmare situation.

It was difficult to determine the time of day. The roads were shaded by mountains and trees that completely masked the location of the sun.

"Bash."

"Yeah?"

"We're about five miles from Franklin. There is a lookout point up ahead on the right. We're going to pull over."

"Got it."

They parked out of sight of the road and pulled off their helmets.

"What's up?" he asked.

"I want to have a look around Franklin and find a place to stay. Make sure our biker friends or your mafia boys aren't a step ahead of us. If nothing sticks out as odd, I'll be right back to get you."

"And if there is a problem?" he challenged.

She met his eyes with intensity. "I'll be back either way. We'll just have to figure out a plan B."

He felt the rise of irritation. "I feel like the schoolboy being sent to timeout so he'll stay out of trouble."

"I didn't mean it that way, Bash. My father thinks I'm a guy, so they will be looking for a guy, not a woman. The mafia guys are looking for you, not me. I've also been to Franklin numerous times. I'm familiar with the town. That's why I assumed I would be the logical choice. I meant no offense. Next time, I promise I will discuss it with you. If it makes you feel better, you can go."

It made sense, and he felt foolish for his bruised ego. "I guess that sounded defensive and unappreciative. It's the right call, but I would feel better if we talked it over in the future. I'm not completely helpless."

"I don't think you are. Again, I apologize. There is a factory on the outskirts of town. I'll tell you right before we reach it so you can break off and park behind it."

Morgan left him at the abandoned factory. She was back within 20 minutes.

"Everything appeared normal, so I went ahead and booked us a room. One will draw less attention. It has two queens. Hope you don't mind."

"That's fine. Are there any shops in town? I hate to complain, but I'm freezing my ass off."

She chuckled. "Yeah. There's an outdoor store. Not sure about the selection, but they should have some fleece lined denim and heavier coats. Boots and wool socks, too. We should do that now before they close."

"Sounds good. Then we can get something hot to drink." He shifted around, trying to stretch his thighs. "My legs are locking up, and my ass is completely numb. That's what happens when I get off my exercise routine."

"Yep. Tomorrow, you're going to be sore. Me too. I haven't ridden much this year. Better pick up some Tylenol."

CHAPTER SEVENTEEN

The motel room was clean but in desperate need of a renovation. They had a productive shopping trip, finding thermal underclothes, down jackets, thick wool socks, and hiking boots. Morgan felt guilty when Bash paid for her clothes. She preferred to pay her own way, but the only credit card she brought had hit its limit when she rented the SUV in Chattanooga. With her on-hand cash dwindling, she needed to check with her bank to see if her inheritance money had been deposited into her checking account.

Pulling her laptop from her backpack, she sat cross-legged on the bed and turned it on. She checked her emails first. An email from Pops' lawyer said he forgot to ask her if she wanted to liquidate all the investments. He recommended she leave them with the current investor, who had done well. The investments had all been set up in her name when she was a child, then transferred into an IRA when she began working. The funds from the sale of his business had been added to the investment portfolio. The profits from the house went into her bank account. The information was being FedExed to her address in Dunwoody. *How the heck had Pops set up an investment account, and me not know about it?* She continued reading until she found an actual dollar amount for the total inheritance—$1,464,739.23. She fell back against the headboard in shock. It couldn't be right. She leaned back toward the screen, wiped her eyes, and read it again. The same amount stared back at her.

"Everything okay?" Bash asked, startling her.

Lifting her gaze from the screen, she met his belly button just above the top of his black knit boxers. Her eyes widened as they slowly moved up the sinewy muscles of his abs to the light sprinkling of hair on his chest. She felt a blush travel up her neck and spread across her face. Her cheeks burned.

"Holy Moley, Bash! Put some pants on!"

"I have on pants. They're called boxers."

"Shorts, maybe?" she suggested.

"Why? I'm going to bed. Don't bitch. You're the one who booked one room. All I can say is if you're offended, don't look," he said, popping down beside her to see what she was reading.

She scooched further up to the headboard. "Do you mind?" she asked, grabbing her laptop. He pulled it out of her hands and sat it on his bare legs.

"Not at all. What is this? Wow! And I was worried you didn't have enough money to buy your clothes," he laughed.

She punched him in the arm and tried unsuccessfully to get it back. "That's none of your business. Pops left that to me."

Bash read the entire email and looked up at her. "It was certainly a successful business. Have you checked your bank account?"

She shook her head and pulled it from his hands. "I was about to before you got all grabby."

A few clicks later the deposit appeared on her screen showed $298,546.18.

"You're fucking rich. He really took care of you."

She couldn't answer, her throat too thick with emotion. He pulled a t-shirt out of his backpack and slipped it over his head. Sitting next to her, he put his arm around her shoulder. She fell against his chest and cried until there was a big wet spot over his heart.

"I'm sorry. There hasn't been much time for me to process everything. The money was too much. We never had that kind of money when I was growing up. Plenty of food, and my clothes were okay, I guess. Nothing fancy. The house was a small two-bedroom, but we had quite a bit of property." She sat up and put the laptop back on her lap.

"How long did Pops have his business?"

"About 23 years. As his business became more established, it attracted wealthier clientele. He bought old bikes and restored them in his spare time. Built racing bikes. He was constantly in demand. A couple of guys worked in his shop, but he handled the specialty work. I guess it added up."

Bash lifted her chin from the screen and held her eyes. "He was saving for you, Morgan."

"I...I guess," she barely spoke.

He handed her a box of tissues sitting on the nightstand. As she wiped the tears from her face and sniffed, she asked, "Want to look at the ledger Pops left?"

He grabbed the ledger off the bedside table and handed it to her. "I was reading through it while you showered. It's interesting. Now I know why they were hellbent on finding your Pops. It's dangerous for you to have this in your possession. For us to even read it. It could be a death sentence if we don't get some serious help."

Bash's comments only doubled the anxiety she already felt. With trepidation, she opened it and stared. *The Dragon Fire Motorcycle Club Income and Expenses*. The pages contained dates, client names, illegal activities, member cuts, banks, account numbers, and locations. The entries ended the day before her Birthday. Reality hit. Everything Pops revealed in his letter was true. She took a deep breath and let it out. When she turned toward Bash, the color had drained from her face.

"You're right. This information is lethal. Even if we gave it back, they would never let us live. We've seen too much. I recognized some of the names. That senator from California is in Washington DC now." Morgan's voice was strained with emotion.

"I recognized him, too. There's more than one elected official on that list of purchases."

"Why would Pops do this to me?"

Bash took her hand and held her eyes. "Morgan, I don't

think he intended that at all. I doubt it even occurred to him. Think about it. He had the ledger for 25 years, and as far as he was concerned, the club left him alone because of it. He assumed it would be the same for you. I think his mistake was in underestimating his son. Maybe Asa's planning to use the ledger as his way back into power with the Dragon Fire. He may know exactly whose names are on the list, and now that those men are rich and high-profile, it's a cash cow. Blackmail is a huge motivator. Those are all reasons for the ledger to become relevant to the club again."

"I'm so sorry I got you mixed up in all of this."

"You didn't get me mixed up in anything. This fell into your lap. Besides, I got you mixed up in my drama first. You are correct about one thing. We do need help. I'll make some calls."

CHAPTER EIGHTEEN

Morgan was sound asleep when Sebastian slipped out of the motel room to call Gray. The night sky was filled with stars and enough moonlight to easily find a greenspace with picnic tables, where he took a seat. The motel parking lot was mostly empty. They appeared to roll up the streets at 8 pm, but it was the off-season. According to his cell, it was almost 10 p.m. It rang three times before Gray picked up.

"Bash. Good to hear from you, man. I thought you were going to call as soon as you got to the cabin. Your follow-through sucks."

"Do you realize every time I talk to you, you're admonishing me like I'm one of your kids? Cut it out. I'm a grown man!" Bash said with frustration. Why hadn't he noticed it before? Maybe because he had relied on Gray too much to keep his life in order. When had he become so co-dependent?

"Chill, Bash. I didn't mean anything by it. Tell me what's going on," Gray asked, trying to placate him.

"I'll get to that in a minute. Did you meet with the security company? Get a background check on Morgan's grandfather, Eli Skylar?"

"Yes, to both. I met with Samuel Barrett of SMB Protection Agency and filled him in on the attack from Fontana's men. He's checking out Maximillian Fontana, too. He ran a more thorough background check on Morgan Skylar. Her record is spotless. Not even a parking ticket."

An image of Morgan pulling guns out of her grandfather's

safe and checking for ammunition came to mind, and he snickered.

"What? Have you found evidence to the contrary?"

"I have not. Go ahead with what you were saying."

"As far as her grandfather, Eli Skylar, he was a highly respected motorcycle and classic car mechanic in closed circles around the country. His personal life was completely invisible to his customers, and his services were word of mouth and through recommendation only. He was a closely guarded secret within the motorcycle who's who. There was no trace of Morgan or any other children in his background check.

"The two mechanics who worked with him for years knew nothing about his life outside of work. Never met one of his friends. Didn't think he had any. A couple of years ago, when they heard Skylar was going to retire, his mechanics talked one of Skyler's wealthy clients into going into a partnership with them to buy the business. As soon as the purchase was closed, they moved the business to Knoxville, Tennessee. That seemed suspicious, so Sam sent a local PI to Knoxville to talk to them. The new owners said the most valuable part of the business had been Eli Skylar himself, but the client list and the recommendations from apprenticing with Skylar for 20 years proved enough to establish themselves. The move out of state was one of Skylar's conditions of the sale. The most interesting thing about Skylar — he doesn't appear to have existed before 1994, a huge red flag. If we had his fingerprints, we might be able to do a better search, but everything seems to fit with what Morgan told you."

"It's not necessary to look further. Is there anything else important before I fill you in on what's happened on our end?"

"Yeah, and it's not good. Maximillian Fontana called me today. On my private cell."

"Shit. How did he get your number?" Bash asked.

"Not relevant at this point. He's determined to meet with you. All he wants to do is make his case. If you still don't want to be involved with his project, he promised to back off."

"Then why the hell is he sending his goons after me? I don't believe shit out of his mouth," Bash yelled.

"I asked the same thing. Since I figured he already knew what went down at the lake, I used that to prove his lack of credibility. Bash, he was truly shocked. I mean, I could tell he didn't know anything about it. He was really pissed. Thinks one of his top guys decided to interfere. Took it upon himself to make a move. If Fontana is lying, he's a damn good actor. It didn't dissuade him. He still wants to meet with you. When and where are up to you. Swears he'll come alone."

"You really don't believe him, do you?"

"My gut tells me he's being upfront. I talked to Alex about it. We think it's our best option. So does Sam Barrett. You can control when, where, and how. Fontana doesn't care if it's Sitka, Alaska. He was that serious. We'll have plenty of security around you. If you don't meet with him, it could escalate."

Bash ran his finger through his hair and rubbed the back of his neck. "This isn't our only problem."

"What do you mean?"

Sebastian spent the next half hour filling him in on everything they found at the cabin and how he and Morgan had made their second hasty retreat. Bash waited in silence while Gray processed the new information.

"This is way fucked up. Just a minute..."

"Gray?... Gray?... Where the hell did you go? If you don't answer..." he bellowed.

"I'm pulling up Google Maps. From what you said about Morgan's grandfather's mountain cabin, I figured that you were somewhere in the Appalachians. Tell me where, and I'll have a helicopter to you in the morning. We'll get you to the nearest airport, and I'll have a plane waiting to bring you home."

"No! No helicopter. No plane."

"What do you mean 'no?'" Gray shrieked. "You do understand you are now being sought by two different criminal organizations? I know this might be exciting and feels like you've stepped in one of your novels, but you are in real danger. We need to get you the hell out of there!"

"I'm not leaving Morgan."

"You know her problems have nothing to do with you, right? I don't want to sound like a prick, but you can get her somewhere safe and walk away."

"Considering she saved my ass in Guntersville when she could have split, leaving her to deal with this alone is not an option for me," Bash said with steel in his voice.

"Is this your dick talking?" Gray asked sarcastically.

"Grayson Lewis, if you were standing in front of me, I would be tempted to pound you into the ground. Her grandfather may have taught her survival skills and how to think on her feet, but she's an innocent kindergarten teacher, for Christ's sake. Unpretentious. Open-hearted. How could I possibly take advantage of her? You'd have to meet her to understand. Call Barrett and get a recommendation on her best options. Leaving her alone with no one in the world to help her isn't one of them. Got it?"

"Got it. This isn't like you, Bash, so there must be something special about this young woman. Do you know what she wants to do with the ledger? It's a ticking time bomb. Has she thought about turning it over to the FBI?"

"We haven't talked specifics. Her grandfather wanted her to keep it for insurance, but I don't see her wanting to spend the rest of her life in hiding. We need to find a way to turn it over to the authorities and stay safe. Get those guys arrested," Bash said with conviction. "Can you have Alex find her an attorney? She lives in the Atlanta area, so maybe that would be a place to start. A good one, Gray. Someone Alex trusts."

Gray sighed deeply, his tell for impatience. "You going to pay her fees too?"

"Now you're assuming she's taking advantage of me. Not true. Pay the retainer for convenience's sake, but she has her own money. Seems Eli Skyler did pretty well for himself."

"What about Fontana? Will you meet with him?" Gray asked.

"If Fontana wants to meet and Barrett's security company can guarantee my safety, it might be the only solution to this mess, but I want to talk to Fontana first. Get a read on him. Give me his private number. I'll ditch my phone after I speak to him. Use one of the other burner numbers if you need to call."

"All right. I'll set up a Zoom meeting with Alex and Sam Barrett to discuss the new developments. How long are you going to be in your current location?"

"We're moving to a larger city tomorrow morning. I'll call you when we get to our next destination."

"Skyler's bagger sounds like a nice ride," Gray joked.

Bash smiled to himself. "You have no idea."

When Bash stood to go back to the motel room, he came face to face with Morgan. She was barefoot in a jersey and sleep pants, her arms folded across her chest.

"What are you doing out here without a coat? Trying to catch pneumonia?" he asked, hoping she hadn't overheard his conversation.

She stared at him, then averted her eyes. He saw hurt in her eyes.

"I woke up and wondered where you were. Just wanted to make sure you didn't get kidnapped or anything," she said, trying to sound light-hearted, but it was forced. Her eyes were focused on the ground as if there was something fascinating to see, avoiding his eyes.

"Checking in with Gray. I didn't want to keep you awake."

She finally met his gaze, shivering in the night air.

"I've been thinking," she began, biting and twisting her lower lip. "As much as I appreciate your help with our getaway today, it might be better for the both of us if we split up. Beth called a few minutes ago. Once I find a place to store my bike in Ashville, I'm going to fly to Nashville and stay at her apartment until I can sort this out. Pops doesn't need his motorcycle anymore, and since you really took to it, it's yours. I know you'll take good care of her. That way, I wouldn't have to think about some stranger owning Roxy. It shouldn't be hard to have it shipped to Chicago. Your friend Gray can send a plane for you, and you'll be home for afternoon tea."

He took a step toward her. "Morgan…"

She held up a hand. "No Bash. It's for the best. You have your own issues, and you don't need mine compounding things. I'm not trying to take advantage of you, and you don't owe me anything." Turning her back to him, she walked back to the motel room.

Shit! She overheard my conversation with Gray. What she suggested might be the best option, but it wasn't one he was willing to accept. It was a lie. She hadn't spoken to Beth. He was sure of it. Not that Beth wouldn't help her if asked, but Morgan would never put her friend in danger. She was taught at a young age to depend on herself, and that was exactly what she was doing. Putting others before herself was what she did.

When he got back to the room, Morgan was tucked in bed, facing the wall. Her phone lay on the nightstand between them. Pushing aside his guilt, he picked up her cell and tried to turn it on. The battery was dead. Confirmation that Beth had not called. She was going it alone.

He fell back on the bed, wondering how the hell he could possibly get to sleep.

CHAPTER NINETEEN

Morgan planned to get up early and be gone by the time Bash woke up. That would prevent any awkwardness between them. She had an internal alarm clock that woke her up within five minutes of 5 a.m. every morning. When she awoke, the room was completely dark. She reached over to grab her phone, hoping it would give her enough light to get to the bathroom, but the battery was dead. She remembered thinking 'why bother' last night, forgetting she might need the light or to know what time it was. With an inward sigh, she felt her way around the bed, found her backpack on the chair, and then made her way to the bathroom. In an effort not to wake Bash, she flipped on the light after she closed the door.

As she washed her face and brushed her teeth, she thought about leaving a note. Decided the motorcycle was thanks enough. She would have to remember to send him the title when she got home. If it was safe for her to go home. The sooner she got out of his hair, the better for him. She looked around the room one last time, barely making out the outline of the rumpled bed where Bash peacefully slept. It broke her heart to leave without saying goodbye, but she knew he would feel obligated to ask her to stay.

Bundled in her coat, fleece cap, and boots, she threw her backpack over her shoulder. When she grabbed for the door handle, she realized she had forgotten Pops' ledger. She felt around the small desk but found nothing. The only other place it could be was on the table beside Bash's bed. If that were the case, she had no alternative but to turn on the table lamp.

The flash of light momentarily blinded her. When she opened her eyes, she saw a fully made bed but no Sebastian Bartoli. Stupidly looking around the room, she couldn't work out where he could have gone. His leather case and backpack were missing, along with Pops' ledger.

"What the heck?" She flung the door open and ran outside.

It was still dark, and it took a few moments for her to get her bearing. Their bikes were parked behind the motel. Running around the side of the building, she stopped dead in her tracks. Bash sat comfortably on the Ultra Classic with one foot propped up while he ate a granola bar and read something on his phone, the soft light outlining his strong profile.

"Bash? What are you doing?" she asked softly, feeling a flood of warmth. He hadn't left her.

He looked up in mock annoyance. Lowering his phone, she could no longer see his expression clearly. "It's about damn time you got your ass out of bed. Let's get moving. I'm not in the mood to dodge bullets this morning." He turned on his headlight and started the engine. Revved it a couple of times. She watched, stunned. "You waitin' for a fuckin' written invitation, Chip?"

Shaking her head, she struggled to keep her voice steady. "No, Bash. I'm asking what you're doing? Aside from using your potty mouth. And you know exactly what I mean. Please don't make sarcastic remarks. Is it pity? Guilt?"

She had heard enough of his conversation with Gray to know they didn't trust her or her grandfather. They had run extensive background checks on them. His friend wanted to send a helicopter to pick him up. The only reason Bash had refused was because she had helped him escape the lake house. Guilt or obligation. She didn't need either.

He rubbed his leather-gloved hand over his face and turned away for a few seconds. When he turned back to face her, his features were hidden in the shadows. She wished she could see if his face reflected his words.

"The truth?" he asked.

She nodded.

"I'm not exactly sure what I'm doing, Morgan, but it's not for any of the reasons you might think. We've both had a lot thrown at us. So far, we seem to be doing okay handling it together. We've formed a partnership. A weird support system. Us against them. As crazy as it sounds, for the first time in a long time, I feel like I'm taking responsibility for my own decisions. I have gotten entirely too comfortable with other people managing my life. It has made things easier for me. My friends are my managers, and I trust them, but I wouldn't have been at the lake house in the first place if it hadn't been for their insane plan.

"Somewhere along the way to success, I stopped thinking for myself even when my gut told me it was a bad idea. Since all this trouble began, I've been the one giving the orders to them. And you've been giving them to me," he laughed. "But that's okay. You know what you're doing and have always had a solid plan. Your instincts are good. I want to see this through for the both of us. You're good at cutting through the bullshit and breaking things down for me. I like that. You tell me the truth, not what I want to hear. Does any of that make sense?"

She smiled and walked over to her Sportster, slipping her helmet over her head. "Only if we can work on some adjectives and adverbs that don't begin with an 'f' and end with a 'k.'"

He snickered and put on his helmet. "Let me clarify something. Just because I'm a successful writer doesn't mean I'm an eloquent one. You obviously haven't read my books. Don't hold your breath on that request."

The drive to Ashville was much more comfortable with the addition of winterwear, but they still took it slow, arriving around 9 a.m. After eating a huge egg and pancake breakfast, they found a two-bedroom apartment rental. The owner, who lived right next door, agreed to keep the rental off the books when Bash offered to pay double the regular rate. Once they got the keys and settled in, he suggested they explore the town.

The picturesque town of Ashville was set in the beautiful Blue Ridge Mountains. It was known for its historic and diverse architecture, art galleries, unique shops, and excellent restaurants.

The sky was vivid blue, and the sun provided just enough warmth to make it a perfect crisp fall day for wandering. They walked, bought homemade fudge, picked up souvenirs, lunched at a microbrewery, and praised and criticized artworks as if neither of them knew a thing about it. For a few short hours, they were typical tourists exploring, eating, drinking, laughing, and having fun while a storm brewed around them. When they got back to the apartment, they both took a much-needed afternoon nap.

When Morgan woke up, she decided to do a little online research. Regardless of the destination they decided on, taking the motorcycles was neither comfortable nor practical. They were going to need to find a place to store them. Bash assured her that her Honda Civic would be transported from the lake house back to her home in Georgia by the time she returned. The SUV rental they had left at the mountain cabin was the current worry on her mind. She hoped Bash would help with a solution. Since she only rode her Sportster in the mountains anyway, she could get it out of storage on her next visit.

"Damn. I over-slept," Bash yawned, lumbering into the living room. He plopped down on the sofa beside her and glanced at his watch. "Shit! It's almost 4 o'clock."

"I haven't been up long either," she sighed.

He leaned over and snuck a look at her iPhone.

"You are so nosey."

"I figured you would jerk it away if you didn't want me to see it. What do we need a storage unit for?"

She frowned. "We? You just assumed it includes both of us."

"Of course. We're partners in crime, aren't we?" He flashed a mischievous grin.

"I guess we are. So, partner, we need to find another means of transportation. There is a storage company in town with climate control that would be perfect for the motorcycles. You can have yours shipped to Chicago at some point. I'll leave mine in storage until I decide what I want to do with it."

He twisted his mouth to one side. "You were serious about

giving it to me?" She nodded. "It's too much. I'll have Gray send you a check."

Her mouth tensed, and hurt bubbled up as she turned on him. "You will not! If you don't want it, that's fine, but don't insult me by trying to pay me for something that meant a lot to my Pops. Seeing you enjoy it makes me happy."

His face sobered, and he placed his hand on her arm. "It wasn't my intent to insult. That bike has got to cost over $30,000, and that doesn't include all the chrome and extras. That's a lot of money to be giving away to a man you just met."

She removed his hand and stood up, glaring down at him with fire in her eyes. "That's right. You can't really trust me, can you? I must have some ulterior motive. Angling for something. If you don't want it, I'll sell it."

"Don't do that," he said quietly. "I don't think any of those things."

"You didn't have me investigated?" That caught him by surprise.

"A lot of people want something from me, Morgan. All the time. The background check merely confirmed what I'd already figured out for myself. Now, can we drop this subject? As far as the motorcycle is concerned, I'm worried about taking advantage of you."

"And you have all the money in the world to buy whatever you want. I'm aware, but I gave it to you because I thought you would appreciate it. Bash, the money doesn't mean that much to me. What Pops left me won't change me or my lifestyle. It will only make things easier."

He reached for her hand and intertwined his fingers with hers. "Then I graciously accept your gift and promise to take good care of … Roxy, did you say?"

She nodded.

"Then I thank you from the bottom of my heart. Better?"

She felt her face flush and slipped her hand from his. "Better."

CHAPTER TWENTY

"Fontana." It was a one-word greeting. Abrupt. No casual friendliness, but then again, Bash hadn't expected it.

"Sebastian Bartoli. Seems you've gone to great lengths to speak to me."

The phone went silent for a few seconds. Was Fontana caught off guard by his abruptness?

"Mr. Bartoli, thank you for returning my call. I'm quite anxious to meet with you in person, as I'm sure Mr. Lewis has relayed to you. This project is personal to me, and I feel you would be best suited to delivering the results I want."

"I'm flattered that you are offering me this opportunity, but I am not a nonfiction writer. I'm probably the least qualified person to take on this project," Bash enthused.

"Obviously, I disagree." It was said like a man used to getting his way.

"You made that point perfectly clear when you sent the welcome wagon to the lake house I was renting," Bash said sarcastically. *Don't poke the bear,* he reminded himself.

"I addressed this with Mr. Lewis. I had nothing to do with an attack. Someone who works for me obviously became over-zealous in the pursuit of your cooperation. I assure you it will be dealt with swiftly."

"We haven't even formally met, Mr. Fontana. I found myself climbing out of an upstairs window in the middle of the night. An innocent young woman, a perfect stranger to me who was staying on the same property, had her cottage vandalized, her car window smashed, and was completely terrorized from the experience." That last part wasn't exactly true, but it felt more compelling to his argument. "If all of that happened before I agreed to work with you, I can only imagine what calamities an actual collaboration might bring."

"There is more to this project than I'm in a position to discuss over the phone. I give you my word, if you are not agreeable after I have presented my case, I will back off. I am doing everything in my power to prevent any recurrence of the threats you encountered. At this point, I have nothing but my personal assurance to convince you."

"Is it safe to assume the men who came after me are no longer in pursuit?" Again, there was silence. It spoke volumes. "What the actual fuck! If you think I'm coming anywhere near you when you still have those gangsters looking for me, you're out of your mind! We're done!"

"Please, Mr. Bartoli! Don't hang up! It's not my doing, and to be honest, I'm not sure who or why they are focused on you. That's one of the reasons we need to meet."

Bash could feel anger oozing from every pore. How could Fontana not know who was after him? The whole thing felt wrong. There was a big piece of the puzzle missing.

"Are you still there, Mr. Bartoli? There is only so much I can say on the phone. My organization has been compromised. I'll text you tomorrow with a number to call me. Tell me the city you want to meet in, and I'll come alone. When I get there, the place will be of your choosing. No one in my organization will know where I am."

"I'm destroying this phone as soon as we hang up. I'll text you a location."

The call ended. When he glanced up, Morgan was watching, her face pale.

"This is a total bullshit," he said.

"I couldn't help hearing you yelling," she said. "Where do you want to meet him?"

"You're assuming I'm going to meet him at all?" Bash said

indignantly. "I could have agreed to throw him off."

She frowned, crinkled her brow, and planted her hands firmly on her hips, just as he would expect her to do when she disciplined one of her preschoolers. It was kind of cute, but he thought better of telling her as much.

"Yes, we are meeting him," she said firmly. "Let me pull up an online map and take a look."

They spent 30 minutes looking over possible sites. Bash decided he needed to get an update from Gray before any decision was made.

"I was about to call you," Gray said. "Just so you know, I've worked harder since you left on sabbatical, than when you are actually here."

"Good to know you're finally earning your paycheck. Any good news for me?" Bash asked.

"I've got you on speaker. Alex, Sam, and I have been working on this all day. Since this involves Morgan too, why don't you put us on speaker," Gray suggested.

Morgan joined them. All the necessary introductions were made.

"I'll start with Morgan," Alex said. "We needed an attorney who has worked and negotiated deals with the FBI, and I think I've found him. Parker Livingston. He has an excellent reputation and is licensed in eight states, including Georgia and California. Since the Dragon Fire Motorcycle Club operates in California, we thought it might be prudent. Livingston is rarely available, but he agreed to a Zoom conference with me. Once he heard the circumstances, his interest was piqued. He agreed to take the case. Bash alluded to Gray that there were some prominent names listed in the ledger. Is that true? It was one of the things that attracted Livingston to the case."

"Yes," Morgan confirmed.

Morgan glanced at Bash, surprised he had shared that. "Some political officials are associated with the purchase of drugs and prostitution. According to the letter Morgan's grandfather left her, Dragon Fire was just getting started in illegal adoptions and human trafficking. There are very detailed notations. Made me wonder if any of the customers were being extorted. None of them would want to be exposed, whether the statute of limitations has expired or not," Bash said.

"That ledger is dynamite, and you need to get rid of it as soon as possible," Alex said. "The sooner Livingston gets the FBI involved, the better."

"If I had somewhere to send it, I could drop it in the mail," Morgan suggested.

"That's not a bad idea," Sam Barrett agreed.

"It's got to be somewhere that wouldn't put anyone in harm's way," Morgan said. "I couldn't live with myself if someone got hurt."

"You didn't cause any of this, Morgan," Bash offered supportively.

"What if you took it to the local police station or FBI office?" Gray asked.

"We want to control the turnover," Alex said quickly. "Morgan needs assurances of protection. Freedom from prosecution should something come to light about her grandfather's more current activities. Then..."

"My grandfather's what?" Morgan boomed with fury.

"What the fuck, Alex!" Bash scolded. "Morgan didn't even know who her grandfather or her parents were until yesterday!"

"Calm down, Sebastian," Alex said in an even voice. "I'm not accusing Morgan of anything. I'm trying to protect her from some hotshot FBI agent trying to find a scapegoat. I guarantee they will start pouring over her grandfather's business for any illegal activities based solely on his past. That's why we want an experienced attorney to control the narrative. They may try to freeze her assets. Her name could become public in the investigation, affecting her reputation by association. Tie this whole thing up in court for years."

Bash glanced at Morgan. Her face was crestfallen. A single tear streamed down the side of her cheek. He felt like crap that he had brought her into the meeting, but she had to know what was ahead of her so she would be prepared.

She cleared her throat. "My grandfather's attorney, Robert Watson, handled the sale of his motorcycle repair shop and all his other assets in my inheritance. Mr. Watson had an accountant audit 21 years of receipts and ledgers. He wanted to be sure that they were thorough before he and the accountant signed off on the sale. In other words, let the FBI look all they want," Morgan said defiantly. "Pops told me a long time ago that he would never do anything to jeopardize losing me, and I believed him.

"I haven't spent a dime of that money. If they find some trumped-up reason to take what Pops worked hard to earn, I'll be sad that he was discredited, but I won't miss it. I can take care of myself. I owe that to Pops. I appreciate y'all finding me an attorney, but I'll take it from here. Goodbye, gentlemen."

Bash's heart squeezed as he watched her walk out the front door.

"Way to go, Alex," Gray said. "For an attorney, you have zero tact. That woman saved Bash's ass, and you made her feel like a criminal."

"She had to understand what she was facing. How the FBI may read the situation," Alex said in his defense.

"Yeah, well, that was for her attorney to explain to her, not you, embarrassing her in front of us. It was a dick move, Alex," Bash said, rubbing his hand over his face. "I got to go. I'll talk to you guys later."

"No! Wait, Bash! We haven't talked about Fontana or your security y…" but Gray didn't get to finish his thought.

Bash disconnected. He didn't give a damn what they wanted to say. He needed to find Morgan.

When he didn't find her on the porch, he looked in the garage to make sure her bike was still there. Even though he saw her Sportster, he had an impulse to touch it just to be sure. He didn't want to examine why there was a sudden pang in his chest at the thought of her disappearing from his life as quickly as she had appeared. He remembered passing a park a couple of blocks away and decided to check it out. Perhaps she needed some alone time to process the possibility that the authorities may try to implicate her or Pops in illegal activities. He hadn't considered it either. It appeared she wasn't the only one who had been naive.

Bash couldn't help feeling his friends had let him down. Their lack of empathy for Morgan, after what she had selflessly done for him, left him cold. They spoke to her in a sterile manner, addressing her possible legal perils rather than the real threats she was facing to her life. When had his friends become so self-serving? All about damage control without regard to the effects on others. When had he?

He spotted her sitting on a wooden-seated rope swing hanging from the branch of a sturdy oak tree. Head down, she swayed from side to side, watching the toe of her boot drag through the dirt. Her back was to him, so she didn't see his approach. When she suddenly stopped, he did too, feeling sure she felt his eyes on her — but that wasn't the case. He stared as she used her feet to turn the swing around and around until the rope was twisted taut against her stomach. With both hands firmly on the sides of the rope, her shoulders and head extended backwards, and her hair barely touching the ground, she picked up her feet and laughed out loud as the ropes unwound at a dizzying pace. All the tension on her face was gone. The last rays of sunset caught the reflection of the golden highlights in her free-flying cinnamon-red hair. The pure joy that exuded from her angelic face was breathtaking. He wasn't sure he had seen anything so moving in his life. In that unguarded moment of release, she was completely free. Lost in whatever memory she was reliving in her head and heart. That's when he knew. He had to leave. His presence was an intrusion. These were her few moments of escape, and he had no right to witness it. Rushing out of the park, he turned back to make sure that he hadn't been seen. The swing had stilled, and her face was lifted toward the setting sun, maybe in prayer. He would never know, but he would never forget it either.

CHAPTER TWENTY-ONE

Sebastian was asleep on the blue sectional sofa when Morgan arrived back at the apartment. She knew her abrupt exit from the meeting earlier must have seemed like a childish tantrum to the powerful men working for Bash. They claimed to be helping her, but she knew they were only doing it at Bash's insistence and were merely trying to mitigate the trouble she might cause him. Their scare tactics were to keep her under control and eventually eradicate her from his life. They had all the answers. Who was she but a silly kindergarten teacher? The daughter of a human trafficker and the granddaughter of a man who they believe never left his criminal past. Their suspicion that she was somehow involved hung over their words. Bash had tried to defend her, but she knew that, ultimately, he would follow the advice and course his friends had set. She would accept the attorney they offered, but she would do so on her own terms without their interference.

"What time is it?" Bash asked, rubbing his eyes.

"After six. You hungry?"

He sat up and swung his legs on the floor. "I could eat."

"How does pizza sound? I'm starving."

"Can we talk first?" he asked with a serious tone.

She eased down on the coffee table in front of him. "If we have to," she said, twisting her lips.

"I'm sorry about what happened before. My friends can be jerks sometimes."

"They're only looking out for your best interest," she conceded.

"Yeah, well, there are two of us in this partnership, and that doesn't work for me."

"*They* are your partners, Bash. I'm just a girl who serendipitously stumbled into your life."

"We've been through this before. I'm getting tired of repeating myself. I'm beginning to think you don't trust me." He put his hands on her knees, then enunciated every word. "We are seeing this through together. Nothing has changed because my overprotective friends think they know what's best for me."

"What do you mean?"

"I mean, you and I will work directly with Sam Barrett, the security consultant Gray hired. Get his advice on the best way to meet Fontana. Next, we call what's his name—Parker..."

"Livingston," she added.

"Right. We call him and get going on a solution for getting rid of Pops' ledger and keeping you safe. The whole 'you could be in trouble thing' is ridiculous. You're the unwitting victim in all of this. We can't prevent the FBI from looking into Pops' activities, but like you said, they won't find anything. I'll take your word for that until I have solid evidence to the contrary. The man gave up everything for you. I don't see him fucking that up after the trouble he went through to save you. I'll share with Gray and Alex on a need-to-know basis, and right now, I don't want them to know shit! We good?"

Relief flooded her. Unable to contain her gratitude, she threw her arms around his neck, slamming him against the back of the sofa.

"Thank you," she whispered against his ear. She felt his body stiffen, then relax as he lightly rubbed her back. Feeling things becoming awkward, she let go and moved back to the table.

"Sorry," she flushed with embarrassment. "I got carried away."

He wiped his hand down his face and cleared his throat. "No problem."

———

Morgan ordered pizza while Bash pulled his burner phone out of his pocket to find the numbers Gray had texted him for Sam Barrett and Parker Livingston. He squeezed his eyes closed and felt a pang of guilt when he found close to 20 missed tests.

Gray: I'm sorry! Don't cut me out, Bash!

Gray: Text me!

Gray: Call me!

Gray: I'll do whatever you want. Tell me where you are. This has gone on long enough.

Gray: We're brothers, man! What the fuck?

Gray: Please tell me you're not dead on the side of the fuckin' road somewhere!

Gray: OK. Agreed. That last one was stupid, but I'm thinking that unless you tell me otherwise!

Gray: I'm only looking out for you like I've done for years. The same way you've had my back. Now you suddenly push me away?

Gray: As your best friend, I deserve better than this…

Gray: If you're in love with her, I'll do everything to help her too.

Every word pierced his heart, but for some reason, the last one prompted a reply.

Bash: It's not like that. We've formed a bond I can't explain. Our circumstances are kind of similar, yet totally different. We're both being hunted. She has no one. I can't leave her until I know she's safe. Sure. This is out of character for me. I'm a selfish prick. Thank you for the resources, but I've got it from here. Love you, buddy.

Gray: What do you mean by "you've got it?"

Gray: Bash?

He could almost hear the crystal tumbler filled with Irish whiskey hit the wall in Gray's study.

Even though it was late, Morgan left a voicemail for Parker Livingston. It shocked them both when he called five minutes later. She put him on speaker, so Bash would know she had nothing to hide. The call lasted over an hour. Bash listened as Morgan told Parker her life story, including anything she could think of that might be relevant. She texted him a picture of the letter that she received from Pops at the cabin. Morgan offered to send the ledger to him, but Livingston didn't think it was safe. Instead, he suggested that she get it out of her hands and somewhere secure as quickly as possible. After Livingston followed up with the information he got from Morgan, he would contact a close friend with the FBI and have her act as the liaison to get the ledger into federal hands. In the interim, his only advice was to stay off the radar and leave no trails.

Next, Bash called Sam Barrett. He answered on the first ring and sounded surprised it was Bash and not Alex or Gray.

"Mr. Bartoli, what can I do for you?"

"I apologize for calling you so late, but we didn't get an opportunity earlier to discuss the phone conversation I had with Maximillian Fontana or get the results of your background check on him," Bash said.

"If you give me your current number, I'll fax the report over to you. Are there any specific questions you have that I might be able to answer? Many of the nuances don't come through in a report," he explained.

"Can you give me some general information first? And your take on what kind of man Fontana is?"

"Up until six months ago, Maximillian Fontana was the VP of the legal department for his family's international real estate and construction company, Fontana Properties & Development. I'm going to add a little background here. Over 80 years ago, his grandfather, Damian Fontana, started a small company, Fontana Construction, with his two brothers. As the company grew, the men brought their sons into the business. The first was Maximillian's father, Julian, and then later, two of his cousins. Julian, who had an advanced finance degree, wanted to expand into real estate. The rest of the family was opposed to diversifying. The cousins had already begun making illegal deals and offering bribes to secure government contracts. They were also using muscle to push smaller companies out of the competition.

"Julian convinced his father that his cousins had gotten sloppy, and it was only a matter of time before the federal authorities would begin an investigation. Julian didn't believe that you had to get your hands dirty to make money. Paper was a much easier and less lethal hiding place. Consequently, Damian and Julian asked the other partners to buy them out. That was when Fontana Properties & Development was born. Four years later, his cousins were arrested on extortion and bribery charges. Once the investigation started into Fontana Construction, it was a house of cards. The family members who weren't indicted lost everything. Obviously, Damion and Julian, no longer being part of the original company, came out unscathed.

"There was plenty of bad blood in the family after that. Damian, who felt guilty about the downfall of his brothers and nephews who were imprisoned, insisted Julian allow their sons, Enzo and Leone, into the business. They were a few years older than Maximillian, so they started before him. Julian held the reigns until 6 months ago when he died. Maximillian was the successor, but let's just say the two cousins weren't happy about it. Enzo called himself Julian's right-hand man. That side of the family has always been suspicious that Damian and Julian had something to do with the downfall of the construction company.

"My sources tell me Maximillian was a reluctant participant in the family business, forced into his role. The international company is worth billions of dollars and employs thousands of people worldwide. An inside informant thinks Maximilian only took over the helm because he was afraid Enzo and Leone, who have questionable ethics, would rape the company of its assets. To keep an eye on the legal side of things, Maximilian promoted Stephen Gallagher, a longtime trusted friend, to head the legal department. Now Maximillian is struggling to deal with the politics and the attempts by his cousins for a hostile takeover."

"I thought he was in organized crime."

"Not in the traditional sense. Everything stays within the Fontana family. There have been rumors for years that they have made their fortune in questionable deals. Skirting the law with legal loopholes. Moving money and business out of the country. Maybe it's true, and maybe it's an assumption because of the legacy of Fontana Construction. Regardless, none of the federal agencies have ever been able to make a case against them.

"On a personal front, he was married in his mid-twenties and divorced 10 years later. Amicably. The marriage produced a highly intelligent daughter, Francesca or Frankie, who graduated from the U.S. Naval Academy in 2009. She's stationed somewhere in the Mediterranean Sea. They have a good relationship, but she has never been associated with the business. He remarried 6 years ago to a New York socialite, Fatima Ethridge, who is wealthy in her own right. There is an ironclad prenup. Rumors suggest it is a marriage of convenience. No children. What else would you like to know?"

"Does everyone really call him Maximillian?"

Sam laughed. "That wasn't the first question I would have thought you'd ask, but I can see it probably tells you a lot about the man. His father insisted he be called Maximillian. He personally hates it. It means 'greatest' in Latin. Julian thought 'Max' was too blue-collar for his son. There are stories of him firing people who called his son 'Max.' If Fontana allowed it now, he would lose respect, so he's pretty much saddled with it."

"Tomorrow, I am supposed to text Fontana with a town and address of where he is to meet me. He says he's coming alone and denies any knowledge of the men who attacked us at the lake. If I hear him out and still decide not to work with him, he'll back off. Should I believe him?" Bash asked.

"I don't know the man or his motivations, but I have a hard time believing he would be speaking to you at all if he wanted you dead. His cousins may take exception to him writing a 'tell-all book,' especially after what happened to their family in the past. A hostile takeover seems likely based on what I've learned. He has nothing to gain from you that he couldn't get from any other bestselling author ... no offense."

"None taken. My gut says he's telling the truth. Next question ... where do we meet? I'll tell you where I am, but I don't want you to share the information or anything we talk about with anyone else, including Gray or Alex. I'll tell them what I want them to know. You can talk to them, just not about anything we have covered. Are we clear?"

"Crystal."

"Is your phone secure?"

"Yes."

"Good. I'm on a burner. We're in Ashville, North Carolina, in a rented apartment. As you probably know, we're traveling on motorcycles. They aren't practical this time of year. We will probably leave them here in storage and rent a car. I'm assuming Fontana will be flying from New York."

"I'm looking at your options as we speak … Most of the roads out of Ashville are remote. You don't want to get boxed back in the mountains. Charlotte is much more accessible to get in and out. It's 130 miles from your location. Would that be too far to ride on the bikes?"

Bash checked the weather. The high was 70 degrees with no rain. His eyes meet Morgan's in question. She nodded.

"That's doable."

"You need a public place to meet with an open space and a storage unit for your bikes, but keep them until you've met with him. They are much more maneuverable if things go south. Take an Uber to the airport and get a rental. I would send you some men to back you up, but I can't guarantee I can get them in place by tomorrow. If you put it off for another day, I'll bring them myself."

Bashed glanced at Morgan, silently seeking her approval. She shook her head from side to side. "We'll handle it ourselves," Bash said more confidently than he felt.

"I'll do some research and text you the best options for the storage facility and meeting place. You can take them or leave them, but let me know what you decide."

"Any thoughts on what the bikers will do next?" Morgan asked.

"I doubt they're going to waste time wandering through

the mountains indefinitely. From what Gray told me, with your rental parked outside the cabin, they more than likely assumed you got out on foot. Caught a ride and could be anywhere by now. I'm guessing they would start at square one and go back to either Topton or Gainesville to see what they can find out about you. The fact that they think you are a man is a big plus, but they do know Morgan's name. Until your attorney sets up an exchange and a deal for protection, stay underground. We'll know more when Mr. Bartoli talks to Fontana. It may be safer for Ms. Skylar to come home with you, Mr. Bartoli."

"You've given us a lot to think about. Thanks. We'll talk soon. And by the way, call me "Bash,'" he said.

"And you can call me "Sam.'"

Bash fell back against the sofa, nervously running his hands through his hair. He had no idea what he was doing anymore. Morgan sat in a lounger, watching him.

"It's a lot, isn't it?" she said rhetorically, leaning forward with her hands on her knees. "Are you sure you want to meet this Fontana guy? I mean, you could just as easily fly back home and resume your life with a security detail."

"That would certainly be the easiest thing to do, but Fontana has my curiosity peaked. For him to personally go to all this trouble just to talk to me seems extreme. There might be a good story there. I know it's risky on my part, but I've got to hear him out."

"Who's been texting you every two minutes?" she asked.

"Gray."

"I thought he is your best friend. Why won't you talk to him?"

"Because he'll try to take over like he always does. I usually take his advice without question, but this time, it doesn't feel right. He's not hearing me. We've been like brothers since kindergarten."

"You need to fix this rift between you. I'm close to Beth, and I'd do anything for her, but you and Gray are truly family. That's rare." She stood up. "Just think about it. There is a balance you and Gray can reach. I'm going to bed. See you in the morning." She surprised him when she tenderly rubbed his shoulder before she left.

He grabbed his backpack, pulled out a new burner phone, and entered Fontana's number in messages.

Bash: Charlotte, North Carolina, tomorrow. Call this number when you arrive for a meeting location and time.

CHAPTER TWENTY-TWO

Maximillian Fontana sat on the tarmac at Hartsfield-Jaxon Atlanta International Airport in a private jet leased under an assumed name, waiting for his pilot to be granted clearance for take-off to Charlotte, North Carolina. He had ditched his security team and taken every precaution to prevent his destination from being exposed. When he spoke with Sebastian Bartoli, he was shocked to learn that someone had sent a hit squad after him. That could only mean one thing: despite all his efforts to keep his meeting with Mr. Bartoli under wraps, someone close to him had leaked the information.

There was never any doubt that convincing Mr. Bartoli to talk to him was going to be a challenge, but with the added threat Mr. Bartoli perceived to his life, it would be almost impossible to gain his trust. That's why he was stunned when Mr. Bartoli agreed to meet him in Charlotte. Of course, it could have been a misdirection, and he was on his way to Malaysia by now, but Max's gut said otherwise.

Max flew to Atlanta last night from Manhattan on the pretense he had a meeting with an international investor who wanted to remain anonymous until a deal was signed. If Max's deception had worked, his two bodyguards were still sitting in the lobby of an exclusive spa northeast of Atlanta. He was supposed to be at an all-day meeting and evening dinner with entertainment, so his guards shouldn't expect to see him until late.

There were only three people who knew of his desire to

meet with Bartoli about writing his biography. His VP of Legal and long-time friend Stephan Gallagher, his assistant Rohan Burman, and his wife Fatima. After speaking to Bartoli, he knew one of them had betrayed him. Although he had a good idea who it was, he needed proof. Now, he was completely on his own with no intention of going back to Atlanta. Let his security team figure it out. For the first time since his college days, he had no clear plan of what came next. Sebastian Bartoli didn't know it yet, but he held all the cards.

CHAPTER TWENTY-THREE

Bash received the call from Maximillian Fontana at 1 p.m. They maintained a crisp, business-like tone throughout their brief interaction. The meeting was to take place at a Mexican restaurant located in an outdoor shopping mall next to a community children's park at 2 p.m. Bash and Morgan had already spent a couple of hours walking the area and checking out the places that would give them the most protection and alternative escape routes. The restaurant was very public, located in the center of the shopping area and directly in front of the park. It had a rear exit in the kitchen that led to an alley. That was where Bash and Morgan stashed their motorcycles behind a dumpster. It gave them a distinct advantage in reaching their transportation quickly because the parking lot was located at the far end of the outdoor mall. Bash paid a substantial fee to the manager for the privilege of using the back exit.

Morgan sat on a park bench immediately adjacent to the restaurant while Bash waited inside at a back table near the kitchen. The plan was for Morgan to text when she spotted Fontana and then meet Bash inside. If he was not alone, they would both leave out the back door. At five minutes till 2 p.m., Bash received her text. Fontana appeared to be alone. A few minutes later, Morgan took a seat beside him.

Bash caught sight of Fontana the minute he entered the restaurant. He was casually dressed in a black leather jacket, khaki wool slacks, a navy sweater, and wore aviator sunglasses. He stopped a couple of feet inside the door and carefully surveyed the large room. Bash wasn't sure if he was looking for him or possible threats, maybe both. It only took a few seconds for their eyes to lock. Fontana did a quick nod of recognition and headed to the table in long, confident strides. Maximillian Fontana emanated power and class. Every eye in the room was drawn to him.

Bash stood as he watched Fontana approach, feeling a need to meet the man face to face. When he stopped on the far side of the table, he pulled his sunglasses off and slid them inside his soft leather jacket. The two men stared at each other for an uncomfortable length of time before Fontana extended his hand, which Bash accepted with a firm grip.

Maximilian Fontana was a handsome man with thick, wavy, dark brown hair streaked with gray. His smooth olive skin showed he carried his age well, which Bash had read was late fifties, but it was his deep green penetrating eyes that held Bash's attention. There was a familiarity there, but he was sure they had never met.

"So, we finally meet. Max Fontana," he said with a pleasant smile.

"Sebastian Bartoli. Please have a seat," Bash said, surprised that Fontana had introduced himself using his nickname.

"Not to be ungrateful for this chance to meet you, but I would feel more comfortable if my back wasn't to the door," Fontana said. "Mind if we relocate outside?"

Bash and Morgan exchanged looks. She shrugged.

"I picked this place for a reason," Bash said, feeling his spine tingling. *Is this a setup?* He struggled to keep his voice even. "If we don't go far, I'll consider it. Where do you suggest?"

"One of the benches in the park. We won't be overheard, and it will be easier to keep an eye out for uninvited company."

He felt Morgan tug on his arm and turned toward her. She cocked her head and pointed to herself. Bash realized he had forgotten to introduce her. Fontana remedied the situation by offering her his hand.

"Max Fontana."

She gave him a confident shake. "Morgan Skylar. Nice to meet you."

"Morgan is the unlucky woman who had the cabin next to mine when your well-armed friends showed up. We've become fast friends," he said, winking at Morgan.

Fontana stood. "As I've explained, not my friends. May I?" Fontana asked, offering to pull out Morgan's chair. She slid back in her seat as Bash observed, amazed at how easily the man had come in and taken over. He wanted to object but couldn't think of a single reason not to agree. *'You're blowing up my getaway plan'* didn't seem to be the appropriate excuse.

"Are you coming, Bash," she smirked.

"Yeah."

They found two benches that sat perpendicular to each other, putting their backs to the long side of a storage container store. In front of them was a set of jungle gyms. The Mexican restaurant was still within sight and easy to access.

"Mr. Fontana, you've gone to a lot of trouble just to hear me say the same thing I've expressed to you in all the communications you've had with my office. I don't do biographies, and I'm not going to change my mind. I have no desire to know about your notorious life. It feels safer that way."

Fontana chuckled. "First of all, please call me Max."

"No offense, but I was specifically told that people who called you anything other than 'Maximillian' have been known to disappear," Bash said warily.

Max burst out laughing. "That is certainly what my father would have wanted people to believe, and I'm sure he was the one to perpetuate the rumors. He was disappointed that his only son wanted nothing to do with his business, and for a long time, he let me believe he would respect my wishes. It wasn't until I graduated law school and was ready to join a prestigious law firm that I learned it had all been a lie."

"What did he do?" Morgan asked.

"Let's just say that any firm who hired me would be financially crushed. I would become a major liability, so I had no choice but to comply. I eventually became head of the legal department and refused to overlook any questionable business practices," Max explained.

"Questionable as in breaking kneecaps or threatening people with bodily harm?" Bash asked sarcastically.

"Bash!" Morgan scolded.

Max held up his hand. "I'm aware of our company's reputation and mine by association, but we aren't the mafia. That is not how my family does business. There are financial ways to make people comply. You can make a lot of money manipulating deals. Edging out the competition. My father and grandfather were certainly unethical businessmen. Fortunately, that sort of violence was beneath them. Not that the methods they used were any less destructive, but they didn't see it that way."

Bash's jaw tightened, forcing down his anger. "I'm having a hard time believing that. Apparently, those two men shooting at us didn't get the nonviolence memo."

Max sighed and leaned forward with his elbows on his knees. "I understand that actions speak louder than words, but I'm asking for a chance to explain. When my father died six months ago, my cousins Enzo and Leone assumed that one of them would step into his shoes, mainly because I'd been so reluctant to immerse myself in the business. Unfortunately for them, my father didn't trust either of them and always kept them on a short leash. Just like their father and grandfather before them, that side of the family has no aversion to doing whatever is necessary to make money or eliminate the competition. That most likely includes me. I'm currently trying to identify the traitor in my company. It shouldn't be too hard to figure out because there are few in my confidence. The only person who should know I'm here is the pilot."

"So why are you so hell-bent on me writing your story?" Bash asked.

"To be honest, I'm not."

Bash sat up straight. His expression turned from confusion to rage. It had all been a deception. He bit out every word. "Then tell me why the fuck we've been on this merry-go-round?"

Morgan put a gentle hand on his arm.

Fontana remained calm. "I needed an excuse to meet with you. We have personal business to discuss."

"What business could you and I possibly have to discuss?" Bash asked incredulously.

He reached into his inside jacket and pulled out some photos. He handed one to Bash. "Do you recognize the woman in the picture?"

It only took a couple of seconds for recognition to set in. Bash felt like his heart had stopped. It was a picture of his mother when she was young. Maybe late teens or early 20s. One he had never seen. All kinds of questions swirled in his head. *How could he possibly have a picture of my mother? Is this supposed to be a threat? Was this how he intends to get me to write his book. Use my mother?* He didn't care how dangerous this man was. He was not going to be able to use his mother for leverage. *Well, the joke is going to be on him.*

"What the hell is this? You think you can threaten my mother to get me to comply? You bastard!" Bash moved to lean toward the man, but Morgan hung on to his elbow preventing him from smashing the man's face in.

"No, Bash!" she shouted, using her weight to hold him back.

"What?" Max said. "No! No! It's nothing like that." He held up his hands in defense.

Bash could feel the heat rush to his face. "Well, it doesn't fucking matter! You can't use a dead woman!" he bellowed. Then he watched the blood drain from Fontana's face as he fell back against the park bench and clutched his chest. His eyes became unfocused. Bash was afraid that he was having a heart attack. Instinct told him to check the man's pulse, but his fury was too acute to force himself to move.

"Oh God," Morgan breathed, falling to her knees in front of him. She wrapped her hand around his wrist and began to monitor his heartbeats. "Are you okay, Max? Are you having chest pains?"

The man didn't answer. Maybe didn't hear her speaking. Bash just watched and waited. Frozen in place.

"His heart is racing," Morgan finally said. "We should call 911."

Max tilted his head to meet Morgan's eyes and offered her a weak smile. "Thank you, Ms. Skylar, but that won't be necessary. I'll be fine in a minute. It was … so unexpected. Finding out that Izzy was … had passed," he choked out his words.

"My mother's name was Gwen, not Izzy," Bash said defensively. "It can't be my mother in your picture. If that's why you came to see me, you have wasted a trip."

Fontana stared at him for a full minute before he spoke. There appeared to be tears in his eyes. "I knew her as Isabel, but she was Izzy to me. And I would never have hurt her, let alone threaten her life."

Bash had no idea how to respond. They couldn't be talking about the same woman, but he couldn't deny the picture looked like a younger version of his mother. Except the woman in the picture had long, honey-blond hair, and his mother's hair had always been midnight black, cut in a short bob.

Max sat up straight and spoke earnestly. "Sebastian, please believe me. My intent is not to intimidate or manipulate you. It is merely to reinforce your belief that I knew your mother."

The wheels turned in Bash's head. When he was old enough to understand, his mother told him that she had run away from home after her parents insisted that she get an abortion. They didn't approve of his father, whose family they believed was dangerous. Bash's mother had never told his father that she was pregnant because she was afraid of his family. When she realized she had no alternatives, she caught a train and disappeared. Her hometown, friends, family, and past were all a mystery to him.

"How do you know my mother?" he asked cautiously.

"Bash!" Morgan clutched his arm and pointed. "There are three men in dark suits entering the park, coming from the direction of the parking lot. They don't look like happy kind of guys, either."

Fontana stood up. "We must leave."

"I thought you said no one knew where you were," Bash barked.

"They don't. I did call my wife this morning to tell her I would be gone for a few more days, but I used a burner phone. It appears I've been tracked."

"How can you be tracked by a burner phone?" Morgan asked.

"I have a stash of burners in my office at home. I bought them myself. My wife is the only one who has access to the numbers in case of an emergency. A tracker could have been placed on them," he said.

"Your wife?" Bash questioned. "What about your pilot?"

"I watched the pilot get on a private 727 headed to Cairo not ten minutes after we landed. That's his home base, so I highly doubt it was him," Fontana confirmed. "Fatima was the only one who had access to the burners. It's disappointing but not necessarily surprising. A marriage of convenience. Now, I need to figure out who she's working with. But we do need to leave before they recognize us. I hope you had an escape route planned," he said to Bash, then reached in his pocket, turned off his cell, and threw it in a trash can.

"Why should we take you with us?" Bash asked.

"Because I'm sure you have a lot of questions, and I'm the only one who can provide the answers," he said confidently. "So, what's it going to be, Sebastian?"

Bash made a split-second decision, hoping he wouldn't regret it. "As long as you don't mind riding on back, we've got you covered," Bash said.

CHAPTER TWENTY-FOUR

Taking Morgan's hand, Bash directed the group through the kitchen door and out into the back alley.

"Where's your car?" Max asked, looking perplexed when faced with an empty alley.

"Behind the dumpster," Morgan said. "Wait here."

A couple of minutes later, Morgan and Bash eased their motorcycles out and stopped in front of Max.

"This explains what you meant when you said I'd be riding on the back," Max said with a grin. "This will be a first."

"I don't have a helmet for you, so if you fall off and break your neck, that's on you," Bash said.

"Don't wreck," Max grimaced, climbing on behind Bash.

The alley had one way out and intersected with the only road exiting the outdoor mall. Morgan led the way. If they had to go off-road, she would be more likely to find the best path. Glancing in her rearview mirror, she chuckled at the sight of the two men, virtual strangers, Max clinging to Bash's waist. She worried that the extra weight might be too much for Bash to control, but there was no alternative.

When she stopped at the street at the end of the alley, Bash pulled up alongside her.

"Morgan," Bash said through her helmet radio. "Casually glance to your far right toward the entrance of the shopping center. We've got company."

Slightly turning her head, using her peripheral vision, she spotted the black SUV Bash was referring to parked on the side of the main road just outside the mall entrance.

"Turkey feathers!"

"Yeah. That wasn't the expression that came to mind, but let's go with it. Regardless, we need a new plan. I don't think we'll be able to slip by with Fontana on the back. He'll be recognized immediately."

"You can let me off here, and I'll call a taxi," she overheard Max tell Bash.

"I'm not letting you out of my fucking sight until I know what your connection is to my mother!" Bash shouted.

"Calm down, Bash. Let's use our inside voice," Morgan scolded. "And don't roll those eyes at me," she added, her assumption.

"No eye rolling here, Morgan," Bash scoffed.

She heard Max laugh.

"She's a kindergarten teacher," Bash explained.

Morgan frantically searched her surroundings for another escape route. She located an empty field on the far side of the parking lot.

"Looks like we're going off-road," she sighed. "We need to turn left. There is a vacant lot at the end of the parking lot. When we get to the last aisle, we'll jump the curve and head across. I'm hoping it isn't muddy, or you guys are going to get stuck."

"You mean that field? The weeds are at least a foot high," Bash said with skepticism.

"Unless you've got a better idea, I don't see another choice. Be sure to slow down and ease over the curve. We'll ride across the field until we reach the used car lot on the other side. Let's hope the guys in the SUV don't notice us. If we're seen, we should be out of firing range unless they have a rifle. Y'all good?"

She heard mumbling between the men.

"We're behind you," Bash replied. "What happens if we get stuck? We have close to 400 pounds between us."

"Don't borrow trouble. We'll improvise. If it slows you down too much, Max can run alongside you."

The ride through the parking lot went without a hitch. The

men in the SUV didn't seem to notice them until they jumped the curb and started across the open lot. Morgan held a thumbs up, confirming the ground was solid.

"The field is uneven. We're bouncing all over the place," Bash complained.

"Give her some more power and see if that helps. If not, Max is going to have to get off."

"I'll try. I feel like I'm riding through a ton of weedy potholes," he said, adding a little bit of speed. "Much better, but we've got company running parallel to us."

Morgan whipped her head to the right and found the black SUV tracking them. Adrenalin shot through her veins, her heart hammering against her chest. Woods filled with pine trees and underbrush blocked their path on the left. Ahead about 20 yards, Morgan spotted a break in the trees where powerlines ran perpendicular to their path. The mowed area underneath it was a welcome site. When she glanced back to gauge where the SUV was located, she saw a rifle sticking out of the window.

"Gun!" she yelled. "Head for that break in the trees on the left."

A shot rang out. It pinged against metal. Roxy was hit. Lowering her body closer to the bike, she asked if they were okay.

Bash didn't answer, but she heard his engine rev as his bike drew closer to her tail. She wasn't surprised when he caught up, pacing with her on the right. He could have used his more powerful engine to get to safety, but instead, he took her out of the line of fire. She cringed when a series of shots peppered the grass around them.

"We're almost there," Morgan panted, her arms and hands burning from the strain of holding the handlebars steady over the rough terrain. She let out a small yelp as another shot took out her taillight. *Just a little further. Come on, baby, almost there.*

When they finally turned down the grass path under the powerlines, she let out a massive breath.

"You okay, Chip?" Bash huffed.

"Just hunky-dory."

"Let's not do that again, okay?" he nervously laughed.

"Roger that," she sighed. "I'm hoping we lost them, but I have no idea where we're going."

"Fontana's telling me they won't give up. They probably have a map and know exactly where we're headed."

"Then we need to get off this path," Morgan suggested. "There is a small break in the trees up ahead. I'm going to stop."

"Got it."

The gap in the trees turned out to be a narrow bike trail that crossed under the powerlines and continued to either side.

"It's going to be tight with that dresser. Think you can make it?"

"I'll manage if Fontana keeps his hands and feet in. Right or left?" Bash asked.

"My guts telling me left," Morgan said.

"Well, mine's telling me right," Bash countered. "Left will take us back to the shopping mall."

"Not if we're behind it."

"Fontana agrees with me."

She shrugged and turned right. "Seats and trays back in the upright position. Turn off your cell phones and hold on to your patooties."

Ten minutes later, they came out on a narrow road with a chain link fence on the opposite side. Beyond was the welcome sight of a highway. They stopped side by side and took their helmets off.

"It's a service road. That's 485 on the other side of the fence," Bash said with relief. He turned to Max. "I guess your instincts were correct."

"Your call. I just agreed. The entrance is up ahead."

"We need to find directions to the storage place," Bash said.

Morgan already had her phone out and was getting their current location. "Five miles. We take the second exit off 485 and turn right. It's three miles on the left. Chesterfield Storage."

"We're right behind you."

With the motorcycles safely stored away, everyone piled in a taxi to get to the closest car rental, avoiding the airport. With one quick phone call, Max's assistant arranged to have a car reserved and prechecked in.

As they stood beside the midsized sedan, Morgan realized they didn't really have a plan. "Now what?"

"I don't know if my opinion matters, but I suggest we get out of the city as soon as possible," Max offered.

Bash's eyes narrowed. "You aren't going anywhere until we finish our conversation."

Max held his hands up in a conciliatory manner. "I was referring to all of us. You're right. You and I have unfinished business. It was merely a suggestion that driving to another town might be the best option. I'm sure the airport is being watched."

"Did you recognize any of the guys in the black SUV?" Morgan asked Max.

"The driver looked a lot like Enzo's right-hand man, Bart Spano. Enzo must be the one working with my wife."

"How do you know?" Bash asked.

"I've suspected Fatima was having an affair for months. It didn't bother me enough to approach her about it if she was discreet. As I said, our marriage is an arrangement. It never occurred to me until now that it might be Enzo. He considers himself a ladies' man. Gets a kick out of pulling one over on his wife any chance he gets. My cousin Leone is basically a troll. That's how I know. Enzo had to have given her the tracking devices to put on my phones, although I'm not sure of her motivation. She is wealthy in her own right due to a sizable trust fund from her father. We have an iron-tight prenup if she did need the money. I called her this morning so she knew which phone to tell Enzo to check."

"Maybe she was blinded by love," Morgan suggested.

"Doubtful. Fatima is too self-absorbed to fall in love. Could be the attention. She's been a good companion. I thought we were at least friends. The betrayal stings."

Bash cleared his throat. "We need to get moving."

CHAPTER TWENTY-FIVE

The closest city in the opposite direction they figured anyone would expect was Winston-Salem. Max drove while Morgan searched for places to stay the night. They stopped at an old-fashioned diner with a sign promising homemade meals guaranteed to remind them of home. Max had to chuckle because his childhood meals had been prepared by a cordon bleu trained chef.

Once they were seated, their server, a round woman named Millie in a pink uniform, set three 24 oz. plastic glasses of an amber liquid with crushed ice in front of them. Max guessed it was tea.

"How you'uns doin' this evenin'?" she said with a toothy grin.

"We're just great," Morgan said, all perky. "This sweet tea?" She held up her glass.

"Yes, ma'am. On the house, too. You don't have to pay for a drink with your meal unless you want a soda. One of the perks of eatin' here," Millie said, pulling three water-stained menus from her apron and distributing them around the table.

Morgan took a long drink. "This is delicious!" she said appreciatively.

"It is, ain't it. Well, I'll give you'uns a few minutes to look over the menu. The special tonight is at the top of the menu — fried pork chops, mashed potatoes with gravy, and turnip greens. I'll be right back now," she said, as she hurried to another table.

Max looked down at the list of cholesterol-ridden meals

and sighed. There was not a healthy choice to be had.

"I'm going to have the special," Morgan said, closing her menu.

"Me too," Sebastian said, taking a swig of his drink.

Max looked at them in disbelief. "You're both eating the pork chops?"

They nodded.

"But they are fried and battered with buttermilk. And the turnip greens are made with ham hocks and fatback. Whipped potatoes with cream. You could have a heart attack right here at the table!"

Sebastian shrugged.

"Yummmm," Morgan said with a wry smile, rubbing her stomach playfully.

Max turned to Sebastian. "Don't look at me. When in Rome..."

Max shook his head.

As Millie approached the table, Max asked, "Could I get a strip steak and a salad?"

"Not at this restaurant, hon."

Max sighed. "I guess I'll have the special." His defeat had Millie chuckling and doing a little jig all the way to the kitchen.

"You mind if I ask something kind of personal?" Morgan asked Max.

He furrowed his brow, not knowing what to expect. "What do you want to know?"

"Are you absolutely sure your wife is having an affair?" she asked. "Like you have proof?"

Yeah, that's personal, he thought, but answered her anyway. "I confronted her, and she didn't deny it. She wondered why it took me so long to figure it out. Didn't think I would notice and asked if I wanted her to end it. I never answered because I didn't want to admit to either of us that I really didn't care. That was three months ago. We have continued our cordial friendship as if nothing has changed, but we are no longer—close."

Morgan shook her head disapprovingly. "Wow. That's no

way to live."

"It is not," he agreed.

"Okay, so…"

"Morgan, that's intrusive," Sebastian interrupted.

"It's okay. Let her continue."

"I understand she betrayed your marriage vows, but how does that imply she would try to help get you killed? Don't you think that's a huge leap to accuse her without evidence? Maybe your cousin got his information from somewhere else. Didn't you say you traveled to Charlotte in a private jet? Was it yours?"

"I leased it in Atlanta. My company jet would have been easily traced."

"Maybe the leasing company verified your identity with someone in your company. They might have wondered why you didn't use your own plane. Your cousin could have had someone place a tracker on your belongings. Had you followed. Those may be terrible examples, but all I'm saying is you immediately assumed it was your wife who gave your cousin your burner number. Shouldn't you give her the benefit of the doubt before you find her guilty?"

Max stared at Morgan for a few seconds rubbing his chin, pondering her words. He had assumed Fatima was guilty, and even though his instincts agreed, Morgan had a point about the need for confirmation.

"You make a good argument, Morgan. I need proof."

They decided to stay at a 3-star, independently owned motel on the outskirts of Winston-Salem, nestled in evergreens against a foothill. Max knew it was the kind of place no one would ever expect to find him. After checking in, they each headed to separate rooms, giving everyone time to decompress.

They were to meet in the self-service lounge just off the motel lobby at 8 p.m. It gave Max an opportunity to devise a plan to expose Enzo and Fatima. He had to be 100% sure his cousin and his wife were the ones who sent the hit squad after them. After eating and grabbing a quick shower, he went to the main office to see if the owner was available.

Gavin Nordstrom, the owner, according to the business license framed on the wall, was seated at a small desk behind the check-in counter, working spreadsheets on a laptop. He was a heavy-set man with a bald spot surrounded by a crown of slightly graying hair.

Max cleared his throat. "I apologize for the interruption, but may I speak to you?"

When the man turned around in his rolling desk chair, a huge, welcoming grin broke out on his ruddy face. "Sorry. I didn't hear you come in." Standing up from his chair, he walked to the counter and stuck out his hand.

"Gavin Nordstrom. What can I do for you this evening?"

Max took his hand. "Max Fontana."

"Nice to meet you, Mr. Fontana."

"Max."

"Okay, Max. What can I do for you?" he repeated.

Max glanced around the small office, looking for prying eyes.

"How long have you owned the motel? It's a nice place."

"Thanks. Been 10 years now. I worked in marketing for a packaged food corporation for 25 years in New Jersey. Stress was unbearable. My wife gave me an ultimatum. Find another career or another wife. She can be a hard ass sometimes, but she's still the love of my life, so staying wasn't an option. Her family lives here. They're the ones who told us the motel was up for sale. The rest is history."

The man is certainly a friendly guy, thought Max. *Threw his whole life out there for me to see. Won't require any more probing to know that he's a 'what you see is what you get' kind of guy.*

"Good for you. I'm glad it worked out." He took a second to collect his thoughts and leaned forward with his elbows on the counter. "I'm a businessman, Gavin, and I have a problem I think you can help me solve."

Gavin's lips tightened. "If this is an illegal problem, I'm afraid I can't help you, Mr. Fontana."

Max stepped back and shook his head. "Nothing like that,

I assure you. I'm going to be honest with you, Gavin." He often used people's given names to establish a sense of familiarity and trust.

"Go on," Gavin said, narrowing his eyes.

"I work in a large family-owned international business. My father recently passed and left me in charge and the majority owner. I left a few days ago for a business trip. Today, someone took shots at me. If I am gone, one of my cousins will take over."

Gavin looked skeptical. "How are you sure it was someone in your family? Did you call the police?"

"There are only a few people close enough to me who could have known where I was at the time. I think I know who it is, but I need to be sure. Obviously, my life depends on it."

The man looked shocked. He wiped perspiration from his face with his large, paw-like hand. "What is it that you think I can do? You can't expect me to put my family or motel at risk."

"That is not my intention at all. First, I need a decoy location to lead them to. Preferably somewhere remote. Maybe a motel or building that has closed. Something abandoned."

"You want me to set them up so you can ambush them?" Gavin said with horror.

"Not at all. All I need is for a burner phone to be planted somewhere in or around the building and someone to surveil the location from a distance to see if anyone shows up. You don't even have to tell me the address. If they do show up, they will realize they've been duped, and I'll know who initiated the attack on me. Then I can get the police involved."

"Not to stick my nose in your business, but why are you using burner phones to begin with? That sounds a bit suspicious to me?"

"That's a reasonable question. I am the CEO of Fontana Properties and Development. You can look me up if you like, but I would appreciate you not sharing this conversation. Many of our clients want total confidentiality until they are ready to announce their intents. If their competition finds out in advance of their announcement, it could cost them millions. I often sign an NDA to guarantee my silence. Personal cell phones can be tracked, so I keep a number of burner phones in my office at home for highly sensitive meetings. Only people closest to me would have access to my home to place a tracker on one of my burners. I'm trying to identify that person so I can contact the police. As I said, my life depends on it."

"Thank you for trusting me with that information. What exactly would you like me to do?"

"In the morning, I'll make a call to the person I suspect is tracking me. It will activate as soon as it is turned on. I need someone to leave the cell phone at the abandoned location and then watch from a safe distance to see if anyone shows up. You can call me tomorrow night, and all you have to say is 'yes' they showed up or 'no' they didn't. They will be there tomorrow if they are coming. You will receive $5,000 for your trouble. Absolutely no one will get hurt. My room is charged to one of my traveling companions, so there is no record to tie anything to you. What do you think? If it's not something you're willing to do, there are no hard feelings. Someone at my next location may be willing to help me. This is strictly about discovering how far the betrayal goes in my company."

"What will you do when you find out?"

"As I said, go to the police."

"If you leave, how do I get paid?" he asked.

"I'm staying in room 212. Call the room phone in the morning by 6 a.m. if you are on-board. I'll give you the burner phone and $5,000 cash before I leave around 8 a.m."

Gavin's mouth dropped open. "Why would you give me the whole amount? How do you know I won't just keep the money and do nothing?"

"I think I'm a pretty good judge of character. If I turn out to be wrong, it's my mistake."

"None of these people will get hurt, right?"

"I won't even know the location or who is placing it there, and I'm certainly not hanging around town to be a target. I'll be miles from here when they show up."

"I've heard a cell phone can set off a bomb."

Max had to suppress the laugh. *Like I would have a clue how to wire a bomb to a cell phone.* "How can there be a bomb if I have no idea where you are placing the phone?"

Gavin studied him for a few seconds, then finally said, "I'll do it."

"Sure you don't want to think about it?"

"I think you're telling me the truth."

"I am, Gavin. Thank you. You may end up saving my life."

CHAPTER TWENTY-SIX

Fontana wasn't at all what Bash had expected. Based solely on the rumors, he had pictured him as an intimidating brute who was rough around the edges, but that couldn't be further from the truth. He was refined, polished, well-educated, and exuded confidence, but there was also a down-to-earth quality about him. Bash could tell Fontana was good at reading people and adjusted his style to fit his audience. Surprisingly, it didn't appear disingenuous or manipulative. He also didn't seem to be a man who would waste his time if it weren't important. There was no doubt the man had an agenda. Bash just hadn't been able to figure it out yet.

"How exactly does a self-service lounge work? You pour your own drink?" Fontana asked, seeming to materialize out of thin air.

Caught off guard, Bash sat up straighter, adjusting himself in his seat. "I didn't see you come in." He cleared his throat to give himself time to put on his game face. "There is a cooler behind the bar with a pad of paper to write down your room number and what you took."

"The honor system. I like it," Fontana grinned, then strode over to the bar. After writing on the notepad, he came back with a Blue Moon and sat back down.

"Are you going to tell me what you're doing with my mother's picture?" Bash asked, impatience in his voice.

"So, you concede that it is your mother?" Fontana reached into his back pocket and pulled out another photo, and handed it to Bash.

He stared at the picture for a long moment before meeting Fontana's eyes. His throat closed so tightly he struggled to force out words. The scene in the photo took his breath away. His mother, stunning in an elegant white wedding gown, stood at the top of the Empire State Building, veil billowing in the breeze alongside a young, smiling Maximillian Fontana, dressed in a black tuxedo. He was looking at his mother as if she were every celestial body in the heavens wrapped into one woman.

"What does this mean? W...Were you married to her?" he asked, feeling his world shift.

A sadness crept over Fontana's face as he cleared his throat. "It never got that far. These pictures were taken around the city in iconic locations on the morning of our wedding day. We wanted to memorialize the d...day," his voice broke.

Bash couldn't comprehend what his eyes were showing him. Seeing his mom so young and carefree, looking adoringly at Fontana, shook him to his core. How was it possible?

His mom had been the light in his life growing up. Although she had been a private person, she had always made their life fun and silly, and completely stable. But she was also extremely guarded. Limiting their associations to only a select few people. Sometimes, Bash felt her overprotectiveness would strangle him, and he couldn't wait until he went to college to gain some freedom. He never expressed that to her because he didn't want to hurt her feelings. Now, he realized there was more to the story.

"What happened?" Bash breathed.

"She ran," Fontana said soberly.

Bash was stunned. The few things his mother admitted to him came flooding back. Her family abandoned her, and his father's family was dangerous. She also told him that his father didn't know about Bash. Was afraid to tell him. Now was the time to find out how much was true and how much was contrived. He couldn't believe what he was about to ask, but before he did, he took a long look at Maximillian Fontana. The same green eyes he had seen a familiarity in. Same nose, cheekbones, firm chin. Similar body builds. The only difference was his own lighter, caramel-colored hair. Fontana was an older version of himself. *How did Morgan not see it?*

"You are my father."

Fontana's eyes widened with shock as he sat back in his chair and took a swig of his beer. "A couple of weeks ago, I was seated in my library reading a book my assistant gave me for my Birthday, *The Deadly One* by Sebastian Bartoli. I rarely have time to read, but I picked it up while I waited for an overseas call. Fatima walked in to tell me she was leaving to have dinner with a friend. Before she turned to leave, she noticed the back cover of your book. She said, 'Oh my God, Max, that man looks just like a younger version of you. Who knew you had a doppelganger?' She left the room laughing. When I turned the book over, I knew. I had to find you."

"You didn't answer my question."

"You didn't ask a question, Sebastian. You stated it as a fact. I have no DNA proof, but there is no doubt in my mind that you are my son. That's why it was a double punch when Izzy ran," he said. "She was pregnant. I've spent a great deal of time and money trying to find you and your mother."

Bash leaned forward in his chair, feeling the need to defend her. "She obviously didn't want to be found. I'm sure she had good reasons." He stopped for a few moments to gather his thoughts. "When I was growing up, Mom never did anything spontaneous. She was a planner … to the extreme. Every decision she made was carefully thought out."

"Your mother and I met at Harvard wh…"

"Harvard?" Bash's voice went up a few octaves.

He nodded. "I was in my junior year studying pre-law. She was a freshman in liberal arts. She wanted to be a writer. It's fitting that you have fulfilled that dream for her."

"How did you meet?"

"She showed up at the wrong building on her first day of class. I noticed her frantically searching the campus map. She was walking in circles with her arms flailing as she scolded herself for getting lost. It was adorable. I couldn't resist offering to help. Since I was free for the next hour, and she was the most beautiful and naturally animated woman I had ever seen, I offered to escort her. There was no way in hell I was letting her out of my sight until I knew how to get in touch with her. Our attraction was immediate. We both felt it. We became inseparable. Best friends. Lovers. Confidants. Explorers of brave new worlds. Everything to each other. We found out she was pregnant a couple of days before I graduated. We were going to quietly get married at the courthouse. There was never any doubt. I couldn't breathe without Izzy. No future if she wasn't in it.

"What we didn't know was that my father was having us followed. His men caught us going into the courthouse and refused to let us go inside. We were manhandled into a limo and taken to my father's office. He had to have threatened or bribed Izzy's doctor because he knew she was pregnant. Izzy was scared out of her mind, but she knew I had no problem walking away from my family. Izzy and I had talked about it at length. We didn't want to be part of that world. When I told my father I was not going to work for the family business, he agreed with conditions. He would pay for law school and not interfere with my choice of firm if I agreed to a traditional wedding so family and friends could attend.

"My mother and aunts pulled out all the stops to plan it. Izzy's parents disowned her. They believed my family would tarnish their social status. They cut Izzy off and basically put her on the street, hoping to force her to cut all ties with me. Everything was fine on the morning of the wedding. We couldn't have been happier. I didn't realize anything was wrong until she didn't show up when the wedding march began to play.

"At first, I thought someone had kidnapped her. There was no way Izzy would leave me of her own free will. But then one of my dad's men said she had asked for $6000 to pay the hairdressers for the wedding party. She left the procession with the pretense of going to the bathroom to fix her make-up. She never returned. We found out the hairdresser had already been paid. Izzy needed cash to make her escape."

Bash was speechless. Dizzy. Light-headed. Suddenly nauseous. Trying to absorb Fontana's words and make sense of them. He knew his mother well enough to know something had scared her. She didn't intentionally hurt the people she loved.

"What happened?" he asked in a small voice.

"She left a note with two words. 'Please understand.' My world stopped. I couldn't function. Something had happened. Panicked her. She never would have left me if it hadn't. My father sent his men to all the bus stations, train depots, and airports. He wasn't concerned in the least about her. It was the baby he cared about. I knew in my heart when things calmed down, she would reach out to me. I frequented our favorite spots. Looked for her in every crowd. After three years passed, my loss turned to anger. Whatever had happened, she didn't trust me to fix it. Trust us. When I graduated from law school and passed the bar, my father made it clear he never intended to let me go. He would destroy any firm I tried to work for. If Izzy and I had still been together, I would have left the city, found a small town in the Midwest, and hung out my own shingle. But she left me. My father eventually had enough of what he called my 'self-indulgent brooding' and started pressuring me to get married. Find an appropriate wife from our social circle. Rose and I were married for eight years. She left me. We have a daughter. Francesca. Her nickname is Frankie. You'd like her. Beautiful and smart as a whip."

So many things fell into place. Why his mother stayed off social media. Would only vacation in remote rural locations. Campgrounds on lakes and in the mountains. She didn't have a lot of friends. Kept a low profile in their small town. Never talked about her past. But it stung. This man had been out there looking for her. For him. Why had she forgotten about him? Not given him a chance.

"Why did your first wife leave you?" It seemed important to know.

"Rose was tired of competing with what she called 'Izzy's

ghost.' She is a lovely woman, and I've always been very fond of her, but I didn't love her. I couldn't blame her for wanting what I couldn't give her. She's been happily married to a surgeon for fifteen years. We've maintained a good relationship. We both adore Frankie and have always wanted the best for her."

Bash rubbed his hands over his face. "It's a lot to take in."

"For me, too."

"Do you still hate her?"

"I could never hate Izzy. She was part of me, and in many ways, she still is. I felt betrayed, but at least now I understand why she left. Not long before he died, my father showed up at my home after having dinner with his brothers. They didn't want him to leave the CEO position and controlling interest to me. Didn't feel I was committed to the business and had no male heirs. He began railing about Izzy and how she stole his grandson from him. Dad was sure our baby was a boy. Then he revealed the mistake he made on our wedding day. He told Izzy he would never let me abandon the family business. It was just a fairytale he had spun so I would get my law degree and remain compliant. He accused her of trying to destroy his relationship with me. Threatened to make sure she never saw her baby again if she didn't stay out of the family business. My father's big mistake was underestimating her. It would have been more prudent to wait until after the wedding to make his threats. I wanted to kill him with my bare hands in that moment.

"All the years of torment I have lived second guessing everything I had done. Wondering where I screwed up. But as much as I wanted to blame him, it was always on me. I was the one who underestimated my father. Let him get to her. She obviously didn't trust that I could protect her. I was hoping when I found you, I would somehow be able to make amends to both of you. But that's not possible now. She's—dead. My failure will haunt me until my dying day."

Bash could see his father's grief. Feel his genuine, raw emotions.

"Can you tell me about her? Did she marry?"

Bash shook his head. "She did not. There were a few nice guys over the years. Some even wanted to make it permanent, but that was the kiss of death for the relationship. I hated seeing her alone, but she always said, 'There is only one great love in your life, and sometimes it just slips through your fingers.' She didn't want that to happen to me. I guess I've never found that 'one.'"

The color seemed to drain from Fontana's face. He looked away, squeezing his eyes shut. It was all so tragic. *Is he remembering? Regretting? Why didn't Mom tell me? Why did she lie? Tell me my father didn't know about me?* It hurt. All of it. The tangle of emotions swirling inside him felt like they would swallow him whole. It was too much.

Fontana suddenly stood up and ran his fingers through his hair. "Where is Morgan tonight?"

"In her room. She wanted to give us a chance to talk alone."

"There's something there, Sebastian."

"What do you mean?" Bash asked, searching his eyes.

"Never mind. I'll meet you at breakfast at 7 a.m. if that's okay?"

"Fine."

When Fontana reached the door, he turned around. "Sebastian?" he called.

"Yeah?"

"You think you could call me Max? Fontana seems so…"

"Goodnight, Max," he said.

CHAPTER TWENTY-SEVEN

Sebastian promised Morgan that he would call her after his meeting with Max. It was now after midnight, and she was worried sick. He wasn't answering his cell. She couldn't visualize them still at the bar sharing drinking stories. She already knew what their conversation would entail. Felt it in her heart. Recognized when Bash and Max sat side by side at the diner. Same eyes. Same nose. Same mouth. Handsome face. Bash was a younger version of Max. She wasn't sure how she hadn't seen it immediately. Max was Bash's father.

It all made sense: The desperate need for Max to meet his son. Using a fabricated story. And Bash was clueless. She had reasoned it wasn't her news to tell. If Max didn't reveal the truth tonight, she would have to voice her suspicions. Her loyalty was to Bash.

Throwing on a jacket over her flannel pjs, she headed out to find him. Three swift knocks on his room door elicited no response. The lobby and the lounge were completely deserted. She walked out the front door, considering he may have gone for some fresh air. The cold mountain breeze reminded her of just how inappropriately dressed she was for a one-woman search party. At the front of the parking lot, she saw a sign that read "Picnic Area" with an arrow pointing to the side of the building.

Bash was seated on top of a picnic table with his feet planted on the bench. He gazed into the night, appearing to be deep in thought. Dried fall leaves crunched under her feet as she drew close, alerting him of her approach. He turned her way.

She was unable to see his expression in the dark shadows, but his slack body language told her what she needed to know.

"Mind if I join you," she asked tentatively.

"I might not be good company, but have a seat."

Morgan sat down and let the silence settle between them.

After taking a deep breath, he spoke. "Max is my father," he declared.

Morgan struggled with how to respond. Admit her suspicions? Console him? Ask how he feels about it? Before she could decide on the correct approach, Bash had already figured it out. He turned sideways to face her.

"You knew, didn't you? Did he tell you?" The tone of his voice betrayed his hurt.

She gently rested her hand on his forearm. "No, Bash. I promise you. I only began to suspect when y'all sat next to each other at the diner. Your features are so similar. I don't know why I didn't notice it immediately."

"Why didn't you tell me?" His voice wavered with emotion.

"That's not fair. Why would I voice something I had no proof was true? Besides, I was sure Max would tell you. Don't you think that's why he's here? The whole biography thing was a ruse. An excuse to meet you. If he hadn't told you tonight, I would have shared my suspicions with you. Please don't be mad."

He grabbed one of her hands. "I'm not mad. Just not sure how I feel about anything right now."

"Do you want to tell me about it?"

In the fall moonlight with both shivering in the night air, Bash relayed to Morgan everything he learned from his father. The only part missing was how he felt about the revelation, but Morgan didn't push.

A thousand questions circled her brain, but the only one she allowed herself to ask was, "Are you okay?"

"I'm somewhere between stunned and angry. Why didn't Mom trust me with the truth? Let me know my father? When I was old enough to protect her? Why didn't she reach out to Max?

Is he telling the truth? Was she afraid of him and not his father?"

"Those are all good questions. Maybe she thought it was too late. If she knew he had married, maybe she didn't want to interfere with his life. Pops used to say that revenge didn't have an expiration date. She could have been plain scared. Unfortunately, you will probably never know, and that must be the hardest part."

He sighed and ran his fingers through his hair. "Yeah."

"Concentrate on what you want to do moving forward. You can't change the past. You need to trust that your mother believed she was doing what was best for you."

"Should I believe him?"

Morgan thought about it for a few moments. "I do. He seems to be an honest and straightforward man. What would he gain by lying to you? I like him, Bash. Do you think your mother would have been fooled and fallen in love with a bad guy?"

"Not Mom. She was a good judge of character and a wonderful person."

"Then she must have realized she was going to have to sacrifice her relationship with your father to keep you safe. It must have killed her inside. I know it would me if I had to walk away from the love of my life. Finding his son after all these years had to have been an emotional bombshell for Max, too. He could have shown up at your office and blurted out the truth, but he didn't. He found a way to ease you into the idea. That had to have taken a lot of restraint on his part."

Bash cleared his throat. Then changed the subject. "Have you heard anything from your attorney about an FBI deal?"

"He's supposed to call me in the morning."

"Good." He glanced at his watch, offering her his hand. "It's 1 a.m. We need to get some sleep. Things always look better in the morning, or at least that's what they say."

CHAPTER TWENTY-EIGHT

Bash tossed and turned for most of what was left of the night, fighting unsuccessfully to eradicate the thoughts in his head. He had to come to terms with his new reality. Not only had he gained an instant father, but he had also been dragged into Max's unsavory world. As if the Dragon Fire gang pursuing them wasn't enough. *Where do we go from here?*

When he got to the motel dining room, he found Max and Morgan seated in a far corner, deep in conversation.

"Good morning," he forced a greeting.

"Morning," Max said with an awkward smile.

Morgan flashed him a warm smile. The kind of smile that assured him she had his back. "Good morning, Bash. Were you able to get any sleep last night?"

"So-so," he said, taking a seat across from Max.

"Morgan was just telling me about her grandfather and your escape from the Dragon Fire bikers. It's quite a story." He turned back to Morgan. "Not a lot of men would give up their whole life for a grandchild ... especially one who had lived such a violent lifestyle. He has my admiration for what he was willing to sacrifice for you. Not unlike what Sebastian's mother did for him. If you think about it, it's quite ironic that you two met."

Bash stared at him for a few beats. "I never thought about it like that. You're right. Similar but different."

"Did your attorney call you yet?" Bash asked Morgan.

"He did, but it wasn't the best news. The FBI can't make a final decision until they complete an extensive background check on Pops and me. You know … in case I'm selling drugs to my kindergarteners," she said, showing her frustration.

"Sarcasm, Morgan. That's highly unlike you. You're usually a ray of sunshine," Bash teased.

"Maybe it's a lack of sleep. Anyway, I expressed my concern about holding on to the ledger. The FBI wants it badly, but Mr. Livingston refused to turn it over until I have immunity from any prosecution they might dream up. He suggested I mail it to a secure location where I could pick it up later. I told him there wasn't anyone who I would burden with that responsibility. Too dangerous. I guess I'm stuck with it until the FBI clears me."

"What exactly is in the ledger? Maybe I can help," Max asked.

Bash glanced at Morgan, whose face read surprise. He wondered if it was a good idea to involve Max, but it wasn't his call.

Morgan described the ledger contents, mentioned some of the recognizable names, and talked about the implications to the high-profile clients listed.

"It has felt like a ticking time bomb ever since Pops left it to me. He called it insurance. Feels more like a death sentence."

"I'm sure that's not what he intended," Bash said reassuringly.

"I wouldn't call it insurance because it makes you a target, but it could have been a multi-million-dollar blackmailing scheme. Still could be."

"What do you mean?" Bash asked.

"I mean, someone went to a lot of trouble to keep track of sales and services made to some very important clients. The information could have been used to extort money," Max said.

"Are you saying my Pops was blackmailing these people?" her eyes widened in surprise.

Max's face softened. "That's not what I'm saying at all, Morgan. For your Pops, it was an insurance policy. If anyone in the club got arrested, all the club had to do was threaten to expose the information. It would encourage influential people with things to hide to keep the authorities at bay. With the ledger in your possession, he probably believed no one would bother you. Your father, on the other hand, must see it as a money-making opportunity. Blackmail being one option. I agree that getting it out of your hands is the best option."

"We haven't been able to come up with a solution," Bash said.

"I know you don't know me, and this is going to take a certain amount of trust on your part, but I think I have a safe place for you to mail it," Max said. "My mother divorced my father about a year after Izzy disappeared. She always believed he had something to do with her disappearance. She loved Izzy almost as much as I did. When Mamma left, she moved back to her hometown, Denver. As soon as my father lost interest in monitoring her whereabouts, I helped her purchase a place of her own just north of Camden, Maine. The property ownership is hidden under a corporate name that my father can never trace. A caretaker and his wife, who are like family, moved with her to Maine so she wouldn't be alone. She has maintained a P.O. Box over the years. It allows us to communicate without her mail being monitored. If you feel comfortable, we can mail the ledger to her, drive to her home, and pick it up when you get an appropriate deal with the Feds. We are all in flux right now. It might be an ideal place for us to land until we get our issues settled."

"But wouldn't that put your mother in potential danger?" Morgan asked.

"No one connected to my family knows this place exists. If I didn't feel it was safe, I would never involve her." Then Max turned to Bash and grinned. "It would give us some time to get to know each other, and I'm sure Mamma would love to meet her grandson."

It might not be a terrible idea, Bash thought. Then, the doubts set in. *Can I trust him? Would Mom trust him? Is he trying to gain control of Morgan's ledger? He did say it was worth millions in extortion money. Is that the motive, or does he really want to help?*

Morgan nervously ran her hands through her hair. "I'm not sure what to do. I need to get back to my life. I have a job. Need to pay bills. My friend Nicole is feeding my fish. She lives next door to me."

"It might not be safe for you to go home," Bash said. "What if your father finds out where you live and tracks you to Atlanta. How can I protect you?"

"That's sweet, Bash, but it's not your responsibility to do that. I can take care of myself."

"Against a motorcycle gang?" Bash's voice elevated with more irritation than he intended.

"Bash? Don't yell at me!" Morgan scolded, jumping to her feet, hands on hips.

Max stood up and spread his arms. "Let's all calm down. There's a lot of emotion on everyone's plate right now. Sebastian is just worried about your safety. I am, too. None of us are a match for a ruthless motorcycle gang, not to mention the men working for Enzo, who I'm sure know your identity by now. It is no reflection on your ability to defend yourself. Have you checked in with your friend to make sure there haven't been any suspicious inquiries about you?"

Morgan's hands flew to her mouth. "Oh my gosh. I never thought of that. I took the battery out of my phone to make sure no one could track me. If there was a problem, Nicole wouldn't be able to get in touch with me."

"Morgan. Stop with the recrimination. Why don't you put the battery in and call?" Bash suggested.

"Nicole and I teach first grade at the same elementary school. I won't be able to speak with her until her lunch break."

"Why don't you leave her a message and let her get back to you. I need to get an update from the security company I'm working with." He turned to Max. "Were you serious about the house in Maine?"

"Absolutely. My offer is to both of you."

"Would you object to having my security team on the property?"

"Who are you using?" Max asked.

"SMB Protection Agency. They are out of Chicago. I'm working with Sam Barrett, the owner."

"I'm familiar with them. If I can be part of the security set-up discussion, I'm good with that."

CHAPTER TWENTY-NINE

Asa Kline leaned on his motorcycle with his arms crossed over his chest, staring at Tree Brook Apartments in Dunwoody, Georgia, waiting for the rest of his crew to arrive. He was pissed. He had ridden all over half of hell's creation, looking for his son, who always seemed to be one step ahead of him. Asa had to admit his old man, the son of a bitch, had done a damn good job of hiding him all those years. When his father took off with his child, it was as if they had vanished into thin air. Unfortunately, his old man died before Asa could properly exact his revenge for the 25 years that he had suffered rotting in prison. He may have lost out on making his dad pay, but he planned to get his money's worth out on his son.

When Asa was released from prison, he headed back to his home with the Dragon Fire MC based in a small town south of Los Angeles. There weren't many of the same guys around, most of them dead, but once a member, always a member. He was surprised by the lukewarm reception. After all, he had taken the fall for everyone involved in the human trafficking ring. The club members still harbored ill feelings about his father's betrayal. The only way to make things right was to find the ledger and return it. Asa had recruited three of the members to help him in the search.

One of Asa's buddies saw an article in a popular motorcycle magazine about the death of some big-deal motorcycle mechanic and what a huge loss it was for professional motorcycle racers across the country. And there it was. A picture of his dad, 25 years older with wrinkled, leather skin, seated on a bike in front of his shop near Gainesville, Georgia. Probably didn't realize the picture was taken.

When Asa and his crew traveled to Georgia, they found the shop had closed and relocated under new ownership. After questioning the locals, no one knew where Eli Skylar (Clark Kline) had lived. When he went to see the sheriff, Asa had to convince him Eli Skylar was his father. The only thing the sheriff had was his wallet with a driver's license and $50. It didn't surprise Asa the old man didn't have anything left. Probably spent his money on women and drugs like in the old days. A note was found in his dad's pocket with general directions to a cabin near Tipton, North Carolina. Written at the bottom was a name—Morgan Skylar. That was the first time he knew his son's name.

When Asa and the guys found the cabin, it was a bust. Groceries sat on the kitchen counter. Little asshole must have heard him coming and ran. They tore the place apart, looking for the ledger, but found nothing. The rental car was bare except for a contract agreement on the floorboard of the passenger side. Name and street address were scratched out until there was a huge hole in the paper. He could still read the renter's city of residence by the indentions of the pen on the back—Dunwoody, Georgia. When Asa searched online, he found a Morgan Skylar listed as a kindergarten teacher at Glendale Park Elementary, not far from Dunwoody.

The conversation he had with the principal was a waste of time. Bitch wouldn't tell him anything. As they were leaving, they spotted a young teacher walking alone to her car in a deserted parking lot. The sound of the motorcycles and the backward glance to see who was coming up behind her were enough of a scare to have her singing like a bird. Didn't have to lay a hand on her. The terror in her eyes was all the coaxing she needed to give up the apartment building where Morgan lived. It was dumb luck that she was one of Morgan's friends.

It was after 4 p.m. when the guys finally pulled up beside him in the parking lot.

"Where the hell have you been?" Asa barked. He wanted to get this over with before people began returning home from work.

"Stopped to get a few burgers," Brutus said, stuffing the last bite in his mouth.

"You couldn't fuckin' wait...never mind. Let's get movin'," Asa said, standing up and heading to the front door.

An older lady carrying a canvas bag with a rat dog stuck in it was opening the door with a code when they stepped behind her. Brutus caught the door and held it open for her.

"You can't..." she didn't finish.

Brutus leaned down in her face. "Can't what?" he threatened, spittle spraying her.

Her mouth flapped open and closed like a swinging doggie door, then she rushed inside.

"Yeah. That's what I thought," he yelled after her.

Asa found the name on the mailbox, 304. They ran up the stairs and banged on the door with heavy fists.

"Open this fucking door, Morgan, or I'll break it down!" Asa hollered.

"Maybe he isn't home," Lance offered.

Brutus beat his fist until the door had a dent.

Asa glanced over at the apartment across the hall. "Knock on that door and see if they know where he is," he instructed Brutus. "We don't have time for this shit."

Brutus did as instructed, using his knuckles like a jackhammer. "Open the door now!"

A few seconds later, a small voice could be heard through the door. "What do you want?" said a quivering female. Then, the sound of a wailing infant drifted through the door.

"If you don't want something to happen to that kid, you better open the fuckin' door!" Asa yelled.

A few seconds later, a trembling woman wearing a robe stuck her head out. She was holding a tiny infant. "Please don't hurt my baby."

"Then tell me where Morgan Skylar is?" Asa demanded.

She clutched her baby to her chest. "I...I...d...don't know a Morgan Skylar. My husband and I just moved in last week."

"You don't know the guy who lives in this apartment?" Lance motioned to the opposite door.

"I...I haven't been out of the apartment since we moved in. Please let me go so I can calm my baby," she pleaded.

"Lance, you stay with her and make sure she doesn't call the police while we search the apartment."

"No!" she screamed, trying to close the door.

Asa stuck his foot in the door to block it from closing. "You keep your mouth shut, and he'll let you go when we're finished. Now move," Asa said, yanking the door open so Lance could force his way inside.

Brutus kicked open the door to 304, and the two other men entered. Asa kept watch in the hall while Brutus and Jax searched for the ledger and signs of where Morgan might have gone. A few minutes later, Brutus came out with a handful of women's lingerie in both hands.

"I think your son is queer," Brutus said. "All I see is girlie clothes."

"You assume all gay men wear women's clothes? You're a homophobic moron. Besides, it could belong to his girlfriend," Jax suggested.

Asa stormed into the only bedroom and rummaged around in the drawers, throwing clothes across the room. Next, he walked into the closet and froze.

"See. Queer," Brutus said, coming up behind him.

Asa looked at him with disgust and shook his head. He walked to the nightstand and picked up a small, framed photo of a young girl with her grandfather sitting on the porch of the cabin. The one they had just left. "Brutus, you're an idiot. He isn't gay. Morgan Skylar is a woman." Shaking his head, he muttered under his breath. "That clever bastard had us all fooled."

There was nothing in the apartment to indicate where Morgan might have gone. His dad had taught her well. There wasn't so much as an electric bill in a drawer. Since her clothes were still there, Asa knew she would return at some point. He just didn't have time to wait around. He needed to find her now.

On the way out, he banged on the door across the hall to let Lance know it was time to leave.

"Don't you fuckin' think about calling the police, or I'll be back for that kid of yours," Asa yelled at the woman cowering in a chair with her infant cradled tightly in her arms. He didn't give her a chance to respond before slamming the door. This time, they went down the fire escape to avoid being seen.

Asa was about to put on his helmet when two men in a black SUV pulled up beside him. The passenger window rolled down, and Asa stared straight into the barrel of a .357.

"What the fuck?" he said, his face going slack.

"Don't even think about it," said a thin-faced, dark-skinned man wearing a black suit and mirrored shades. The bikers released their grip on their weapons.

"Look, man, we don't want any trouble," Asa said, trying to keep his wits about him.

"What is the Dragon Fire doing here?" the man with the gun demanded as he and the bulky, older guy who was driving eased out of the vehicle.

"None of your damn business," Brutus shouted.

Asa shot him a scathing glare. "Back off, Brutus. I'll handle this."

"Don't make me ask again," the man holding the gun barked.

Asa decided he needed to play nice to defuse the situation. He didn't trust Brutus not to pull out his gun and start shooting.

"Feels like we got off on the wrong foot. We've got no beef with you guys. I'm Asa. These are my buddies Lance, Jax, and Brutus. We're here on family business," Asa said with more calm than he felt.

The driver took a few steps closer to Asa. "If it's personal, why are all of you wearing your insignia. Looks more like you're making a statement to me. Sure as hell not trying to fly under the radar. The fact that you are in an obscure location in Georgia,

2000 miles from your home base at the same time we are, can't be a coincidence."

"This has nothing to do with you. I don't even know who the hell you guys are," Asa said, beginning to lose his patience. "I came a long way to visit my son…daughter."

The suited men exchanged looks. Then the younger guy asked, "Wouldn't be Morgan Skylar, would it?"

Asa narrowed his eyes. "You after my daughter?"

"Yeah. We think she can lead us to a couple of men we're looking for," the older guy said.

"Maybe we can help each other," Asa said thoughtfully.

"Now, why the hell would we do that? Let's just say we don't have your daughter's best interest at heart," the driver grinned.

"Neither do I," Asa said with a sardonic smile. "I've got information about her that I'm sure you don't. She's been a ghost her whole life, and she's good at it. If she's traveling with someone you're looking for, you obviously have information I don't have. Makes sense we should work together."

The driver rubbed his chin and said, "Let me make a call." A few minutes later, he disconnected his cell and looked up at Asa. "My boss has authorized me to make a deal."

"Who's your boss?" Asa asked.

"Not your concern," the driver said.

"Fine. Do it without us. You wouldn't be here if you had any ideas where to look, and I guarantee there is absolutely nothing in that apartment that will help you. Not so much as a scrap of paper. If we're going to work together, I need to know who I'm working with. You could be the FBI for all I know," Asa said testily.

"If you repeat this to anyone, including one of those assholes," he said, pointing to his partners, "you are a dead man."

Asa had a feeling this was bigger than he imagined and wasn't sure how a kindergarten teacher had gotten mixed up in it unless she used her occupation as a cover for illegal activities. Being raised by his old man, he wouldn't be surprised.

"No one will know," Asa agreed.

"Enzo Fontana."

Asa nodded, almost swallowing his tongue.

CHAPTER THIRTY

Early the next morning, Max quickly showered and dressed. It was time to get his plan to expose the traitor in his life into motion. He drove to the center of Winston-Salem and parked on an empty side street. Using the same burner phone as the day before, he called his VP of Legal and longtime friend, Stephan Gallagher.

"Max, where the hell have you been? And why aren't you calling from your cell? I've left you at least ten messages. Didn't recognize the number. You're lucky I picked up. I thought you were going to try to sell me an auto warranty," he laughed.

"It's a long story. I'll happily share it with you over a bottle of Scotch when I get home. What was so urgent that warranted all the messages?" Max asked.

"Enzo's up to something. He showed up at my office yesterday morning with some guy named Carter Pullman. Introduced him as the building inspector assigned to the Fontana School Revitalization Project in Harlem. Your personal baby."

"I've never heard of the man, and you know I've overseen all the initial start-up details personally," Max enthused. "We're still four weeks from breaking ground. What did he want?"

"Enzo said Pullman needed copies of the final plans with the revisions you made. Since you're out of town, he wanted me to turn my files on the project over to him."

"What? That is bullshit! There were no revisions. The city has had copies of those plans for months. It has been approved, and the permits have been issued. I'm not going to ask if you gave him anything because I know you didn't. But what do you think he's after?"

"My guess is he's trying to mess with the project. Maybe set you up for cutting corners or making changes under the radar. Hell. Who knows what's in that slimy little bastard's brain? You need to come home."

Max fell silent. There was no way he would leave Sebastian and Morgan. Not while they were in danger.

"Are you still there, Max?"

"I am. Got lost in my head for a few seconds. It's not possible right now. There's a lot going on. I'll be in touch soon. Thanks for watching my back, Stephen."

"Stay safe, Max."

Max's next call was to his assistant, Rohan Burman. He learned Enzo and Fatima had both been by the office on separate occasions with ridiculous excuses to access Max's office. He wasn't worried. If they tried to open his desktop without his password and retinal scan, it would fry itself. All his files were backed up and encrypted. After speaking to Steve and Rohan, he felt he was closer to confirming who had betrayed him.

His third call was to Fatima to tell her he had just arrived in Winston-Salem and would be staying the night. She feigned indifference. Their conversation was brief. She was rushing off to a breakfast meeting. Max turned off the phone and drove back to the motel.

Max dropped off the burner phone and $5000 cash. He instructed Gavin to make sure the phone was not turned on until it was taken to the remote location. Whoever was monitoring the scene should take extreme care to remain hidden, and under no circumstances should they try to retrieve the burner. Max insisted their safety was paramount over anything else. If no one showed up after today, the assignment would be concluded. Max gave him a number to call.

After collecting his few belongings from his room, Max ran through the parking lot in the pouring rain to meet Sebastian and Morgan at the rental car. Morgan was already seated in the back, so he sat up front with Sebastian.

"Ready to go?" Sebastian asked from the driver's seat.

"Just a minute," Morgan said. "I have a voicemail from my friend Nicole. She must have tried to call me back while I was in the shower."

They both turned toward Morgan when she began to speak.

"Hi Nicole, it's Morgan. How's everything going? Are the fish behaving? They like to fight over the food sometimes. ... What? ... Say that again?"

Max watched her smile fade and her cheerful voice fall flat. He and Sebastian exchanged worried looks. Morgan's eyes squeezed shut as she listened. Something terrible had happened.

"I'll call her tomorrow. ... I understand. ... We'll talk about it when I get home. Tell the maintenance guy I appreciate him putting in a new door."

After Morgan hung up, she covered her face with her hands.

"What happened?" Max asked.

Pulling her trembling hands from her face, she hugged herself for support. She was doing her best to stay calm, fighting back tears. With a quiver in her voice, she detailed her father's visit to her elementary school to speak to the principal, then recounted the destruction of her apartment and the terrorizing of a mother and her infant across the hall. Nicole relayed a message from the principal that it wasn't safe for the kids for Morgan to return to work until the situation was resolved. Morgan was to call her if she had questions.

"Christ," Max said, his voice tight. He felt the heat rise in his neck at the thought of the innocent mother and child being held against their will. His thoughts flashed to Izzy and how she must have felt when his father threatened to take her child from her. "They're animals. All of them."

Sebastian practically climbed between the seats to reach Morgan's hand. "I'm so sorry, Morgan."

Max could see the fear and guilt in her expression. She

held herself responsible for the sins of her father. He knew there was nothing he could say at that moment to change how she felt. It would be a process.

"They tore the place apart. I assume they were looking for the ledger. Maybe money, too. Pops left me his assets in his will, but Asa wouldn't know about that. I only learned about the will last week. Now I'm basically suspended from my job."

"Asa?" Max questioned.

"My biological father's name is Asa Kline, but he is nothing to me."

Max nodded understanding.

"Thank God you weren't home," Sebastian said with relief. "He's a dangerous man."

"Oh goodness. What am I going to do now?"

"You're coming with us," Max said emphatically. "You'll be safe at my mother's home for now. We'll figure the rest out later."

She looked up with watery eyes. "They killed my fish."

"Why don't you let me drive?" Max whispered to Sebastian. "You sit in back with Morgan until she wraps her head around this. We can stop in the next town and mail the ledger. I also need to buy some clothes and toiletries."

"Are we driving all the way to Maine?" Sebastian asked, opening his door.

"I'm still working that out," Max said.

CHAPTER THIRTY-ONE

They were about 100 miles northeast of Winston-Salem when the sun finally peaked out of the gray rain clouds. They stopped in a small town with two traffic lights, a discount store, a gas station, a grocery store, and a tiny post office. Bash waited in the car while Max and Morgan took the ledger inside. They purchased the appropriate size box and sent the package express mail to Max's mother's P.O. Box in Maine.

As they were walking back to the car, Max said, "You doing okay?"

She gave him a weak smile. "It's a relief to get it out of my hands, if only temporarily." He nodded in agreement.

After a trip through the discount store, where Max was surprised to learn you didn't have to pay $500 for a pair of jeans, they headed to the car with their arms loaded with packages.

"Just to be safe, we need to change our vehicle," Max said.

"What about an RV?" Morgan said, pointing to a large billboard.

Max followed her finger with his eyes. The sign read *Mountain Road RV Sales and Rental*.

"That's a damn good idea, Morgan," Max said with enthusiasm. "Five miles down the road. This should be fun!"

Bash started the car and turned to Max. "What will be fun?"

"Figuring out the sleeping arrangements," he smirked.

Max would have preferred the 44-foot class-A recreational vehicle due to the additional space, but Morgan reminded him they didn't need to draw attention to themselves. According to the salesman, the smaller version had more than enough space to accommodate three people comfortably. Max listened to the sales pitch and agreed to purchase a barely used 2020 model at a reduced price. A quick wire transfer from an untraceable account he shared with his mother and the traveling motel was all his. He mused that his friends would find his new acquisition quite out of character for him.

As a condition of the purchase, the salesman agreed to drop off their car rental at the nearest airport. After the paperwork was completed, the salesman did a brief orientation of the amenities and how to operate and maintain the vehicle. As Max stared blankly at the keys in his hand, it dawned on him that he had no idea if he could even drive the thing. Morgan must have seen the sheer panic in his eyes because she swooped to the rescue.

"I've got this, y'all. Let's get loaded."

Morgan explained that her Pops had allowed her to help drive an 18-wheeler across the country to deliver classic cars. She reasoned the RV would be much easier to maneuver. Max had a ton of questions about how that was even possible but decided he preferred not to know.

Who is this woman? He knew the story of the sheltered life Morgan lived with her Pops, the ex-motorcycle outlaw, but the skills she possessed could rival some of his best security guards. For some reason, that didn't jive with the whole kindergarten teacher thing. He liked her and wanted to believe she was exactly who she appeared to be, but the cautious side of him hoped he wasn't being played. Except for his mother, he had grown up in a den of vipers. It was hard for him to stop expecting to find them in the most unlikely places.

Although it would make the trip longer, they decided it would be best to stay off the major interstates. They mapped out obscure routes through the mountains and foothills through Virginia, West Virginia, Pennsylvania, and western New York. Then, they would head northeast toward Maine. It would keep them off the main Atlantic coastal highways and selfishly give

Max time to get to know his son and get a better read on Morgan.

Max admired Morgan's independent and guileless nature. Sebastian, who he felt had come into his success too easily, needed someone like her in his life to keep him grounded. From what he had gathered, his son had become entirely too dependent on his inner circle. Max understood how easily it could happen when people tried to run interference and insulate you from conflicts and dealing with the tough issues. He had been there himself, and it had cost him the only thing that truly mattered—Izzy.

The shock of learning she had died gutted him, but he refused to dwell on it. He had prayed he would see her again. Happy. Enjoying her son and grandchildren. He imagined she had married years ago, but he refused to believe anyone could replace what they had shared. He was secretly glad no one had. There was no way he could make up for the years away from Sebastian. He would never let that happen again. Building a relationship with his son and protecting him from the Fontana family was his highest priority. And because Morgan had risked her life to save Sebastian, Max would help her find a way out of the crosshairs of the biker gang and the FBI.

Max received a call from Gavin Nordstrom at 5 p.m. on a new burner phone he had purchased.

"Max."

"Mr. Fontana, this is Gavin." His voice was shaky, his breathing rapid.

"What happened?" Max asked, sensing the worst.

"Well... I let my son Shawn take care of planting the phone and watching the building for you. He and his wife need the money. There is a small ten-room motel on the outskirts of town that's been abandoned for close to fifteen years. Rumor is the owners skipped town to avoid a foreclosure. Been sitting with a condemned sign on it for years. It fits your criteria. Shawn said the doors and windows were boarded up tight. Probably didn't want squatters in there causing trouble. He turned on the cell and wedged it inside a broken light fixture under one of the outside eves. He was 100% sure no one could have been inside.

"The motel is across the road from a steep wooded foothill. Shawn took his backpack with supplies and settled on a ridge behind some evergreens. Two black SUVs with six men in dark suits showed up around 1 p.m. Some were carrying AR-15s. They broke down the doors with an ax and searched every room. Didn't find the burner phone until they called it. That's when the hollering started. I guess those men figured out they had been bamboozled. One guy made a bunch of calls.

"An hour later, I got an interesting phone call at the motel from a man looking for you and a male and female companion. Said he was an FBI agent, and they had a warrant for your arrest. Suggested you guys could be traveling under assumed names."

"That wasn't an FBI agent," Max said dryly.

"I figured. Shawn said none of those men had any law enforcement gear on. I called a buddy of mine who runs the Briarwood Motel and asked him if he got a call from the FBI. He received the same call about ten minutes before I did. Looks like they were going down a list. Made me feel better knowing they hadn't singled me out."

Max scrubbed his chin nervously. "It makes me feel better too. Did they give you a number to call in case you saw us?"

"Yeah." He gave Max the number. He didn't have to look it up. He knew exactly whose number it was. Enzo Fontana.

"Is that it? Did your son get home okay?"

"That's not all. Before they left, they lit some rags soaked with gasoline and tossed them in some of the rooms. That place went up in flames and was mostly gone when the fire trucks arrived. Shawn walked a half mile through the woods to his car and got out of there. He didn't want to be charged with arson."

"I'm sorry Shawn got stuck like that. It never occurred to me that they would burn the place down," Max said with regret. "I just wanted to see if my suspicions were correct. Tell Shawn not to put that money in the bank. He doesn't want to bring any unnecessary attention to himself. The only thing he did was put a phone in an abandoned building. No one will ever know. When I get home, I'll send him another $5000, but it may be a week or two."

"That's not necessary. I'm just glad you got out of here, okay," Gavin said with sincerity.

"Yes, it is. I always pay my debts. Thanks a lot. I won't forget what you and your son did for me."

As he was about to hang up, Gavin said, "I almost forgot something. When Shawn was on his way home, he passed a diner. Both of those vehicles were parked outside. They haven't left town."

CHAPTER THIRTY-TWO

Morgan took a county road through the mountains of West Virginia, thinking it would be the least likely route anyone would expect them to take. It turned out to be a bad decision. The narrow road hugged cliff edges, making it downright scary. Max sat in the passenger seat, white-knuckling the dashboard. She inwardly laughed at his offer to drive. Bash sat quietly on the sofa with his eyes squeezed shut, practically hyperventilating.

She regretted embellishing her driving experience with the 18-wheeler. Relieving Pops for an hour while he took a cat nap was more accurate to the truth. And that was only because he had fallen asleep, almost running them off the road. He was on a critical deadline, and she had been his only alternative. Unlike the curvy mountain roads, the interstate had been straight and flat, and it was the middle of the night, so it was highly unlikely the highway patrol would catch a 17-year-old driving a big rig.

"Don't you think we need to find a place to stop for the night?" Bash asked with a nervous tremor in his voice. "Not sure navigating these roads in the dark is the best idea. It's already dusk."

"I agree," Morgan chimed in.

Five miles down the road, they found a place to stay called Ryder Campsites. It had water, electrical hookups, and a bathhouse with restrooms and showers. With the campground only a few days from closing for the season, there were only a few campers on site. Max specifically asked for a secluded spot. Their scenic campsite was nestled in a valley right next to a rushing creek.

"Hey, look!" Morgan called excitedly as she stepped out of the RV. "We have our own firepit with a grill! Anybody up for barbeque steaks? Those ribeyes and potatoes I picked up will taste great cooked over an open fire."

Max and Bash were in full agreement.

The rain held off just long enough to get the steaks off the grill. They shared an excellent meal, and it turned out to be a perfect opportunity for them to get to know each other in a relaxed atmosphere. Her heart warmed listening to Max and Bash share stories about his mother. The tension between them seemed to dissipate. It was a good time to find the bathhouse for a long, hot shower to wash away the road.

The light rain had stopped, but the cloud cover remained, blocking the moonlight. There was a crisp bite to the air, and remnants of the burnt hickory aroma still lingered. It was uncommonly quiet, with no noises from fellow campers. Once she got to the end of their campsite, she realized there was only a dimly lit deserted gravel road lined with dense trees between their site and the bathhouse. The reminder of every scary camp movie that she had ever seen quickened her pace.

She sighed with relief when she reached the log cabin-style facilities. Men on the right and women on the left. The motion lights flicked on the instant she opened the door, revealing a large room with toilet stalls, sinks, individual showers with cloth curtains, and wooden benches. Undressing hurriedly, she pulled her pjs out of her backpack and laid them neatly on the bench. The rubber-grid lining covering the cement on the bottom of the shower was a welcome sight. She wouldn't have to stand on the cold concrete in puddles of dirty water.

As the warm water with a heavy sulfur smell hit her shivering skin, Morgan thought back to her conversations with Bash. They had developed an easy and comfortable rapport. Ever since Max came into the picture, she noticed Bash withdrawing from her. If he was frustrated with her, she understood why. They had both barreled into Bash's neatly organized world and tossed it up in the air. Now, her problems only compounded his own. Though Bash insisted she stay, she wasn't sure that was what was best for his safety or his ability to adjust to having his father in his life.

As she was drying off with a cheap, thin towel, she heard a car engine.

"Turkey feathers," she muttered. Hastily dressing, she grabbed her backpack and crept to the door, flipping off the light. It could be another camper, but she doubted it. On the way in, they passed a restroom much closer to the only other RV that was parked on this side of the campground. Cautiously listening at the door, she heard two car doors slam.

"You had better make this quick," a man with a gruff voice barked. "They could be gone by the time you get showered and changed."

"No one's going anywhere. It's after eleven, and the owner said everyone's in for the night. Besides, they probably aren't even here. You heard the man the same as me. Three retired couples and one family with toddlers. They're closing for the winter. That RV Fontana bought could be halfway across the country by now. No damn way they'd be wasting time in these mountains. The sooner we're out of here, the better. We're going through the motions to satisfy Enzo that we've looked everywhere," grumbled a younger male. The voices were getting closer. "One of the other teams has a better chance of catching Fontana on the interstate."

"Don't let Enzo hear you say that."

The door to the men's restroom opened and closed as the men carried on their conversation. Morgan knew she needed to warn Bash and Max, but she couldn't help the need to see if she could learn anything useful. Creeping silently out the door, she stopped outside and listened to the muffled voices.

"Yeah. Yeah. Now let me get cleaned up."

"Boss isn't going to like you going around in jeans. That's not the image he wants us to project," an older man said.

"I doubt he wants me to stink either. If he'd let us get a

hotel room instead of sleeping in the car, maybe the suit would have made it a little longer. Unless you tell him, he'll never know. Now take a fuckin' load off and let me get cleaned up!"

Morgan was stunned. *How did they find out about the RV? Had to be the salesman. But why? It had only been hours since Max purchased it.*

When the shower began running, Morgan assumed they would be occupied for at least a few minutes. Seeing no one else, she ran to the far side of a black SUV. New York license plate. It was too dark to see inside the vehicle, and she didn't want to use the light on her phone. If they planned to check all the RVs, theirs would be the closest. That thought sent chills through her. She had to slow them down.

Pulling a small pocketknife out of her untied boots, she crouched down in front of a back tire. Raring her hand back, she rammed the knife between the tire tread. When she pulled it out, she didn't hear air escaping. Reinserting the blade in the same place, she took off a boot and hammered the heel against the hilt of the knife. After a few hard hits, she heard a faint hiss. Time to go.

"What the hell are you doing to my car?" shouted a man coming out of the bathhouse.

Without looking back, Morgan turned and ran.

CHAPTER THIRTY-THREE

Max was giving Sabastian a tutorial on how to load and shoot his 9mm when his burner phone rang. They both stared at it. *Who in the hell?*

"You going to answer?" Sebastian asked.

"No one has this number but Grayson Lewis. I purchased three burners at the airport in Charlotte to make sure they weren't compromised."

"What about when you checked us in earlier? Did you put it on the registration?"

Max nodded. "I paid the owner $500 extra to stay off the books. I forgot I gave him a number to call if anything looked troublesome. He knew what I meant."

The cell stopped ringing.

"Maybe you should call him back?" Sebastian suggested.

Max pulled up the last number and pushed enter.

"You just called? …. What do they look like, and what are they driving? … How long ago? … Me either. Thanks for the call. We may be leaving sooner than expected."

Sebastian's face fell. "What's wrong?"

"Grab your stuff and anything Morgan left behind. Be sure to turn off the lights. I'll tell you once we are out of the vehicle."

Bash nodded and rushed to the bedroom. Max began to grab anything that would identify them and packed it in the duffle bag that he purchased at Walmart. He picked up the Colt .45 Morgan gave him before she left to take her shower and couldn't help wondering about the timing. *Did she know someone was coming? Was it a coincidence? If it was, it was a fortuitous one.* But Max didn't believe in coincidences. *Maybe it was intuition she picked up from her grandfather? I want to believe in her.*

"Are you okay, Max?"

The question shook him out of his head. He looked at Sebastian, who was now in his coat with his arms loaded with bags.

"Morgan took her backpack with her. I picked up everything else."

Max looked on the table for the 9mm Ruger. It was gone. Max stuffed the Colt .45 in his coat pocket.

"I've got the Ruger," he confirmed.

"Good," Max said, reaching for the keys on the coffee table. "Let's go. We need to find Morgan. They are coming for us."

Sebastian's eyes went wide. "What the hell?"

Max flipped off the remaining lights. After they stepped outside, he locked the door.

"Now, can you tell me..." The sound of a vehicle approaching halted Sebastian.

Within seconds, the vehicle would reach them. Max grabbed Sabastian by the arm and yanked him behind the RV. They watched a dark-colored SUV whizz past their site toward the restrooms. Max knew from the sitemap the road was a dead end.

"Christ," Sebastian gasped. "They're headed straight towards Morgan."

They began running. "Hopefully, she'll hear them and stay out of sight," huffed Max.

The bathhouse was at least 100 yards from their campsite. When they were within sight of the SUV parked in front of the bathhouse, they stopped.

"You think they already have her?" Sebastian whispered, as they stooped behind an evergreen.

"I'm guessing there would be a loud ruckus if they did ... unless they caught her off guard," Max said.

A figure suddenly popped up behind the SUV.

"Can you tell if that's a man or woman?" Max whispered.

"What the hell are you doing to my car?" yelled a large man in a suit who was coming out of the men's restroom. Max detected a Jersey accent.

When the figure turned to run, they realized it was Morgan.

"Get out here, you asshole! Some woman was messing with our vehicle!" the suited man screamed back through the restroom door.

Seconds later, another equally muscled but younger man pulling a sweater over his head burst out the door. They ran full speed after Morgan.

Sebastian jumped out in the road to follow, but Max pulled him back and covered his mouth.

"You are going to get Morgan shot. We'll follow them and catch them by surprise. She's heading to the RV. The door is locked. Just calm down. We'll get her back."

"She didn't take her gun!" Sebastian stage-whispered with panic in his voice.

"Please trust me, Sebastian," he pleaded.

"Let me go!" they heard Morgan scream.

"Shut your fucking mouth and tell me what you were doing to our tires," one of the men shouted back.

Max and Sebastian moved swiftly through the trees running parallel to the road. They stopped when they reached a position with easy access to Morgan. The younger guy was standing in front of her, while the suited guy held her arms behind her back. The streetlight next to the campsite made it easier for Bash and Max to see what was happening.

"We need to wait for the right opportunity. I believe Morgan will provide that. She can see the lights are off in the RV. Flip the safety off on your gun, and don't put your finger on the trigger and shoot yourself," Max whispered in his ear.

"I wasn't doing anything!" Morgan shouted.

"Then why the fuck did you run," the suited guy barked.

"Helllllloooo," she singsonged sarcastically. "Two strange

men. One female. The middle of the night. I'm not stupid. I was trying to see if I recognized the car. Then this guy." She moved her head in the direction of the man behind her. "Unless suits have become the new camping gear, I doubt y'all are here for the trout. So, of course, I'm going to run."

"She's trying to throw them off," Sebastian said. "I've seen her do it before."

"Where is your campsite?" Sweater guy stepped forward, grabbing her jaw and squeezing.

"Well, it doesn't look like it's working this time," Max said under his breath. "Those guys are hardcore. When I move, you come behind me with the gun in hand. And try not to shoot me in the back."

Morgan jerked her head and attempted to bite the man's hand. It got her a slap across the face. It all happened in the blink of an eye. Morgan collapsed to her knees, dropping her weight, and went down as if she had been hurt. When the suit guy grabbed her under her arms and yanked her back up, Morgan threw her head back and busted the suit guy in the nose. She drew her knees upward into her body, then pushed her legs out, slamming her feet firmly into sweater guy's chest. The momentum and shock sent him backward to the ground. Despite the blood flowing from his broken nose, the suit guy still held his grip on Morgan, but by then, Max had his .45 against the back of the man's head.

When the guy on the ground reached inside his jeans for what Max assumed was a gun, Sebastian fired his 9mm near the guy's feet. Sweater guy flew back three feet and threw his hands in the air.

Max couldn't help wondering if Bash was trying to scare him or shoot him. It didn't matter. His choice would have been the latter.

"Let her go nice and easy," Max demanded.

Suit guy released Morgan, and she quickly moved beside Sebastian.

"Are you okay?" he asked, rubbing his fingers lightly down her cheek.

"I'm fine. Just smarts a little."

Still holding the gun to suit guy's head, Max reached around and relieved the man of his weapon, handing it to Morgan. She held the gun on him while Max patted him down, finding a knife strapped to his ankle. The same process was done to disarm the sweater guy. Both men were instructed to lie face down with hands and legs spread.

"How are we going to tie them up?" Sebastian asked. "It's not like we have handcuffs."

"If you can get me their keys, I'll see what I can find in their SUV. I'm sure they had a plan if they found us. What self-respecting kidnapper wouldn't?" Morgan asked with a little shrug.

Max found the keys in a suit pocket and threw them to Morgan. A few minutes later, she returned with plastic zip ties. "Yeah. These guys are planners," she said, handing them to Max.

After securing the men, they moved them to the backseat of the SUV and zip-tied their feet and hands. Ignoring the threats and groans, Max searched the car for information. Morgan insisted Max put their jackets over them so they wouldn't get cold. He couldn't help but laugh at her concern, commenting that they wouldn't have done the same for her. When the threat was neutralized, they returned to the RV.

"Are we leaving?" Sabastian asked.

"At sunrise. Let's try to get some sleep. I'll give the owner the keys to the SUV in the morning. He can call the police," Max said.

"What if those men give our names to the police?" Sebastian asked.

"Not a chance in hell. They screwed this up badly, and they know it. They'll probably spend the night trying to figure out what to tell Enzo that won't get them killed."

CHAPTER THIRTY-FOUR

Morgan startled awake to the sound of her phone ringing. She hoped it was Parker Livingston. As she fumbled around for the cell, she tried to wipe the fog from her head. Her fingers found the cell tucked under a t-shirt on the floor by the bed. Trying to focus on the screen, she noted the time as 6:12 a.m.

"H...hello?" she answered.

"Morning, Ms. Skylar. Parker Livingston. Sounds like I woke you. Sorry about that, but I felt it important enough to contact you immediately. I secured an agreement with the FBI."

Morgan sat up, wiping her face. "Really? Is it a good thing or something I'd rather know when I'm more fully awake?"

He laughed. "No worries. It's good news. They have agreed to hold you blameless for anything to do with the Dragon Fire or the ledger left to you by your grandfather. They did a thorough investigation of Eli Skylar, your grandfather's alias, for the last 25 years and found no criminal activity. His business was clean. For a multitude of reasons, one being his insistence on only accepting cash for payment, the FBI assumed his business was being used for money laundering. Mr. Skylar cleverly employed a reputable bookkeeper who he insisted audit his books monthly."

Morgan felt her eyes sting. "T...thank you."

He cleared his throat. "Then there was the matter of the guns in your father's mountain cabin. They were all confiscated to check the ballistics against any firearm-related crimes. Those tests came back negative. Although your grandfather had a bill of sale for all the weapons, the fact that he used an alias when he purchased them makes them all illegal. There were three guns missing, based on the purchase receipts. You wouldn't know anything about that, would you?"

Morgan swallowed hard and used her sweetest voice to respond. "Mr. Livingston, I've led a very sheltered and isolated life. What in the world would a kindergarten teacher need with a gun?" Not exactly a denial nor was it an admission.

He chuckled. "Now that I think about it, it is farfetched. Anyway, there wasn't anything else of consequence in the cabin. Mr. Watson, your father's attorney, had the paperwork for everything in his office, which made it easier for the FBI. They could tell you how much he spent on your tennis shoes when you were five years old."

"Why would he keep all that paper?"

"My guess is he wanted to make sure he would never come under suspicion. Particularly if anyone found out his real identity. And by the way, there were no outstanding warrants for his arrest when he kidnapped you."

Morgan bit her lip. "He didn't kidnap me. He saved me from being human trafficked."

"I know, Morgan, but it was still illegal. He would never have been granted custody of you. Social services would have found you a home."

"That's a big 'if,' Mr. Livingston. Who would want a kid from a drug-addicted mom and a dad who was a convicted child trafficker? Bad seed and all. I understand why Pops did it, and I'm grateful."

"I am too, Morgan. He didn't want to risk losing you. He apparently did everything in his power to walk the straight and narrow. By isolating you, he kept you out of harm's way. You are now set up for a good life without being saddled with his past."

"Until now," Morgan sighed.

He cleared his throat. "Yes. It appears his past finally caught up to you."

"Are they going to take his money from me? It doesn't seem fair to his legacy."

"There are no legal grounds for anyone to do that. Mr. Skylar proved he earned every dollar. Although he used an alias to pay taxes, he did pay them. The Feds are willing to overlook it in exchange for the ledger."

"It's a conditional arrangement?" Morgan asked. She wondered what would happen if the ledger got lost now that it was out of her hands.

"It's how the agents are writing up the agreement. A justification for removing the penalties for the falsified tax returns. Since your grandfather has passed, he can't be made accountable. Getting the ledger smooths over a lot for the FBI. Regardless, you have no liability for any of it. Every dollar you've earned and spent is accounted for."

"I assure you if my Pops was still alive, you and I wouldn't know anything about the ledger."

"I'm sure you are correct."

"What next?" she asked.

"Do you still have the ledger?"

"I mailed it to a friend. I'm on my way there to pick it up. We figured it was safer in the U.S. Post Office than it was with us. I'll be there in a couple of days. I'm staying off public transportation." She then told him about her biological father and his motorcycle buddies visiting her employment and breaking into her apartment and threatening her neighbor.

"Are Fontana's men still after you and Sebastian Bartoli?"

"I guess it depends on which Fontana you are talking about?"

"What does that mean, Morgan? This is serious. I didn't mention anything to the FBI about Fontana sending his men to the lake cabin to find Sebastian Bartoli, and how you became involved. I was afraid it would muddy the waters. Would Fontana's men have any way of knowing about the ledger?"

Morgan felt a sinking feeling in her stomach. *There is no way anyone else could possibly know about it. Bash and I only found out about it when we went to Pops' cabin. Enzo Fontana couldn't have known about the ledger when his goons came after Bash at the lake house. Bash and I had never met until I knocked on his cabin door in Guntersville. Max didn't send those men after them. Enzo Fontana did.* A chill ran through her.

If the ledger really is Max's motivation, I just mailed it to him. No fuss. No muss. It is headed to a P.O. Box that I can't legally access. Am I really the dumbest person on earth? No, I'm not. I know people, and Max wouldn't do that to me. I trust him. Besides, Beth and her father were the only ones who knew I was going to be at the cabin.

"It wasn't Maximillian Fontana who sent the men after us. It was Enzo Fontana. Sebastian and I met with Maximillian Fontana in Charlotte, North Carolina, at a very public place. We were shot at by some men who Mr. Fontana recognized as employees of his cousin Enzo. It's a long story, but Enzo Fontana is trying to take over the Fontana business. We've been on the run ever since."

Her attorney was silent for a few minutes. Morgan wondered if they had gotten disconnected. Finally, she heard him take a deep breath. "Let me get this straight. You have Enzo Fontana, a reputed gangster dressed in a fancy suit, and Asa Kline, a violent ex-con and outlaw motorcycle gang member, both trying to find you. And you think they have two different motivations? And Maximilian Fontana, the CEO of Fontana Properties & Development, who employs Enzo Fontana, has nothing to do with it? You strike me as an intelligent young woman, Morgan. You can't believe it's a coincidence."

"I…" words escaped her.

"Hold on a moment, Morgan. I have another call from the FBI coming through. It could be an update, and I need to tell them to contact the Dunwoody Police Department and get the information about the break-in at your apartment. See if they have an APB out on Asa Kline. Don't worry. I won't mention the Fontana involvement. I don't want our deal to go up in smoke."

Morgan felt the blood drain from her face. Pops had always been there to protect her. Made these kinds of judgement calls on her behalf. Kept her safe. Livingston made a lot of sense. How could it be a coincidence? If Max was only interested in getting the ledger, and it was all some elaborate plot, then why was he still here? In a small RV? Eating steak and Twinkies? All he had to do was hop a plane to Maine, pick up the ledger, and use it for whatever purpose he saw fit. Her heart sank. If Max planned to use the ledger to gain power over the men in influential positions, then she and Bash were threats. Her attorney had already contacted the FBI. She doubted Max would hurt his own son. *But I'm nothing to him. An inconvenience.* Her whole body began to shake. Her imagination ran wild. She couldn't think straight. *Get away. Get away. Get away.*

"Morgan? Morgan? Are you there?"

The sound of her name pulled her back from her thoughts. "Yes. Sorry. What were you saying?"

"It's not good news. The FBI was already fully aware of the incident in Dunwoody. Your neighbor and her infant were held hostage and terrorized while the Dragon Fire gang broke into your apartment. They were able to identify three of the four men, including Asa Kline, who all have felony records."

"I already knew all of that," Morgan said, wanting to get off the phone. She needed space. A place to think. Figure out a new plan.

"There is something else. The outside cameras picked up two men in suits approaching the gang members on their bikes in the parking lot of your apartment complex immediately after the attack."

Morgan felt lightheaded. "W…What?"

"After the FBI analyzed the tapes, they believe the initial contact appeared adversarial. As they began speaking to Asa Kline, the temperature seemed to settle down. One of the suits made a phone call and spoke for a few minutes. He exchanged a few words with Asa. Then everyone leaves, heading in the same direction."

Morgan's voice was tight. "They have been working t… together?" The thought made her skin crawl.

"There is no way to know for sure, but from the dynamics of the conversation, they appeared to be strangers. The FBI is doing facial recognitions on the men in suits, but I think you and I both have an idea who they might be or at least who employs them. They may have found a common goal and decided to work together. Because of client confidentiality, I am not obligated to volunteer information to the FBI on my suspicions. But Morgan, if these two groups of thugs are coordinating their efforts, no matter how it happened, the situation just became extremely volatile. Maybe we should tell the FBI about Fontana's involvement."

"No!" The word shouted from her lips before she could contain it. She felt faint. Shook it off. Had to get her head on straight. *Get out. Now.* "Mr. Livingston, I've got to go."

"There is just one other thing. Maximillian Fontana's wife reported him missing today. Swears he's been kidnapped."

"What? That's not true... I mean, he's fine. Why would she do that?" Morgan whispered.

"I don't have a clue what games these people are playing, but his picture has been on the national news all afternoon, asking the public to call in any information. You and Sebastian don't want to be caught up in whatever twisted power struggle the Fontana's have going. And you certainly don't want to be accused of kidnapping. My ultimate priority is you. You're my client. My advice is to distance yourself from all of them. Get the ledger back and call me immediately."

"I'll call you back," she said with a quivering voice.

"Morgan? Don't hang up? I'm worried about you. Tell me where you are?" he sounded panicked.

"I'm fine. I promise I'll call later. I've got to go."

"No one who says they are 'fine' actually..." She never heard the rest.

After several steadying breaths to calm herself, Morgan threw on her clothes and slipped on her boots without bothering to tie them and her coat. Looking around for her phone that had disappeared in the covers, she gave up and quietly pushed open the door. Max and Bash were sleeping as she eased outside.

Then she ran. And ran. And ran. With no idea where she was going. Tears stung her eyes. The cold air burned her lungs.

It was still dark, with the only light coming from a few scattered lampposts along the road. The sound of rushing water reminded her she must be running parallel to the creek, swollen from the night rain. *Get away. Get away.* The words pounded in her head in time with her footfalls.

She didn't notice the road had veered to the left until she was slapped in the face with an evergreen branch, but it barely slowed her down as she swung her arms wildly to block the foliage. Suddenly, she felt her right boot sinking, the ground shifting under her foot. The forward momentum of her body sent her flinging forward, landing face down in the freezing water. The shock took her breath away. It wasn't that deep on the edge, but with her feet elevated (her one boot still stuck in the muddy bank), her head and upper body were underwater. She frantically felt around the creek bottom for something solid enough for her hands and arms to be able to support her weight, allowing her to get her head above water. Feeling a collection of stones, she was able to lift her head enough to catch a full breath of air but then slowly sank back into the muddy silt, pulling her head back under. The frigid water seeped through the armholes and neck of her waterproof coat. Her body shivered from the shock.

She had to get herself out before she went into hyperthermia or drowned. There was no one to rescue her. Allowing her panic to override her common sense, she had foolishly fled without telling anyone. By the time Bash and Max even realized she was gone, she would be dead. A million thoughts swirled through her head. A cluster of emotions. Longing. Sadness. Regret. Clarity. She didn't have time to sort them out, but she never would if she didn't save herself.

"Evaluate your situation with a calm head, then decide your best options," she heard Pops' words in her head. *My right boot is stuck solidly in the mud, so no help there.* Then she remembered. With her laces untied, her boots should have a looser grip on her feet. The angle of the right foot made it impossible to move her leg, but maybe her left foot could slip free with a little maneuvering. If she could wiggle her left foot out, she might be able to use her

toes to push the lip of the right boot down enough to ease her right foot out. At that point, her legs should drop level with her upper body and allow her to get up on her feet. If she could make it back to the bank without cutting her bare feet on the jagged rocks, she would be safe.

Readjusting her hands to another pile of rocks, she pushed up enough to get her mouth above the water to take a few deep breaths. As her head went back under, she concentrated on working her left foot out of the boot. A small surge of relief shot through her as it pulled free. Once her foot released, she wedged her toes under the shoestrings on the stuck boot, trying to loosen them. Pushing against the tongue of the boot, she felt its grip on her right foot loosen and then release. As her legs began to fall, she bent her knees just before they hit the bottom of the creek. With her arms pushing against handfuls of bottom silt, she thrust herself backwards and upright onto her knees, gasping for air. She shakily got to her feet and carefully made her way to the bank, grabbed a branch, and pulled herself out of the water. As exhaustion took over, she fell to the ground and rolled over on her back. Looking up into the now dawning morning, red streaks of light breaking through, her body began to tremble violently as she sobbed.

CHAPTER THIRTY-FIVE

Seconds after Morgan stealth routine out the door, Bash was out of bed, pulling on his jeans.

"Why didn't you stop her?" Max asked, getting out of his bed.

"Why didn't you?" Bash shot back, buttoning his flannel shirt and tying his boots.

"I didn't want her to know we heard her whole damn conversation. That attorney said something that scared her. He planted doubts. Made her second-guess herself. Maybe us or at least me," Max suggested.

Bash grabbed his coat and flew open the door. Max caught his arm and peered deep into his son's eyes. "I wouldn't do anything to hurt either one of you. I swear on my life, Sebastian. Initially, I just wanted to meet you. See who you grew up to be. But now... I'd forgotten what it was like to connect with someone you truly care about. Laugh. Share jokes. Work together. Those things aren't part of my world and probably never will be if I don't make some major changes in my life. I don't want to lose this...ever. If it means giving up my place in the family company, I'm willing to do that. Sell my shares. But first, I must insure my employees are not subjected to men like Enzo and Leone. Men who will force them to break the law. Leverage their families' safety as motivation. They deserve a leader who will have their best interest at heart. Once that's done, I'm out."

"Do they ever let you go?" Sebastian asked skeptically.

"As I tried to explain before, we aren't the mafia. My

cousins are unscrupulous, dangerous members of our wealthy family. Enzo and Leone are the last of the instigators. Their grown children want nothing to do with the company business and are all estranged from their fathers. It is a lot to ask, I know, but please believe me. I'll do everything in my power to fix this mess. Morgan's, too. If she'll let me."

Bash nodded and rushed out the door.

The sunlight barely peeked through the clouds when Bash stepped on the grave road in front of their campsite. He watched the lights on the automatic lamp posts slowly turn off one by one as the sunrays grew brighter. Looking both ways, he saw no movement. Even though he doubted she had gone to the restroom, he checked there first. He couldn't resist a quick look in the SUV when he passed by. Both men were snoring but still secured.

Seeing no sign of Morgan, he headed in the opposite direction toward the main campground. He had gone about a quarter of a mile when he caught sight of a red pickup with a camper attached. A young woman with a small shovel was cleaning soggy ashes out of a firepit.

"Good morning," he called.

She looked up in surprise. "Hi."

"I didn't mean to startle you," Bash said.

"It's okay. After we got visited by two men in the middle of the night, I'm a little jumpy."

Bash winced at the thought that they might have been hurt. "I'm looking for a friend who went for a walk. She left a little while ago. I wanted to make sure she didn't get lost."

"Like in the dark?" she asked, furrowing her brows.

"Yeah."

"Did the owner give you a map?"

"He did."

"Did she take the map and a flashlight?" she asked.

Now Bash was worried. "Don't think so. Why?"

She let the shovel drop and held her arms out to form a large u shape. "This is how this side of the campground is shaped.

We are in a large crescent flanked on the outside by the stream. The campsites are spaced out along the bend. In other words, if you get off the road and walk beyond any of the campsites, you'll end up in the water. It's wider and deeper around the crescent. That's why this is a prime spot unless there's a lot of rain and it floods. We've been coming here every fall for the past five years."

"Shit. It's been raining too! Thanks," he called back to her as he ran, screaming Morgan's name.

When he reached a sharp curve to the left, he stopped. Did she come this far, or did I miss her? Turning in a slow circle, it occurred to him that had he been running in the dark, he might not have stopped and would have plowed right into the woods. As the blood pounding in his ears began to slow, he thought he heard something muffled. Coming from the trees. He isolated the sound of the rippling water in the stream. Walking to the edge of the road, he strained to hear the sound coming from the brush. It was crying. Morgan. He fought panic as he pushed branches out of the way. Only a few more steps, and he found her. Laying on the ground, crumpled in a fetal position. Soaking wet next to the edge of the water. He fell to his knees and pulled her into his arms. Instead of the relief he hoped she would feel, her sobs increased until she was gasping for air. Her body was shaking uncontrollably. He pulled her into his lap, tucked her head into his neck, and held her close.

"It's okay, baby," he said in a soothing tone. Holding his cheek against the top of her head, he gently rocked her in his arms. "I've got you. It's going to take more than falling in a creek to get rid of me." Her arms squeezed around his waist as she violently shivered against him. She was freezing, but he didn't want to move her until he knew she wasn't physically hurt.

Morgan had been the strong, level-headed soldier who had kept him safe. Every step of the way, she had been a positive ray of sunshine, refusing to let his grumpy ass get away with anything. He had been so wrapped up in how his life had been upended that he hadn't noticed how broken Morgan must be. She guarded herself, not letting anyone get close enough to see her pain. Masking it with her sunny disposition. He had selfishly ignored it. Despite his drama, he still had his home, friends, and a career to go back to in Chicago. Morgan wasn't so lucky. Her Pops had sheltered her. Isolated her. Taught her all the survival skills he thought she would need to stay safe. Unfortunately, she had little experience with building relationships and trust, things her Pops didn't have the personal experience to teach. Now that he was gone, so was her support system. Her only friend, who had been granted access to her life, was now married and moving on. Bash wanted to be there for Morgan, but would she let him? Believe she could count on him?

"I...I'm sorry," Morgan whispered.

"There is nothing to apologize for. Your life has been a train wreck ever since you met me."

"M...my f...family brought its own level of dysfunction into the mix. I think we're even," she tried to force a smile despite the chattering teeth and blue lips.

"I'd love to continue this discussion on a deeper level, but you're drenched and appear to be freezing to death. Seems you're also missing your boots. Can you walk? Or do I need to carry you?"

"You're not carrying me. M...My boots are stuck on the side of the creek bank."

"Got it."

Bash gingerly sat her on the pine straw and pulled off her soaked jacket, replacing it with his dry one. He stood up and located her muddy boots. She had just slipped them on when they heard a car pull up, a door slam, and Max screaming their names.

"Over here," Bash called. Within seconds, Max appeared in front of them.

"My God, Morgan. What happened?" Max asked in disbelief.

"I...I..." Morgan struggled with where to begin.

"We'll let her tell us after she gets a hot shower and some dry clothes. Where did you get a car?" Bash asked.

"When neither of you came back, I called the owner. He offered to help me look for you guys."

"I...I...I'm o...o...kay," Morgan stuttered.

"Sure you are, baby," Sebastian said, then scooped her up in his arms and carried her to the car.

CHAPTER THIRTY-SIX

Wrapped in a blanket and dressed in dry clothes, Morgan sat on the fold-down sofa, drinking hot tea. Max and Bash patiently waited for her to tell them what happened after she fled the RV. They deserved the truth, but she struggled with how to best explain the conversation with her attorney. How it had made her feel. The fight or flight instinct Pops had instilled in her had taken over during the phone call. His words thundering in her head. *"You can't trust anyone but yourself, Chip. Whenever you're in doubt, run as fast and as hard as you can. If you can't run, you fight."*

"That's silly, Pops. I can trust you," she remembered saying the first time he imparted that Popsism.

"Not everyone tells the truth all the time," he had answered.

His response had been confusing. Only after reading his letter did she understand what he had meant. The one person she had loved and trusted above anyone had lied to her, too.

His words may have protected her when she was a child, but now that she was an adult, they were preventing her from living a full and healthy life. Except for Beth, she had never developed any meaningful relationships, nor was she sure how to tell who was genuine from who was deceitful. She never seemed to shake the feelings of suspicion with every attempt anyone made to get close.

As she lay face down in the stream with her head underwater, she believed she was going to die. In that moment, she thought about Bash and the realization that she would never see him again. Wondered if he would miss her. If he would give

Max a chance. She wanted to find out. That's when her fight reflex kicked in. She wasn't sure what she meant to Bash, but she wanted to know.

"I shouldn't have run out like that. It was foolish. There was no preparation. It was dark. I was unfamiliar with the terrain. And worst of all, I let my emotions get the better of me," Morgan said contritely. "I'm sorry I disturbed your sleep."

Bash leaned forward with his elbows on his knees. "You honestly think we were worried about losing sleep? Christ, Morgan." He squeezed his eyes shut, holding his temper back, then opened them. Softly whispering with raw emotion. "I was worried about you." His glance flicked toward Max as he added, "We both were."

Tears threatened to fall.

Max cleared his throat. "What Bash is trying to say is we couldn't help but overhear your side of the conversation with your attorney. The door to your bedroom must not have been completely shut. We felt guilty for eavesdropping. It didn't seem to go well. Not that we planned it, but we both had the same response… pretended to be asleep so it wouldn't become awkward for any of us. If we hadn't taken the cowardly way out and lent our support instead, you would never have ended up in the creek. I apologize for that," Max said with sincerity.

"My head has been up my ass ever since we left the motel, Morgan. You've been nothing but supportive of me from the first day we met. I got up to come after you the minute you closed the door. It should never have gotten that far. Can you tell us what happened to make you run? Why the heck was Livingston calling you so early, anyway?"

She shared all the information related to the final agreement.

"That all seems to be good news. I still don't understand why you ran," Bash said.

"It was about me, wasn't it? He made you doubt my motives. Suggested I wanted the ledger for myself," Max said.

Morgan's momentary silence said it all.

"Mr. Livingston said he didn't tell the FBI about you or your involvement with Bash. He thought it would add suspicion and sour the deal," Morgan finally explained.

"Does he know Max is my father?"

"I didn't tell him anything else. He has no idea I sent the ledger to Max's mother's P.O. Box in Maine or that Max is traveling with us. Or even where I'm going or how I'm getting there. Only that I'm not using public transportation. He reminded me that Enzo Fontana works for you, Max, and that you are all dangerous." Morgan lowered her head. "It … made me feel foolish. Naïve. Like maybe it wasn't all some big coincidence, after all. Meeting Bash. Then… meeting you." She looked at Max for a split second, then dropped her eyes to her hands.

"You honestly think I somehow plotted to meet you at the cabin to obtain a ledger that you knew nothing about? This was all some elaborate set up between Max and me?" Bash asked with indignation. He stood up and looked down at her.

She could feel the disappointment.

"*You* came to my vacation rental for *my* help, not the other way around. *You* invited me to your grandfather's cabin. Christ, Morgan! I thought we had built trust. I guess I was wrong." He ran his hands through his hair and walked to the door. Now, he was the one escaping.

"Don't leave. Please," Morgan pleaded in a small voice.

Bash turned around to face her. "I'll be back."

"I do trust you, Bash. But at the time, I was confused. Mr. Livingston's words … it was like listening to Pops. The fear. The paranoia. I suddenly felt like a minnow swimming with sharks. I had to get away to clear my head." Tears began to fall freely down her cheeks. "I have spent so much of my life alone. I'm friendly with people, but it's all surface. They don't really know me, nor do I know them. This is all new. Believing in someone unconditionally."

Max stood up and put his coffee cup on the counter. "We probably need to get out of here, but you guys should talk. I'll be back in fifteen minutes. If we need to adjust our plans, we can talk about it then." He grabbed his coat and left.

Bash and Morgan stared, neither speaking or breaking eye contact for a full minute. She was at a loss. The right words eluded her. Maybe she never learned them. Bash made the first move when he sat down beside her and turned to face her. He pulled her into his arms, her head resting against his shoulder. It felt natural.

"When I realized this area of the campgrounds was surrounded by water and knowing the emotional state you were in, I completely lost all rational thought. I was terrified you might fall in… I had to find you. Make sure you were safe. Then discovering you lying on the ground, soaking wet and completely hysterical…"

"I'm fine, Bash. I can take care of myself." She said the words but wasn't sure if they were true.

He used his index finger to lift her chin to meet her eyes. "There is no doubt in my mind that you are self-reliant. But I don't want you to have to do everything by yourself. I'd like you to rely on me. I care, Morgan. A lot. We may come from different worlds, but we have a lot of important things in common. I was cocooned as a child, too. And now, as a successful writer, I've allowed my team to coddle me. Handle my life. It's about time I learned to manage myself. The important parts, anyway. You are independent and exceptionally good at taking charge when you need to. Maybe you can help me. I'm good at knowing who to trust. Identifying those I can count on and build close relationships with. Maybe I can help you with that. See win-win."

She gave him a tentative smile. "In theory, it sounds like a good idea, but aside from the geographical division, we live different lives. You're an international celebrity. I'm a country girl from Georgia."

"That's true, but it doesn't have to stop us."

"And what does that mean? I get added to your inner circle of friends? We do FaceTime? Text? Visit every now and again? I become one of your new BFFs?"

Bash shook his head and gave her a shy grin. "There

are obstacles, but I'm not looking for a new friend unless that's all you can offer. If that's the case, I'll accept what you think is appropriate to keep you in my life."

Her eyes went wide. "I don't understand. What do you want from me, Bash?"

Gently caressing the side of her cheek, he rubbed his thumb lightly over her lips. Goosebumps sprung up across her arms. "Aside from the physical distances, I'm nine years older than you. It's not a big deal for me, but it may be for you. Morgan... you are beautiful inside and out. You're smart and witty and compassionate and caring and a complete badass. Everything feels different with you. Real. If you're willing, I'd like to see if there can be more. If you don't feel the same, be honest with me."

She was stunned into silence. Her mouth opened a few times, but no words left her mouth. He was attractive, and she felt drawn to him. But in her mind, he was like a magnificent planet revolving around a brilliant sun in another galaxy. A phrase from a Rudyard Kipling poem, *The Ballad of the East and West*," came to mind... "*Oh, East is East and West is West, and never the twain shall meet.*"

"Like a couple kind of relationship?" she asked, not wanting to misinterpret his meaning.

"Only if it's what you want too."

"B...but why me? I'm nothing special," she said, feeling her throat tighten.

He cupped her cheeks in his hands and stared into her eyes. "You are so wrong, Morgan. You are the most amazing woman I've ever met. Is there any part of you that feels...?"

Sebastian never finished his sentence. Morgan leaned in to capture his lips into a soft and gentle kiss as she wrapped her arms around him. A myriad of emotions and warmth burst through her core, confirming it felt right. Kissing him. Being in his arms. Knowing the unnamed feelings she felt were reciprocated. When they finally pulled away, Bash smiled and kissed her on the forehead. She felt her face flush.

"You set the pace, baby," he said earnestly. "To be honest,

all my relationships with women have been temporary. There was never any real connection other than sex. I'm telling you this because I want you to know this isn't temporary for me. Do you understand?"

She nodded. "It's not for me either."

Suddenly, the door flew open, and Max stepped into the RV. He stopped short when he noticed their embrace. Morgan could feel her already heated face redden.

"Glad we got that settled," Max said with a smirk.

CHAPTER THIRTY-SEVEN

After a quick breakfast, they stopped by the registration office to drop off the weapons and keys belonging to two angry men. Max had done an early morning check and found them both asleep. The owner agreed to call the local police as soon as they left.

It was a magnificent morning with clear azure skies and lush mountains covered with tall evergreens and brilliant gold, burnt orange, and crimson colors from the changing leaves on the oak, birch, and hickory trees. They selected an obscure route to avoid the Baltimore and Philadelphia metro areas as they made their way northeast.

Max was shocked when Morgan told him her attackers knew they were traveling in an RV. It didn't make sense how they had learned that information until Morgan explained his wife had reported him missing. Then it all fell into place. It appeared that Enzo and Fatima used the ruse of Max's disappearance to utilize the national news and the public to find him. The RV salesman probably saw the report on the news and contacted the authorities.

After they stopped for gas and lunch, Bash went back into the bedroom to take a short nap. Max was glad for the opportunity to speak to Morgan alone.

"Are you still okay with the arrangements we made for the ledger? I don't have to go to Maine with you guys. You can drop me off in Harrisburg, and I'll drive back to Manhattan. My mother would be more than happy to go with you to pick up the ledger. I care too much about Sebastian to jeopardize our relationship over suspicions. We have enough barriers to overcome without adding to them. Gaining his trust means everything to me. I would like to have yours, too."

"Maybe I'm the one who should leave to give y'all a chance to get to know each other," Morgan offered, suddenly feeling like the obstacle to their bonding.

He gently put his hand on her arm. "That's just it. The three of us seem to be the right combination."

"You mean I'm the buffer?" she asked innocently.

"Not just that. You are a healer of sorts, natural and unpretentious. So unimpressed by either of our wealth or fame. Mine being more notorious," he chuckled at the last part. "You speak your mind, and in turn, it inspires others to do the same. You are also a lot of fun."

Morgan grinned. "Thanks. I think. I don't want you to leave, Max. I've chosen to trust you and believe you're willing to help me. In the same token, I'm here to support you just as I am Bash."

"I take it you two worked things out?" Max asked, lifting one eyebrow.

"We did. He wants more in our relationship, which is hard for me to understand."

"Why is that?"

"Isn't it obvious? I'm not his type," she said.

Max shook his head. "Why? Because you don't have dyed-blond hair, weekly spa appointments, and a closet full of Christian Louboutin heels? Well, I married that woman. Twice. The first one being the nicer of the two. If I were twenty years younger, I'd give ten of them for one of you. You remind me of Izzy in many ways. She was a natural beauty who wore little make-up. Didn't care about designer fashions even though she came from a wealthy family. Shopping in thrift shops to find interesting clothes was her hobby. Compassionate toward others. Authentic. Like you. My advice would be to let things develop organically, as they already have. If it's right, you'll know. Don't try to label it or force expectations."

"Male relationships are new to me."

"Not surprising."

By late afternoon, the weather had shifted. Gray storm clouds hung low over the mountaintops leaving only a small clear gap of green before it met the fog that covered the valley in a blanket of eerie white. Max and Bash took turns copiloting as Morgan maneuvered the narrow roads with low visibility. Once the rain began to come down in sheets, driving became a nightmare. When they arrived in Albany, New York, Morgan decided she was at her mental limit. Max found a small RV park to stop for the night.

CHAPTER THIRTY-EIGHT

"Were you able to get in touch with Stephen Gallagher?" Bash asked Max.

They were talking over morning coffee while Morgan showered.

"I did. Stephen had already told the authorities I was not missing or kidnapped. He called Fatima, too. She was quite unhappy with his interference. I'm sure Enzo instigated the kidnapping claim to use the media and authorities to flush me out."

"Maybe Enzo will concentrate their energies in the mountains now that we are clear," Bash suggested.

"We can only hope. Did you call Sam Barrett?" Max asked. "I don't want my mother to be in danger."

"Just got off the phone. Sam assured me they are already set up at your mother's home. He was very complimentary of the security system and cameras you had installed. The ten-foot spiked iron fence is a bonus. The only real exposure is the open water on the bay side. Six of Sam's most experienced men are with him. He said to tell you that despite his protests, your mother made them Barciole with homemade linguine and marinara sauce. A huge salad and homemade Italian bread."

Max's face softened. "She isn't just my mother, Sebastian. She is your grandmother."

Bash nodded. "It's still hard for me. Did you tell her who I am?"

Max shook his head. Their relationship was tenuous, so

he had to be careful not to push too hard. His biggest fear was that his son would bolt. It was a lot for him to absorb. Especially when Izzy was no longer alive to confirm Max's account of what happened all those years ago.

"I want to ease Mamma into it, but she will be thrilled. Her name is Gia, but she also goes by Linda. Or you can call her Nonna … if or when you feel comfortable."

"Why does she go by Linda?"

"When Mamma asked for her divorce, my father had one condition. She had to keep her married name, Gia Ravalli Fontana. He was a control freak, and it was his insidious way of warning off other men. Mamma bid her time until Dad would lose interest in having her monitored. It took three years. When she moved to Maine, I helped her change her name, buy the property, and disappear. She picked Linda Martin because it was a relatively common name. She decided if Izzy could vanish, she could too."

"Was she that scared of your father?"

Max took a deep breath. "In the back of her mind, she was afraid that Izzy may not have run. Someone could have 'handled' her."

Bash's mouth dropped open. "Did you ever consider that?"

Max shook his head. "If I had let my thoughts go there, I would have lost my mind. When I figured out who you were, it was a huge relief. Even though Izzy has passed, at least I know it wasn't by his hand."

"I'm sorry. I've been so wrapped up in the shock of finding out you exist and how it makes me feel I haven't really considered what you have gone through all these years. Not even knowing if we were alive."

"I've had more time to get used to the idea of having a son than you have of having a father. We can take this new relationship at whatever pace you like."

Bash nodded in agreement.

"There is something I've been worried about, and I hesitate to mention it. We seem to be finding some common ground and…" Bash trailed off.

"And you don't want to say something that will break what trust we have established?" Max finished.

"Something like that."

"Our circumstances don't call for a lot of diplomacy. Say what's on your mind."

"Once the FBI is aware of your involvement, I'm worried Morgan's deal with them will go to hell. What if they think this was some master plan you and I set up to get the ledger, and she is somehow involved? Her attorney suggested as much to her."

Max stood up and put his hand on his son's shoulder. His head was down, unable to meet his father's eyes.

"Look at me, Sebastian."

Bash blew out a breath and looked up.

"I will not allow that to happen to either of you. You have my word. I unknowingly made you a target. If I had only handled this differently. Sent you a letter or called you personally. Been honest from the beginning. None of this would have touched you."

"You honestly think those guys would have left me alone the minute they found out I was your son? I'm guessing if there was a possibility of me becoming an heir, they would have been damned worried. And how do you know your wife hadn't already figured out who I was from the picture on my book and told Enzo. Hell! Morgan figured it out before I even told her. Did your family know my mom was pregnant when she ran?"

"Only my dad and his closest associates. Enzo's father was one of them. After Izzy left, the secret became common knowledge. So, you are probably right. Fatima would have told Enzo her suspicions."

"Second-guessing the past at this stage of the game seems fruitless. All we can do is move forward," Bash said.

"I agree."

CHAPTER THIRTY-NINE

Bash hung over the back of Morgan's seat as she stopped in front of the ivy-covered iron gate at the entrance to Gia Fontana's home. He didn't want to miss a thing. He caught the deep sigh of relief escape Morgan's lungs. It had been a long journey, and she had shouldered the burden. Although Max and he had offered to try their inexperienced hands, she insisted they couldn't afford the loss of time. They knew she was correct.

The anticipation of meeting his grandmother was mounting. His thoughts drifted to the past. He remembered the sadness he had felt as a kid listening to his friends talk about holidays and Birthdays spent with aunts, uncles, cousins, and grandparents. His holidays had always been Gray, their moms, and him. And even though their moms provided plenty of surprises and fanfare, it never stopped him from wondering how things might have been with a dad.

"Do you know the code?" Morgan asked Max. Before he could answer, a tall, middle-aged man with close-cut blond hair, wearing a charcoal gray suit, appeared inside the gate. Bash assumed it was Sam Barnett. Seconds later, two additional suited men stood behind him. Holding up a remote control, the first man opened the gate. A few seconds later, there was a sharp knock on the door.

"Mr. Bartoli, it's Sam Barnett," the man in the gray suit called, holding up a pictured ID.

Bash reviewed it, opened the door, and extended his hand.

Sam stepped inside, motioning for his team to wait. Bash

made the introductions.

"I wanted to make sure you were all okay and didn't need any special assistance before we go inside," Sam said.

"I think we are all good," Max confirmed. "Why don't you ride with us to the house."

Sam nodded.

It was a short ride to a circular driveway in front of a beautiful white Victorian three-story home with turrets, a tower, and a veranda that spanned three sides. It was nestled in the woods. The only patch of grass in the front was within the circular drive.

Sam stepped out first, introduced two of his men, and then led the weary travelers into the house. "There are four more men stationed in various locations around the property. They are all either former FBI, military police, or special forces. Your mother is in good hands."

"I appreciate the care you've taken to protect her," Max said. "I've booked Mamma a flight to Ft. Lauderdale to spend a couple of weeks with an old friend. As soon as we pick up the package at the post office, I would appreciate it if a couple of your guys could escort her to the airport in Portland."

"That's not a problem," Sam confirmed.

They stepped into a spacious foyer with an open ceiling that gave a clear view into the top of the main tower, with glass windows surrounding the top. The foyer had off-white walls with ornate walnut trim, dark hardwood floors, and a staircase that made two turns before it reached the second floor. A huge living room was on one side of the foyer, and a formal dining room on the other.

Bash watched Morgan with amusement. She appeared to be in awe of the elaborate details of the home.

"It's so beautiful. Like a fairytale house," she said with a wide grin. Her eyes roamed the rooms until they reached the inside of the tower. "My goodness. I sure would hate to have to clean those windows."

Max chuckled good-naturedly. "Mamma contracts

professionals for the tough jobs."

That was what Bash liked about Morgan. She was always so comfortable in her own skin. Saying whatever was on her mind, never worrying about what others thought. Appreciating whatever the moment might bring with an open mind and heart.

"Max! You get over here and hug your Mamma!" came a stern but loving female voice.

Bash turned toward the sound and watched a petite, attractive older woman with white hair piled neatly on top of her head walk into the foyer. She wore a plum floral maxi skirt with a cream-colored blouse and a gray cable-knit sweater. The things that immediately struck Bash were her infectious smile and the mischievous twinkle in her forest-green eyes, the same color he shared with his dad. Max strode across the floor and lifted his Mamma off her feet and into a bear hug. When he sat her back down, she grabbed his cheeks and gave him a quick kiss on the lips.

"I've missed you so much, Maximillian. We've barely spoken since your dad's passing."

"Not now, Mamma. We will talk later. I promise."

Sam had discretely left the room, leaving Bash and Morgan standing in the foyer feeling like intruders.

"Maybe we should wait in the living room," Morgan whispered a little too loudly because it caught Mrs. Fontana's attention. When she spotted them, her eyes flicked past Morgan and landed on Sebastian.

When Max realized where his mother's attention was drawn, he said, "Mamma, let me intro…"

Gia Fontana cut him off with the lift of her hand. Her eyes locked on Bash as she slowly crossed the room toward him. He stood frozen in place, barely able to breathe. No one moved. His heart pounded. When she finally stopped in front of him, she reached up and touched his chin, lightly turning his head to the left and then to the right, scrutinizing his features. Her lips began to tremble.

"Y…You look like my Sebastian," she whispered.

Bash was stunned. Max told him his Mamma didn't know who he was. How could she know his name? He glanced at Max, pleading for answers. *I don't understand. What do I say? What did you tell her?* But Max just smiled and shrugged.

He turned back to his grandmother. "I am Sebastian," he confirmed.

Her hands flew to her mouth, tears springing from her eyes. Turning to Max, she said in a breathy voice, "She named him Sebastian? … And Izzy?"

Max's face fell, shaking his head. That's when she threw her arms around Sebastian and cried. "Mio nipote." (My grandson)

Instinct prompted Bash to gently hold her while she fell apart. Even though she was a stranger to him, he felt her warmth seep all the way through his bones. Swallowing hard, he struggled to stop the flow of his own tears burning behind his eyes.

Gia looked up at him and smiled sweetly. "My papa was named Sebastian. Isabelle really did love us. I knew she did. You are such a handsome man. So much like Maximillian and his Papa. I would have recognized you if I had passed you on the street."

Max walked up behind his mother and gently pulled her away. "Mamma, you're going to scare him. He just discovered he has a father. Let's let him get used to the idea of a Nonna before you maul him to death."

Gia nodded and pulled a laced handkerchief out of the pocket of her sweater. She wiped her eyes, then smoothed non-existent wrinkles from her skirt. When her eyes found Morgan, she grinned. "And you must be the extremely brave young woman who has brought my son and grandson safely to me."

Morgan wiped her eyes with the back of her hand. "I'm not sure how safely I got them here, but at least everyone's in one piece," she said in her charming Southern accent. "Y'all sure have a beautiful home, Miss. Gia."

"Thank you, dear. I love that adorable accent of yours." Gia took Morgan's arm and intertwined it with hers. "Why don't we sit on the sunporch and have some tea. You can tell me all about yourself and give me the inside scoop on my grandson. Are you two a couple?"

"Mamma!" Max scolded, before a shocked Morgan could speak.

Morgan cleared her throat, obviously grateful for the intervention, and asked, "Y'all have any sweet tea?"

Gia padded her hand. "I'm sure you can teach me how to make it, dear."

"Yes, ma'am."

Sebastian had a feeling his life was about to change forever.

CHAPTER FORTY

The late afternoon sun cast an eerie golden glow across the room in the five-star hotel where Enzo Fontana was staying in Portland, Maine. He leaned against the bar, feeling pure aggravation. He watched Asa Kline take in the luxurious accommodations with appreciation. The man turned out to be everything Enzo had feared—a con artist and an absolute waste of time and space. Faded, grease-stained jeans, beat-to-hell black boots, an old flannel shirt, and a worn black leather jacket. The scruffy, unkept beard, unwashed dark red hair, and bags under his eyes only reinforced everything Enzo had already figured out. Asa Kline was a desperate man, which meant he would say or do anything to get what he wanted.

Kline had blatantly lied to Enzo's men about the information he had to offer about the location of his daughter, who was traveling with Max and his newly found son. Bluffed his way into the search so he could utilize Enzo's resources for his own gain. *You will find out the hard way, Mr. Kline, I don't like being made a fool.*

When Enzo realized he had been deceived by a man who had spent the past 25 years in prison, his first impulse was to kill him and his biker buddies. Then, something occurred to him. Why would four bikers from a club in California ride all the way across the country in search of a woman? There had to be more to the story, and before he put the man in the ground, he was going to find out what it was. He wasn't a man to let an opportunity slip through his fingers.

"Nice place," Kline said. "I guess you're Enzo Fontana. The boss man."

Enzo cringed at the cocky grin on the man's face. "Have a seat, Mr. Kline. We have some things to discuss." He motioned to a brown leather chair next to the sofa. Asa took a seat, then looked up in surprise when the two suited men who had escorted him into the room stood sentry on either side of him.

"I thought this was supposed to be a friendly discussion," Kline said, casually leaning forward, his hand slowly inching toward his boot.

With lightning speed, one of the men grabbed Kline's arms and pulled them behind his back while the other guard retrieved a small derringer from his boot.

"You said you didn't have any weapons!" the guard with his gun bit out, smacking Kline in the head with it.

Kline groaned and rubbed his temple.

Enzo's face hardened. "And you took his word for it?"

"No, sir. I searched him, but I didn't see how a gun could fit in his boot," the guard said defensively.

"You let anything like that happen again, and that will be the last mistake you make," Enzo growled between clenched teeth.

"Yes, Sir," the guards said in unison.

Kline's head lobed around a few times, but he was still conscious. Enzo grabbed a glass of water from the bar and threw it in his face. He sat up straight, wide-eyed.

"Now, Mr. Kline. You are going to tell me what is so important about finding your daughter, who my informant assured me you have never met. What would motivate you to drive across the country and worm your way into my organization under false pretenses? And don't give me any bullshit about Daddy just wanting to make amends."

Asa peered up with defiance on his face. "It's club business. I'm sure you can appreciate my loyalty to the Dragon Fire."

Enzo shook his head in disbelief and stepped in front of him. He stuck his hand out to the guard who held Asa's gun, wiggling his fingers for it to be handed over. Once firmly in his grip, Enzo placed it against Asa's forehead.

"Tell me what you are expecting to get from your daughter, or I will pull this trigger. Your choice."

Asa's face paled. He sucked in a big gulp of air. "Okay! Okay!" He threw up his hands. "B…but how do I know you won't kill me anyway?"

Enzo's voice was emotionless. "You don't. It's a chance you'll have to take."

Asa's eyes frantically darted around the room, searching for an escape route. When the futility of his situation finally hit, he told Enzo about the ledger. Thirty minutes of probing questions, and Enzo had everything he needed to know — the ledger would be his. If what Kline told him was true, some very influential politicians would soon be in his debt, and it wouldn't cost him a dime.

"I could help you get the ledger. I mean, my buddies and I can take the risk. If we knew where Morgan was… I mean, you must have some idea. Portland isn't exactly New York. Gotta be a reason you're here. You tell us where she is, and we'll get the ledger for you. All I want is the girl," he added.

"The girl? Why would you want her? It's always been about the ledger and money. Don't pretend you care anything about your daughter."

"If I'm taking all the heat and you're getting the ledger, why I want her is my business."

Enzo rubbed his chin. "And I'm supposed to believe you're doing this out of the goodness of your heart for no fee?"

"My heart's got nothing to do with it. I'm just trying to stay alive."

Enzo thought about it for a few minutes. He didn't trust Asa Kline as far as he could spit. The man was buying time, hoping to get the ledger for himself. But the bikers taking all the risks was actually a good idea.

Earlier that morning, Enzo received a phone call from one of his informants with the FBI who had recently been transferred to Portland, Maine. He had information about Morgan Skylar but insisted Enzo meet him in person. Enzo was still pissed about making the trip. The informant had come across an expense advance request for a couple of agents who were traveling to Cliff View Harbor, Maine. They were meeting with Morgan Skylar, the two people who were traveling with Max and his son. The agents were to pick up a package at the local post office and interview potential witnesses. Now that Enzo knew about the ledger, it answered the package question, but not what they were doing in Maine or why the girl was traveling with Max and his son in the first place.

When Fatima called him about seeing Max's doppelganger on the cover of a bestselling novel, Enzo figured she was up to something. She was a manipulative bitch, and he never knew what game she was playing. He only began the affair to get inside information about Max. It had been easier than he had anticipated.

His Uncle Julian had spent over twenty years trying to find Max's child, and the idea that he could have been in the public eye for a good portion of that time was pure irony. Besides, no one was sure about the sex of Max's child or if it was still alive. One look at that picture on the back cover of Sebastian Bartoli's book, and Enzo knew without a doubt. He was a younger Max, and that fact screwed up all of Enzo's plans for taking the company away from him. Sebastian would inherit Max's controlling interest in the company. Now Enzo had two people to eliminate. Asa and his buddies were excellent scapegoats for the theft of the ledger and the murders of Max and his son. Enzo's men would shadow the bikers to Cliff View Harbor. As soon as Max and Sebastian were dead, his men would retrieve the ledger, and the bikers would meet a tragic end.

"Okay, Mr. Kline. You've got yourself a deal."

After Kline left, Enzo punched in a speed dial number on his cell phone.

"Have my plane ready to leave for New York within an hour. I don't want to be anywhere near this place when this all goes down."

CHAPTER FORTY-ONE

Morgan lay awake in a lavish Victorian-styled bedroom decorated with dark-polished wood, taupe walls, and fabrics of satin and chiffon in colors of cream and moss green. The delicately embroidered quilted bedspread and piles of decorative pillows made her feel like a princess. Her beat-up backpack looked out of place lying in the corner. She didn't dare set it on the furniture for fear of getting it dirty.

The afternoon and evening had gone well. Mrs. Fontana turned out to be a gracious, down-to-earth, and giving woman despite her wealth. If she hadn't known the truth, Morgan would have thought Ms. Fontana had been a grandmother to Sebastian his whole life.

In the late afternoon, Morgan received a call from Agent Miguel Perez with the Portland office of the FBI. He was the local liaison agent for the Washington DC FBI office that was handling the Clark Wayne Kline case. After a call to her attorney for verification, she agreed to speak to the agent on speaker while Max, Bash, and Sam silently listened to the conversation.

The agent took the explanation that Linda Martin of Cliff View Harbor was a family friend at face value. If they had run a background check, it certainly would have revealed her identity as Gia Fontana. Agent Perez and his team should arrive at Ms. Martin's address by 10 a.m. They would explain the release documents Morgan was to sign, then escort Ms. Martin to the post office to retrieve the ledger. The agent didn't see a reason for Morgan or anyone else to accompany them for the retrieval. The call took less than ten minutes.

As soon as Morgan's phone disconnected, everyone began speaking at once. Sam was upset with the casual attitude the agent displayed, leading him to believe the FBI didn't perceive any threats. Max refused to let his mother be escorted anywhere without him and a security detail. Bash was concerned with the dismissive attitude the agent had toward Morgan and couldn't believe no one openly voiced objections.

Sam explained that arguing with an FBI agent on an open and most likely recorded line was a bad idea. It might have jeopardized Morgan's deal. They agreed to wait until the federal agents were present to voice their concerns. Once the agents arrived, they would be more likely to negotiate rather than waste a trip. No matter how many agents showed up, Sam and his team would keep everyone safe.

During the whole conversation, no one asked for Morgan's opinion or even glanced her way. She suddenly felt irrelevant and wasn't sure why she no longer mattered. Her experience with men was limited, but they all seemed to be competing to be the alpha. Well, she sure as heck wasn't about to be their beta. The worst part—it hurt. Sam Barrett worked for Sebastian and Max. The last thing she wanted was to sound like a whiny female. It wasn't her house or her family. She was the sole reason they were all forced to be involved with the FBI. She would only sound ungrateful if she spoke up. The reality was that without Pops, she had no family on her side.

After taking ten calming breaths to clear her mind, she asked herself what Pops would tell her to do. Things always felt better when she had a Popsism to fall back on. A few minutes later, Pops' words came to her. *You can't let yourself be at other peoples' whims, Morgan. If you feel you have lost control, find a way to take it back. Ultimately, you must look out for yourself because no one else will. You do you. Let them do them."*

Morgan would control what she could control. Herself. *Thanks, Pops.*

CHAPTER FORTY-TWO

Morgan was showered and dressed by 6 a.m. the following morning. She wasn't sure what to wear to a meeting with the FBI but figured it didn't matter anyway. Her choices had dwindled to unwashed jeans, a few dirty thermal tops, and one clean sweater she had picked up in Ashville. It would have to do.

When she walked into the kitchen, her stomach did an audible growl from the smell wafting through the air. Her face flushed with embarrassment when she noticed Mrs. Fontana look up from her magazine and smile.

"Good morning, Morgan. I don't have to ask if you're hungry," she laughed. "I'm told I make the best blueberry and lemon scones in Maine. They are here on the table. The coffee is on the counter unless you would prefer tea."

"Thank you, Ms. Fontana. Coffee is fine," Morgan said, walking to the counter. After filling her cup, she added cream and sugar and sat at the table.

"Please call me Gia," she said, handing Morgan a small plate with a scone. "If we are outside the house or in front of the FBI agents, Linda would be best."

"Thank you, ma'am. I mean Gia."

"I hope you got a good night's sleep."

"I did a bit of tossing and turning, but not because of the accommodations. That guestroom is so elegant. And that bed—I felt like I was sleeping on a cloud."

Gia looked at her with concern. "A lot on your mind, dear?"

"Yes, ma'am."

Gia reached over and took her hand. "Why don't you tell me what's got that worry in your eyes? I know it's not from this meeting with the FBI. Max told me what you guys have gone through these past few days, so meeting a few agents should be a piece of cake. It's something else, isn't it?"

Morgan put her coffee cup down and met her eyes. She had nothing to lose by telling her the truth.

"The agent in charge called me last night to let me know what to expect from the meeting this morning. They need my signature on the release agreement, and then their team will escort you to the post office to pick up the ledger. My phone was on speaker, so Sam, Max, and Bash heard everything. As soon as the call ended, the guys began to make plans. Who would go? Who would stay? Kind of assigning roles. Things like that," Morgan explained.

Gia nodded slowly. "And they totally left you out of the conversation, didn't they? Went into macho mode, with everyone putting in their two cents. Let me guess. You are supposed to stay here with your hands folded in your lap while they take care of business," Gia said with sweet laced with sarcasm.

"Yes, ma'am. I guess I'm just a kindergarten teacher again."

The sound of footsteps tapping against the back staircase leading to the kitchen halted their conversation. Before anyone entered the room, Gia leaned close and, with a gleam in her eye, whispered, "Regardless of what the FBI or anyone else thinks, this is your show, Morgan Skylar. Don't let them forget it. And by the way, my keys are in my car."

To cover the Cheshire cat grin on her face, Morgan shoved a scone in her mouth as Max and Bash entered the room.

The FBI arrived fifteen minutes late. Bash answered the door and escorted them into the dining room to a large mahogany carved table where Morgan, Gia, Max, Sam, and four security guards were seated.

Agent Perez was a tall man with dark brown hair, almost

black eyes, and a serious but handsome face. From the look of the worry lines around his mouth and eyes, Morgan guessed he was in his mid-forties. Agent Miranda Scott looked more like a nerdy librarian than a federal agent. She was shorter than Morgan, wore thick horn-rimmed glasses, and her hair was in a blunt-cut bob. Both agents wore solid navy suits. Before Sebastian could introduce the people seated at the table, Perez chimed in.

"This isn't a dinner party, folks. There are only two people I need to speak with, the first being Morgan Skylar." His eyes roamed the table and landed on hers. "I'm assuming that is you?"

Morgan was so stunned by his rudeness that all she could do was nod. She had already gone over the final agreement in detail with Mr. Livingston. He had insisted she faxed a copy of the agreement the agent presented to verify they had not made any last-minute changes. It took thirty minutes to email the new document and receive confirmation the documents had not been altered from the original. Her signature on the page gave her a sense of relief.

Agent Perez pointed a finger at Gia. "You must be Linda Martin. You can stay put until we are ready to leave for the post office. The rest of you good people can vacate the room," the agent said, making a sweeping motion with his hand.

Max sprung to his feet and glared at him. "Agent Perez, do you have a warrant that allows you access to this house? Or for the arrest of anyone in this house?"

The agent was taken aback, staring at Max for a few moments. "Why would I need a warrant? This is a simple agreement, and we will be on our way to pick up the ledger?" Agent Perez said indignantly.

At that moment, Morgan realized the people sitting around the table had a totally different perception of the volatility of the situation than the two agents.

Gia stood up, clearing her throat. "Let me explain what my son Maximillian is saying. You are a guest in my home, Agent Perez. You have no legal authority to be here. I don't remember receiving a request for permission from you or any representative of the FBI to have a meeting in my home, nor did I receive a request to accompany you to pick up a ledger. If it hadn't been for secondhand information, I wouldn't have a clue that you were going to appear at my door. As I see it, the only legal documents you possess are related to an agreement with Ms. Skylar. I did give Ms. Skylar permission to have your meeting in my home, but you have no right to tell me who can sit at my table. After this meeting is completed, we can discuss your little trip to the post office."

The agent's lips parted in surprise, then quickly closed. After Gia sat down, there was no further comment about the people seated at the table.

After Morgan's portion was completed, Bash introduced Sam Barrett as the CEO of SMB Protective Services and Max as simply Linda Martin's son.

The agent appeared flustered when he realized he was getting pushback for what he must have assumed would be an in-and-out assignment. Without legal authority to force Linda Martin to go to the post office with him, he became more amiable to Max's request to drive his mother and meet the agents at the post office. If Agent Perez didn't have Gia's (Linda Martin) cooperation, the whole deal would be on hold until he could get a warrant for the post box.

The tense expressions on the faces of the men around the table reflected their concern from the lack of FBI agents to handle the task. To make matters worse, Miranda Scott wasn't even a field agent. She was an analyst who was asked at the last minute to accompany Agent Perez.

"Are you not aware that the Dragon Fire outlaw motorcycle club has been looking for Morgan to get their hands on the ledger? Have those men been apprehended? Is that why you aren't concerned about security?" Max bellowed across the table.

"Asa Kline, Morgan's biological father, would do anything to get that ledger. Are you not aware of the break-in at her apartment in Georgia? A woman and her baby were held against their will," Bash added.

The agent purses his mouth in irritation. "Everyone calm down. I'm not familiar with all the details. The agents working on this case are from the Washington, DC office. I'm from the Portland office, so we were the closest for the retrieval. The DC agents assured me no additional security would be necessary. You can have your little entourage of security tag along if it makes you feel better. Ms. Scott and I must be back to the office by three o'clock this afternoon, so we need to get moving."

Morgan listened to Sam Barrett try to convince the agents of why things weren't as simple as they appeared, but to no avail. All Agent Perez was concerned about was getting to his next meeting.

As soon as the caravan of cars left, she and Bash stood alone in the foyer. She had kept her mouth shut all morning, only speaking when asked. Their plans were made. Now, she would implement hers.

"What's wrong, Morgan?"

"Everything's peachy. I'm going back upstairs to lie down," she said, turning toward the stairs.

He caught her hand, pulling her toward him. "That was a blatant lie, Morgan. Not once have I seen you take a nap, and you certainly wouldn't under these circumstances. What's up? You have barely spoken to me or anyone else since we got here."

Morgan bit her bottom lip, trying to hold her temper. "I could say the same thing about you."

"What is that supposed to mean? I just had a whole new family dropped in my lap. I'm entitled to be a little distracted," he said defensively.

She softened her face. "You are right. This is all new to you, and you should spend time getting to know your family. I don't want to interfere. You seem to fit right in. If you don't mind, I'm going to lie down." Pulling away, she ran up the stairs.

"I'll be in the den if you need me," he called after her.

She ran to her bedroom and pulled her 9mm out of her backpack, and stuffed it in her coat pocket for easy access. With a bulky coat, scarf, and knit cap, she would be less recognizable. The FBI agents might not believe there was a threat, but she did, and there was no way she was going to sit by and watch anyone else get hurt.

Listening for sounds, she crept down the stairs. The faint hum of the television confirmed Bash was preoccupied. The kitchen was attached to a portico leading to the garage. Fortunately, she had overheard Sam giving Agent Perez the code to the gate, so getting out wouldn't be a problem. Her only worry was the two guards watching the perimeter, but it wasn't like they would shoot her.

As she was about to open the back door, she saw a post-it note attached to a windowpane near the handle. It had four numbers and said, *Enter code off* and *Enter code on*. She stared at the post-it, wondering what the heck it meant. As her eyes roamed the door, she noticed the alarm panel, and it clicked.

"Oh, hockey sticks! I almost set off the alarm!" That got her blood pumping. Gia left it for her. She hurriedly entered the code to turn the alarm off, then immediately reentered the numbers to turn it back on. Scurrying to the garage, she fumbled for the light.

"Aren't you a cutie patootie," she mumbled when her eyes landed on the only car in a four-space garage—an electric mini car. On the passenger seat lay a remote control with a sticky note saying, *Front gate #8646.*

"Thank you, Gia," she whispered.

When she passed the circular drive, a man in a green coat and baseball cap ran out from behind an oak tree, frantically waving his arms. Looking straight ahead, she buzzed past him. As she approached the gate, she entered the code into the remote. Chancing a look in the rearview mirror, she realized the man in the baseball cap was Bash.

"Morgan, stop! You can't go without me!" he screamed.

Before she could decide whether to let him in the car, he had already yanked the door open and plunked down in the passenger seat. All she could do was stare in amazement.

"What? You think I didn't know what you were planning?

I've been waiting outside for five minutes."

"You knew Gia loaned me her car?" she asked dumbfounded.

"Of course not. I expected you to hot-wire it. Honestly, I'm a little disappointed, but at least we won't have to deal with a grand theft auto charge." He looked out the back window. "Damn! You better get moving. We've got company."

Morgan didn't look back; she knew it was the guards. With the petal to the metal, she pulled out onto the road.

"I'd bet my next royalty check those guards are on the phone to Sam."

CHAPTER FORTY-THREE

The post office was in the center of the quaint tourist town of Cliff View Harbor, twenty minutes south of Gia's home. The FBI's black SUV led the caravan, with Sam, his mother, and Max behind them in Sam's silver SUV. Sam's four security guards rode in two additional vehicles. Currently, everyone was stuck at a railroad crossing with a stalled train blocking the only road into town. It had been an excruciating fifteen minutes for Max.

The plan was simple. Agent Perez would meet them in front of the post office and escort him and his mother inside. The agent hadn't been keen on Max being part of the equation, but he refused to allow his mother to go inside without him. Once Gia picked up the package and handed it to Agent Perez, Sam would escort Gia to the bodyguards who were driving her to the airport. Max hoped that would be the end of the matter, but he was not that naive. He was still stewing about the lack of FBI presence. Sam assured him that his men, who would be parked on the street to surveil the area, had them covered if there was trouble. Sam had just opened his internet browser to check for another route when the train began to move.

"About time," Gia mumbled.

Ten minutes later, they pulled into the post office, finding two parking spaces not far from the front door.

While Max waited for Agent Perez, his phone rang. "Max."

"It's Sebastian. Where are you?"

"Just pulled into the post office. Got stuck by a damn train. Why? Anything wrong?"

"Morgan and I will be there within 10 minutes."

"Mamma's car?" he asked calmly.

"Yeah. She offered it to Morgan this morning."

Max turned around and looked at his mother, seated in the back seat. She must have known who it was because she plastered an innocent expression on her face.

"I was afraid Morgan wouldn't be willing to sit this one out. Let her silence fool me," Max chuckled.

"Not me," said Sebastian. "I was waiting for her outside when she blew right past me. Had to chase her down. We'll be parked down the block to watch for anything unusual. She's packing. Perez was extremely clear about federal property and firearms. Neither one of us want to be somebody's prison bitch. Talk to you soon."

"Tell her not to do any of that hero crap," Max growled before hanging up.

"Don't have to guess what that was about," Sam said.

"Suppose this is what we get for not including her. I just hope this goes as smoothly as our overly confident FBI agent believes."

Agent Perez knocked on the passenger window. "Let's go people."

"He's a real charmer, isn't he?" Gia mumbled under her breath before scooting out of the car.

"I like your Mamma," Sam whispered to Max.

"She can be a pistol," he said, shaking his head. "She gave Morgan her car."

Sam burst out laughing.

The U.S. Post Office was a typical, small-town single brick building. The parking lot held twelve cars, six spaces in front of the building and six on the opposite side of a one-way drive that ran parallel to the street. Max hoped Sam's men were close.

In the small lobby, there were three stations for customers to do their mail transactions. Nearing lunchtime, it was quite busy. As they headed down an adjoining hall to the post boxes, Max noticed Agent Perez scan the room for potential threats.

Except for a few retail catalogs, his mother's post box was empty. The agent's expression transformed into a scowl.

"Guess we will..." Gia began to say but stopped when Agent Perez stepped into Max's personal space.

"Do you realize that any deviation from the agreement Ms. Skylar signed will be null and void if we do not gain procession of the ledger today? If she's trying to hold out for something more, she is not going to like the consequences."

"Look, Perez..." Max began.

Gia held up her hands in frustration. "Cool your jets, Agent Impatience. If you weren't so busy expecting the worst of people, you would have noticed a ledger would never fit in the box. The clerks usually leave me a note directing me to the counter for anything too large. Either they forgot to leave a note, or it fell out when they stuffed it with catalogues."

Max bit back a snicker.

"Wait here," the agent said, then walked back into the lobby. When he came back, he said, "It's clear, but the lines are long. The middle counter is the shortest."

The longer they were exposed to the public, the more nervous Max became. His mother grabbed his hand and squeezed, her eyes focused on his fists, clenching and unclenching. It seemed that every person in front of them had a problem.

"Next," a perky twenty-something woman finally called. The trio stepped up to the counter.

"Good morning, dear. I think I have a package that was too big for the box. The name is Linda Martin, P.O. Box 112."

The clerk did a few keystrokes on the computer and glanced up. "Sure do, Ms. Martin. I'll go get it out of the back. Be right back."

"Thank you."

Turning to the FBI agent, Gia snidely raised one eyebrow. "See."

Max almost jumped out of his skin when his cell rang. Sebastian again. "What's wrong?"

"You need to get out of there now!" Bash screamed. "I

mean right now!"

He heard Morgan in the background say, "Give me the phone, Bash. Take a breath."

"Max?" It was Morgan.

"What's happening?" Max whisper-shouted into the phone. Agent Perez's head swung toward Max, his hand instinctive resting on the gun.

"Bash is right. You need to get someplace safe. Are you still in the post office?" The strain in her voice was palpable.

"We're in line at the counter. What's going on?"

Agent Perez craned his head toward Max to hear the conversation.

"We were looking for a place to park near the post office when we passed a black sedan with New York license plates with two men inside. After we parked, we casually walked past the car. The two men had bullet holes in their heads. We're thinking they might be Enzo's men. Suits. Looks like guns under their jackets. As soon as we got clear, we spotted one of Sam's SUV's. We're with two of his men, Flip and Riley."

"Which means the Dragon Fire guys are probably on top of us. Looks like Asa Kline double-crossed Enzo. Did you see any motorcycles?" Max asked, while Agent Perez tried to grab Max's cell phone.

"Just a damn minute," he huffed to the agent. "Not you, Morgan."

"It's too cold for bikes, and the engines would announce their arrival from blocks away. I'm betting they rented a car. Maybe you should find a back door." She hung up.

"Tell me!" Agent Perez demanded.

"Morgan and Sebastian are here. They found a black sedan with two dead men with bullets in their skulls. Obviously, this isn't as easy-peasy as you were led to believe. The Dragon Fire are here somewhere. We need to get the hell out the backdoor unless you want to hand them the ledger and pick bullets out of your teeth."

The clerk walked back to the counter carrying a brown

wrapped package. "Here you go, Ms. Martin."

The second it was in Gia's hand, the agent snatched it from her and stuffed it inside his coat. He reached into his jacket and pulled out his FBI shield, and flashed it at the clerk.

"We need a back way out of here before someone gets hurt."

The woman's eyes widened, color draining from her face. "Oh my. I...I..." She couldn't speak.

Max pointed to a door at the end of the counter. "If you can let us in that door, all you'll have to do is lead us out the back."

"It...it's our loading dock," she said. "It requires a code to get out. I can't give you that. I'll get fired."

"Just open the door..." the irritated agent barked.

"Don't worry. You won't get in trouble. This man is a federal agent," Max explained. "You can put in the code yourself."

Gia pulled on Max's sleeve and pointed to the door where two large, bearded men in jeans and leather jackets pushed through the doors."

Max nudged the agent and nodded his head toward the door.

"Well, damn," Agent Perez said under his breath. "Get to the door before they spot us. I hope to hell they didn't see Miranda sitting in the car. She's not a field agent."

Max did an inward sigh of relief when they made it through the door without being seen. The clerk motioned them back toward the counters, where they would be visible from the lobby.

"Isn't there another way to get to the loading dock without us being seen?" the agent asked.

"I'm afraid not." She pointed down the hall in the opposite direction. "The offices and breakroom are down that way."

"Well, hell," Max said, exasperated.

"Let me look," Gia said, peeking around a clerk.

Max yanked her back.

"Maximillian," she admonished.

"Mamma, you have to be more careful."

"Those men don't know me from Adam's house cat. I'll just walk past the counter with the clerk to see if those men are still there. Wait for my little wave to give you the 'all clear,'" Gia said.

"I guess you would draw less attention," Agent Perez agreed.

Max wasn't happy but nodded.

Once Gia strolled past the clerks' stations and was no longer exposed, she frantically waved her arms for them to join her.

The agent went first, keeping his head turned away from the lobby. He was halfway to Gia when a bullet whizzed past his head, slamming into a cabinet behind him. Everyone dropped to the floor. Screams rang out. Then, it was pandemonium in the lobby. People pushed and shoved to get to the doors. Some stood frozen in terror. The counter clerks dashed past Max, heading to the back offices. He ducked low and used the chaos as an opportunity to move through the open space. When another shot rang out, he dove for the concealed area where Gia and the agent waited.

Gia grabbed the clerk's hand when she began to cry. Gia spoke calmly. "Dear, we need you to get us out of here. We'll keep you safe."

"O…okay."

More shots were fired as they made their way to the back door. With trembling fingers, it took the clerk four tries to enter her code correctly. They hurriedly made their way down the back steps of the dock and around the postal trucks to find Sam Barrett in his SUV with the engine running. He was a welcome sight.

"Get in!" he screamed out the window.

Max practically threw the two women into the backseat. He looked up at the agent, who now held his gun firmly in his right hand.

"Aren't you coming?" Max asked.

"I have to help those people," Agent Perez growled.

"You're outgunned, Perez. Get in the vehicle till we can get some backup," Sam said in a calm voice. "My men and I will help until the police get here."

The words had barely left Sam's mouth when shots blasted against the back loading dock door, holes appearing on the outside. The agent jumped in the backseat while Max slid in the front. As Sam was turning left toward the front of the building, a bullet shattered the back window. The clerk screamed.

"Get in the floorboard," the agent yelled.

"It's going to be okay. We're out of range, but stay down," Max assured them.

When they reached the front of the building, they realized escape wasn't going to be easy. The front parking lot resembled a scene from an apocalyptic movie. In their panic to leave, drivers were recklessly slamming into each other, blocking the exit. Terrified people abandoned their cars and fled the parking lot. Some ran screaming down the sidewalk. Others headed across the street to the city park.

Sam opened his door. "This is as far as we can go. Everybody out. Max, my men are parked on the street to the left of the exit in two silver SUVs. If you can get the women to the vehicles, my men will get them to safety. We are going to need the others for backup."

"What are you planning to do?" Perez asked Sam.

"I'm coming with you," Sam said, reaching into the console and pulling out a .45."

"You can't have that on federal property," Agent Perez huffed.

Sam raised his eyebrows and narrowed his eyes to slits. "Minutes after Morgan advised me there were dead bodies in a car down the street, I observed two armed men get out of a black van and head toward the front doors. I had my team call the local police for backup but found there were only a couple of deputies at the station. The other three on duty are 50 miles away with the sheriff at an officer's funeral. My team is all you've got for at least another 30 minutes. From what I understand, there were four DF members in Georgia. If those are the men we are dealing with, you just met two of them. The other two could be anywhere, probably in the black van that sped off. Now you want to quibble about my gun? Plenty of innocent bystanders need protection unless you want hostages."

"Don't you guys coordinate with the local police when you're working a case in their jurisdiction?" Max asked, not masking his irritation.

The agent shook his head. "As I said earlier, this wasn't even my case. I got minimum information. It was supposed to be low risk."

Max resisted the urge to ask him how that was working out for him.

The agent turned to Sam. "I guess I don't have any choice but to accept your help. At least until I know everyone is safe," the agent sighed with resignation. "Do you know if anyone inside is hurt?"

"I don't. The first thing I did was swing around back to pick up you guys, assuming that would be your emergency course of action. My men and I have no authority to go inside with weapons. The team is waiting for my instruction."

"Let's take a look inside," the agent said, grabbing the door handle. "I don't want a gunfight with innocents getting hurt."

"I want to help," Max said quickly. "I'm experienced with a firearm."

"Sorry, I'm all out of guns," Agent Perez said sarcastically.

Gia cleared her throat. As they turned toward her, she was holding a 9mm pistol.

"Mamma. For Christ's sake."

Agent Perez rolled his eyes.

"What?" she shrugged. "I'm a senile old woman. I didn't know it was against the law." Then she handed the weapon to Max. Taking the clerk's hand, Gia pulled her out of the car. "I'll find your men myself, Sam. Run like the wind, dear." And the women took off.

"Well, hell," Perez said under his breath. Then he turned

to Max. "Do not use that firearm!"

CHAPTER FORTY-FOUR

Finding the dead men in the black sedan was a shock. Morgan knew in her heart they were Enzo Fontana's men. What she couldn't understand was how her outlaw father had gotten the best of such a sophisticated and powerful man.

"Never underestimate nobody, Chip. Especially a highly motivated opponent. People are rarely what they seem. No matter what you think you know about someone, there is always something you don't. That's what'll get ya," Pops warned. It turned out to be the most important Popsism of all, Morgan thought with newfound appreciation.

Pops knew this day would come. It was why he trained her to take care of herself and always be vigilant. She felt bad for resenting his paranoia and blaming him for her inability to have a normal childhood. He had isolated her. Engrained a mistrust so deep in her psyche that she had never been able to develop a meaningful relationship with the men she dated. Now, she fully understood why. He had always known her father would come for her. To punish her for what Pops had done all those years ago. Put him in prison. Stolen his child.

Asa Kline was here, and she wasn't going to shy away from him. Her presence had jeopardized the people she cared about. She would do everything in her power to make sure no one got hurt.

"T...that's one of Sam's SUVs parked up ahead," Bash said.

Picking up their pace, they reached the vehicle within

seconds. The driver's window rolled down, and a voice called out, "Get in the back." Morgan pulled the door open, and they slid inside.

"We heard you guys decided to come along for the ride," Riley chuckled from the driver's seat. Morgan had met the muscular, dark-skin man earlier that morning at breakfast.

The man in the passenger seat turned around to greet them. "Sam told us to keep an eye out for you guys. I'm Flip... short for nothing remotely related," the blond man with brown laughing eyes joked.

"We need t...to get help," Morgan said between gasps for breath. "There are two dead guys in a car a couple of blocks from here. Probably Enzo Fontana's men."

"Whoa. That's a game changer," Flip said, putting his hand to his ear. "Did you get that, Sam?"

That's when Morgan realized they were all wired to communicate on open mics.

"Will do, boss. I'll let her make the call. ... Just say the word," Flip said. He turned to Morgan. "Sam wants you to call Max and tell him about the bodies. I'm calling the local police for backup."

"I'll make the call to Max," Bash said, punching in his number.

"You need to get out of there now!" Bash screamed into his cell. "I mean right now!"

In a calm voice, Morgan held out her hand and said, "Give me the phone, Bash. Take a breath." He reluctantly handed it to her.

Morgan filled Max in on finding the dead bodies. When she hung up, there were two conversations going on simultaneously. Flip was talking to the local police while Riley was in a conversation with Sam.

"...Got it. We'll keep our eyes open. Just give us the word," Riley said to Sam.

"What's going on now?" Bash asked anxiously.

"A black van just pulled up front and let two armed guys

out…" Riley stopped mid-sentence and pointed out the front window. "There's the van exiting the parking lot."

Morgan rolled down her window to get a better look.

"It's not good news, folks. The local police said their backup is at least 30 minutes away," Flip said. "We're on our own for a while."

"Boss said to hold tight until we hear from him," Riley said.

"We don't have to worry about following the black van," Morgan said tightly. "It's double-parked in the street on the right side of the exit."

"Seriously?" Flip said, getting out of the vehicle for a look.

"Oh, my heavens, I can't…" No more words would come. Morgan watched a medium-built armed man step out of the back of the van carrying a gun tucked in the front of his pants and an AR-15 in his right hand. When her eyes reached his face, she felt like her heart had stopped. Early 50s, red hair, light freckles, dark shaggy beard. It had to be him. Her father.

"Morgan? Is that him? Is that Kline?" Flip asked, leaning in her window.

"I…I think so," she shuddered, momentarily stunned.

"Jesus Christ," Bash breathed.

"Riley, you stay here with Morgan and Sebastian. I'm going to follow him. The driver is still in the van, so keep your eyes on him," Flip called in the window.

"Wait!" Riley yelled. "You can't follow him on government property with a firearm. Sam was adamant about that."

Flip ran his hand through his hair in frustration, then crouched next to the SUV.

Suddenly, muffled shots rang out from the direction of the post office building. Seconds later, people ran screaming out the front doors, pushing and shoving to get to their cars.

"What's going on, Sam?!" Riley screamed in his mouthpiece. "We heard gunshots."

Morgan leaned closer to Flip, hoping to hear Sam's response.

"Sam saw two armed men enter the post office," Flip told Morgan. "He swung around back to pick up Gia, Max, and Agent Perez."

The next few minutes were pandemonium. Hysterical people collided into each other's vehicles and then abandoned them entirely when the parking lot became impassable.

"I can't stand by and do nothing. It was a mistake for me to come here. All these people are in danger because of me. I've got to do something before someone gets killed," Morgan said. Not waiting for a response, she jumped out of the car.

"You aren't going without me," Bash barked, but was met with the door slamming in his face. When he tried to wedge it open again, he heard a click.

"Safety locks, Mr. Bartoli. Sam doesn't want you getting killed. I should have done it before Morgan slipped out," Riley said with aggravation.

Morgan heard the exchange and knew Bash would be safe. Searching through the chaos around the parking lot, she felt a hand grab her elbow. Jerking her head around, she met Flip's eyes.

"You aren't going anywhere. Those men don't give a damn that you're an unarmed, innocent woman," Flip said harshly.

Morgan narrowed her eyes. Flip stepped back when she pulled a 9mm out of her coat pocket. She didn't recognize the commanding voice that came from her mouth. "I am neither unarmed nor innocent. The only way you are going to stop me is to shoot me. And at this point in my life, there is no one left to care." With that, she turned and headed into the chaos.

CHAPTER FORTY-FIVE

Morgan lost track of her father between the screaming people and the abandoned cars. Thankfully, she had not heard any rapid fire from the AR-15 he was carrying. As she frantically searched for a way to stop them, her eyes landed on the black van parked in the street. The least she could do was prevent their escape.

Squatted behind a red pickup truck, she almost jumped out of her skin when she felt a hand on her shoulder.

"Sorry," Flip said.

"Please don't do that," she whispered.

"Why are you watching the van?" he asked. She figured Sam sent him to keep an eye on her. Make sure she didn't do anything stupid.

"It may be their only transportation out of here. If so, we need to separate the driver from the getaway vehicle."

Flip chuckled. "That's a good idea but not a simple task."

"Yeah. I may need help once he's out of the van," Morgan said.

"You have a plan to get him out of the van?" Flip asked.

She looked over her shoulder and gave him a confident look. "I can get him out of the van. The problem is stopping him once he's out."

"What did you have in mind?" Flip asked, narrowing his eyes with skepticism.

She pointed to a 15-foot evergreen across the street in the park adjacent to the van. "If someone was behind that tree, they could catch him off guard."

Flip's eyes widened. "You want me to ambush him?"

"You don't have to shoot him. Yell 'hands up' or 'get down on the ground" or whatever you guys do. I just need you to be ready when he gets out."

"And you're going to sweet-talk him out of the van?" His tone was condescending.

Morgan rolled her eyes. "In a manner of speaking. Are you helping or not?"

Flip surveyed the area. "Give me three minutes to get over there."

Morgan took the Harley cap off her head and handed it to him. "Put this on. You scream cop."

She watched Flip backtrack down the block in the opposite direction and work his way back up the other side of the street, weaving behind the parked cars. He stopped about twenty feet from the designated evergreen tree, where there was an open area with nothing to hide his approach. He looked at Morgan and shrugged. She held up her finger for him to give her a minute. With Flip approaching from the left side of the van, she had to find a way to get the driver's attention focused on the right side long enough for Flip to get in position.

She looked on the ground for a rock or something she could throw. Feeling in her coat pockets, she found the apple she had tucked away for later. Making her way to the front of the truck, she stood up and threw it against the right side of the van. As soon as it smashed against the side panel, Flip sprinted toward the tree. She barely made it behind the truck when the driver's wiry-haired head stuck out of the passenger window, his eyes nearly bugging out of his head. Finding no one near his van, he tucked himself back inside.

Morgan stood up and waved to Flip. She ran out into the street, stopped about fifteen feet from the van, and fired two shots into each back tire and two at the driver's side mirror, shattering it into pieces.

Within seconds, a giant of a man with a ruddy face and a long beard jumped out of the van with a 9mm in his hand. His jaw clenched, his eyes searching for the threat.

"On the ground," shouted Flip, moving in from across the street.

That's when the plan fell apart. The burly man turned his gun toward Flip and fired. Flip got off one shot, hitting the driver in the chest, then grabbed his side and fell to the ground. The driver stumbled into the van but righted himself, preparing to take another shot. Morgan fired twice, taking the driver to the street. She kicked the assailant's gun away and rushed to Flip.

"Oh, please, Lord. Let him be okay," she cried, falling to her knees. She lifted his head in her lap.

"I...I'm okay. K...Kevlar vest," Flip struggled to speak.

"We're sitting ducks out here," Bash said, coming up behind them.

Morgan looked up in surprise.

"Yeah, Riley let me out of the car since the guy was down. I'll get Flip to the SUV."

Bash put his arms under Flip's shoulders and helped him to his feet.

"I'm so sorry, Flip," Morgan said with remorse.

"N...not your fault," he said. "Getting him out of the van was a good idea. I just assumed you were going to scream at him. Shooting up his van never crossed my mind. I put you in danger. And I...I underestimated you. I'll never make that mistake again."

"Once we get to the van, Riley's going to pull the driver out of the street," Bash said.

"Yeah, boss. I'm okay. Probably bruised ribs," Flip said to Sam over his mic. "I got him in the chest, and it looks like Morgan got him in the leg and hip. He's not going anywhere. I'll let you know as soon as we get to the SUV."

After Riley moved the perp onto the sidewalk, he filled them in on the status with the other team. Two of the Sam's men dropped the female postal worker at the police station and were on their way with Gia to the airport in Portland. Perez wounded one of the gang members who had followed Sam's car around the building. He was now secure. When the gunmen went out the back door, the quick-thinking postal workers secured the building from the inside. There was no information on the extent of injuries, but at least the gunmen couldn't get back in the building. That left two men at large. One was Asa Kline.

"Damn!" Riley said. "Agent Perez's partner is missing." He turned toward the back seat. "Flip, do you think you'll be okay if I go help Sam?"

"We'll be fine," Flip said, still holding his side. "If Kline has the female agent, they are going to need more help. I've got two more clips, so I'm good."

"Miranda Scott," Morgan whispered, feeling the weight of responsibility on her shoulders.

"Who?" Riley asked.

"The woman agent. That should be me."

Before Riley could respond, she slid out of the car with Bash behind her.

"You can't keep doing that, guys! Sam's going to kill me!" Riley yelled after them.

"You need to help Sam! Let them go. There's nothing you can do," Morgan heard Flip tell Riley.

Instead of heading to the building, Morgan hurried across the street to the park, trying hard not to glance at the man bleeding out.

"Where are you going?" Bash asked, hurrying behind her.

"I couldn't live with myself if anything happened to you. Please go back to the car."

He caught her wrist and stopped her.

"What are you doing?" she huffed.

"Let's get one thing straight. I'm not leaving you. You have been by my side since this whole screwed-up drama began. You've saved my ass more than once."

Morgan felt emotions welling up but shook them off. "You don't owe me anything. We've helped each other. You can go back to Chicago with a clear conscience. Now let me find Asa and see if I can negotiate a release for Agent Scott."

"You mean trade yourself? It's not happening, Morgan."

She stopped. "Agent Scott could have a husband. Kids. I have no one. It's just fate. I was never meant to get away from him."

He pulled her into his arms. "Do you know how asinine that sounds to me? There is no world in this universe where you are fated to end up in that man's hands. And you are wrong about so many things. People do care about you, Morgan. I care about you. A lot. This isn't the time or place to talk about it, but I want you to come back to Chicago with me."

"But…" He put his finger to her lips.

"We can argue about it later, but you are *my* fate."

Her eyes turned to saucers.

"Now, tell me where *we* are going so I can help."

She pointed to a children's play castle with a tower that stood in the middle of the park. "Everything is flat. I wanted to climb up in the tower and see if I could spot Asa and the other DF member."

Grabbing her hand, they ran to the children's play castle and crawled through the cramped tunnels. It was a tight fit for Bash. When they reached the top, they had a 360-degree view of the park and post office. Riley was positioned on the far-left side of the building, while Sam and Max were stationed on the right side. Perez was searching the abandoned vehicles. As if he could feel their eyes on them, Max glanced in their direction until he spotted them. Morgan was waving at him when they heard a shot.

A blond-headed man blasted from the bushes near the front doors and began firing random shots as he maneuvered between the vehicles heading toward the street, probably expecting to reach the getaway van. Sam and Max dashed from the right corner of the building in pursuit. As they drew closer, Agent Perez aimed his gun and shouted, "Stop. Drop your weapon and put your hands behind your head."

The man turned to fire at Perez. Riley, who had been making his way from the left, took a couple of shots to draw the man's fire away from Perez. When the blond guy turned his attention to Riley, Perez fired, hitting the blond guy in the right shoulder. Sam jumped out from behind a truck and had him on the ground with his hands behind his back within seconds.

Morgan was paralyzed, watching the scene play out in front of her. Bash squeezed her hand. The guilt bubbled up inside.

CHAPTER FORTY-SIX

Bash found sliding down the tunnels much easier than climbing up had been. He insisted on going first. He was afraid Morgan would hit the bottom and take off without him. The sense of guilt she felt for the whole situation was weighing on her. The carefree, perky, glass-half-full kindergarten teacher he'd met at Guntersville Lake seemed to be slipping away from him. She refused to believe she didn't bear responsibility for something that happened before she was born.

Morgan began withdrawing as soon as they arrived at his grandmother's house. She had not wanted to interfere with his reunion with his new family despite their attempts to include her. After dinner the previous evening, she stayed in her room. When she realized she had not been included in the plans to retrieve the ledger, she took it as a dismissal. It had been their attempt to protect her. She had already done far more than her share. It probably felt like another abandonment. Her Pops died. Her apartment was destroyed. Her teaching position was suspended. Her best friend married. He had handled it all wrong.

How she had crept so far under his skin was still a mystery to him. They had only been together for a short time, but he knew in his heart he did not want to let go of her. They were nowhere near making a long-term commitment, but he could visualize it down the road. They needed to take it slow. Like normal people do when they date. The best-case scenario, they become lifelong lovers. Worst-case longtime friends. In other words, there was no worst case. She would be in his life one way or the other. They just needed to be in the same location to give themselves a chance.

"Bash! Wait!" Morgan said, grabbing his hand to stop him.

When he glanced at her, he realized they were at the edge of the tree line. He had been lost in his thoughts, running on autopilot without being conscious of where he was going.

"We can't go barreling blindly into the woods. Asa could be anywhere. Two shots, and we're dead. We need a plan."

"What we need is backup. There is no plan where I'm one damn bit of help in a shootout. Besides, my ego can't tolerate you saving my ass again," he said, pulling his cell from his pocket. He tried Max's cell, but it went to voicemail. Then he sent a brief text explaining where they were and what they were about to do. "I'm texting Max. Hopefully, he'll see it and bring the cavalry."

"You wait here, and I'll go in," she said.

He took her hand and frowned. "No way, Morgan. We either go together, or I'll hog-tie you right here until we get help. And for the record, I think we should wait."

She shook her head.

He reached in his pocket and pulled out the 9mm she had given him at her Pops cabin. "Well, I guess I'm as ready as I can be."

"Do you feel comfortable shooting that? I mean, I'm hoping it's not necessary, but just in case?"

"Max gave me a few pointers. I checked it this morning. It's got a full clip. Aim and shoot. What's to know?"

Morgan shook her head. "If you say so. Just don't you dare get behind me!"

Bash couldn't help the feelings of trepidation the further they wandered into the wooded area. It was mostly red spruce trees with no bushes or underbrush for cover. They were fully exposed. Walking side-by-side, they stopped every 15 feet to listen.

"This isn't safe. We need to get out of here," Bash pleaded.

"Maybe there is something on the other side of this little forest area. I mean, we are in the middle of town. It must end somewhere."

"Let's go back and get Agent Perez. I've got a bad feeling about this."

"Give me a minute." He watched her turn around in a circle, trying to find some evidence to indicate which direction Asa may have taken Agent Scott. "There!" she pointed toward the ground on the right. "It looks like someone slipped."

Bash followed her a few feet further to find a muddy shoe print. He took her hand and turned her toward him. "Good job. Now, we have a direction, but this is as far as we go. I'm not risking your safety."

They did a stare down for a full minute before she relented. As they reached the edge of the park, they heard their names being called. Bash dropped Morgan's hand to wave at the three men across the road heading toward them: Agent Perez, Max, and Sam. The sound of sirens caught Bash's attention and filled him with hope. *Help is on the way.* In his excitement, he turned to hug Morgan. His heart fell into his stomach. She was gone.

CHAPTER FORTY-SEVEN

Morgan sprinted through the trees, trying to put as much distance between herself and Bash as possible. This was her mess, and she was going to fix it. The only option she could think of was to trade herself for Agent Scott. Then, she would have to hope she could find a way to escape. If Asa's plan was to take her back to California, it gave her a lot of trip time to catch him unaware.

It only took a few minutes to reach the footprint she had shown Bash. What she did not show him was the white plastic zip tie she spotted on the ground a few feet away. That was the only breadcrumb she had to follow, but at least she had a direction. Looking back over her shoulder, she saw no sign of Bash. He would not risk hollering her name for fear of revealing her location. As she ventured further into the woods, she noticed the ground gradually descending. She admonished herself for not pulling the area up on Google Earth to get an idea of the topography.

Eventually, she came to a small clearing in the middle of the trees with a 20-foot-long rock formation that stood at least 12' to 15' tall in places. Its entire surface was rough and jagged from erosion, so climbing up to get a better view was out of the question. She closed her eyes and listened. No footsteps, voices, or sounds of any kind.

I'm too late. He's gone. I might as well go back, she told herself, slowly retracing her steps.

"Didn't take you long to give up. I'd expect more from a girl raised by Clark "War Dog" Kline," came a grating male voice.

Morgan spun around and was met by the smirking face of an older, male, red-headed, blue-eyed version of herself, pointing a gun at her chest. She held in the gasp, threatening to escape her throat. Her heart went into overdrive. Despite the dryness in her mouth, she forced herself to speak calmly.

"Where is Agent Scott?" she asked.

"Oh, don't you worry about that FBI woman. She's taking a little nap, so we can have a chat," he answered with an obnoxious singsong in his voice. He did a little chop motion with his free hand to indicate that he had knocked her unconscious.

"Where is she?"

"Not far. And not dead ... yet. She's my bargaining chip to get that ledger back." His eyes narrowed with a dark menace. "No thanks to your meddling. But don't you worry, I'm going to get my pound of flesh from you. You can bet your skinny little ass." He looked her up and down. "Funny. I never believed Patrice when she told me you were mine. She was just one of the ole ladies we kept around when we need a to get our rocks off. Said she caught feelings for me. I wasn't the first and sure as hell wasn't the last man she latched on to. Looks like she wasn't lyin'. You couldn't be nobody's but mine." His snicker turned her stomach. "But don't get your hopes up, girlie. I've had twenty-five years to ponder what my dad and you did to me. He may be gone. May he rest in hell, but you aren't. And I'll get my revenge one way or the other."

She held her head high. "How can I possibly be responsible for something that happened before I was born?"

His lips flattened, and his jaw tensed. "Don't matter to me. You lived your life. I got robbed of mine. And you are gonna pay."

Morgan straightened her back. The conversation was almost exactly as she had expected, and she didn't want to hear anymore. "Now that you have me, you can let Agent Scott go. Kidnapping a federal agent carries a lot of penalties. I'll go with you willingly. If they get Agent Scott back, it may be a reduced sentence if you're caught."

His burst of laughter made her wince. "As if shooting up a United States Post Office is a misdemeanor. You are either one dumb bitch, or you think I am. Which is it? As soon as I meet my DF brothers, we're heading to Canada. By the way, thanks for making this so convenient. Your location couldn't have been better. Couple hundred miles north, and we're over the border. With you and Miss. Federal Agent with us."

He was obviously unaware his men had been shot. She debated telling him. Would it make him more violent? More determined for revenge? She decided on another approach.

"The ledger is gone. On the way to the nearest FBI office."

The smug expression on his face fell. "What are you talking about? There are only two federal agents here, and I've got one of them," he growled, stepping closer to her. "There is no way in hell he would leave her."

"Agent Perez handed the ledger off to one of the contracted security teams with instructions to take it to the FBI office in Portland," she said.

Asa glared at her. He wanted to rip her head off. "I don't fuckin' believe you. The FBI don't hire contract security."

It was a lie. As far as she knew, Agent Perez still had the ledger. She had to convince him the situation was hopeless. Maybe he would release Agent Scott. Before she could answer, he drew his own conclusion.

"That Fontana guy? Or was it Bartoli? Had to be one of them who hired the rent-a-cops."

It was Bash, but she wasn't volunteering that information. "I'm not sure. It could have been either of them. I don't know them that well."

As he walked toward her, she mentally fought to stand her ground and appear unafraid. When he was within striking distance, he backhanded her across the face. Her head flew back, pain ripping through her jaw, the force sending her to the ground. He shouted commands, but her ringing ears couldn't make out the words. She rolled over on her right side and curled into a ball. The tears she had been holding back threatened to spill. She decided it would be in her best interest to let them flow, so she did. She needed to appear weak. Defeated. No longer a threat. *Always let them underestimate you, Chip. Gives you the advantage,* Pops spoke in her head. *They will never see it coming.*

"Get up and stop blubbering! I can't believe you've got my blood running through your veins," he scoffed, spitting the words.

A sharp pain radiated through her face when she tried to speak. Slowly, she maneuvered herself into a sitting position, her knees bent, hands holding the sides of her thighs. She leaned her head between her knees to stave off dizziness.

"Look at me when I talk to you, or you'll get it worse next time," his voice oozed with contempt.

Morgan took a ragged breath and watched his feet from between her partially spread knees. She wanted to be ready if he made another approach.

"Are you fucking deaf? I guess you didn't learn your lesson?"

"No. No. Please don't hit me again!" she cried. She began rocking back and forth like a wounded child.

"I've had enough of this shit," he said, storming toward her.

When he was almost close enough to grab her with his left hand, she pulled the 9mm she had maneuvered out of her coat pocket and pointed it up in his face. He froze. They stared at each other for a few seconds, him assessing how serious this new development was. Her tears were gone. Her face stone. She caught the flinch in his right hand that held his gun at his side.

"If your hand moves one inch, Kline, you're not going to like the new shape of your face," she said between gritted teeth. And she meant it. This man was the monster her grandfather had warned her about without exaggeration. And she realized in that moment that Asa Kline was nothing to her. A calm resolve came over her. He would not hurt anyone else. It was like she had shed her skin and become someone else. Harder. More determined.

"Big talk for a little girl," he mocked with a forced laugh. "You didn't even take the safety off the gun."

He was trying to trick her, but it wouldn't work. "This gun doesn't have a safety. I'd think the son of Clark Kline would know that," she said, volleying the taunt right back. *Who was she?*

His eyes narrowed to slits. Her lips puckered. He slowly began inching backwards but never raised his gun.

She wanted to get to her feet. Sitting below him was a vulnerable position, but the awkward movement it would take to get off the ground would leave her more susceptible to attack.

"Drop the gun," she commanded.

"You won't shoot your own father." He stated it as a fact, attempting to soften his face with sincerity.

She quirked a brow, confidence dancing across her unrelenting face. "I guess we'll see."

Shaking his head dismissively, he said, "I don't believe you can pull that trigger."

Morgan's eyes bore into his unblinking ones, tightening her grip. "You ready to bet your life on it? Mr. Bartoli went for backup. I'm fine waiting."

"You don't fool me. You're trembling in your boots. It takes balls to pull a trigger."

Mentally bracing herself, she watched with dread as his right hand began to inch upward toward her. The challenge in his eyes never wavered. He was going to kill her in cold blood. Her own father. She felt a paralyzing fear trying to take hold. Then, it all happened as if they were in slow motion.

"No, Morgan!" Bash screamed from behind her. The ground almost vibrated with the steps approaching, but she never took her eyes off Kline.

With his gun almost level with her middle, Morgan held her breath, bracing for impact. Then she heard him again. Her protector. *Take the shot, Chip. Now!* And she did.

Two shots rang out simultaneously. Hers and another that came from behind her. One shot hit him square in the chest, knocking him backwards. The other hit the tree behind him, exactly where he had stood moments before. She was filled with adrenalin and raw emotions, barely able to decipher what had just happened.

Bash flew past her and stopped beside Kline's prone body. He swiftly kicked the gun out of the wounded man's hand. Picking it up, he stuffed it in his coat pocket.

"Sebastian?" Morgan softly called his name, not sure if her eyes were deceiving her.

He knelt beside her and pulled her into his chest. "It's okay, baby. He can't hurt you anymore."

Feelings warred within her. She wanted to scream and cry and laugh and fight all at the same time. Maybe crawl out of her skin. Outrun her insides. But she was paralyzed. An invisible weight seemed to be bearing down on her. She glanced at Bash. He was beginning to blur. Her vision narrowed.

"Look at me, Morgan," Bash instructed. His eyes searched her unfocused ones. "Oh, baby, you're going into shock."

Someone sat beside her and gently rubbed her back. "Morgan," the voice said tenderly. "Can you hear me?"

Was it Max? She wanted to see who it was, but her body wouldn't cooperate. She detected movement around her. Agent Scott was still missing. *Tell somebody. Find her.* None of the words would come. Her vision became pinpoints. Then nothing.

CHAPTER FORTY-EIGHT

"Morgan passed out," Bash shouted. "We need help."

"Shock or possibly a concussion," Max suggested, lightly running his finger over Morgan's swollen right cheek and jaw. "Kline hit her pretty hard. He may have broken her jaw, the bastard. The police said a couple of ambulances should be here within the next ten minutes. The first two left with the wounded MC members and a police escort."

Perez suddenly appeared behind Max. "We found Miranda in a ravine just north of here. She's alive but not in good shape. Blunt-force trauma to the head. Awake but barely responsive. Sam and one of his men, who was a medic in the military, are with her until an ambulance arrives. How's Ms. Skylar?"

Morgan began to groan, her eyelashes fluttering. When her eyes fully opened, she stared at Bash. "Agent Scott?" she asked.

"They found her. She's alive. An ambulance is on the way. Just lie still." Lightly rubbing her lips with his thumb, he fought back his own tears. He thanked God she was safe in his arms.

Bash rode with Morgan to the hospital in Bangor. She was lucid but had emotionally shut down. He intertwined his fingers with hers.

Tests verified Morgan was not concussed. There was swelling, bruising, and lacerations on the right side of her face. The worst damage was a hairline fracture on her cheekbone. Bash never left her side unless forced by medical personnel. He was more concerned about the mental injuries than the physical ones.

"Sebastian," someone called his name through a fog.

He sat up quickly, rubbing his eyes. He had dozed off in a chair, watching her sleep. Glancing toward the bed, he met her gentle blue eyes and a slight grin that warmed his heart. He reached for her small hand. Seeing her face continue to swell and change colors broke his heart.

"Are you in pain?"

"My cheek is throbbing, but it was nice to get a little nap."

"I can call the nurse to get you some pain meds," he offered.

She shook her head. "I'll be fine. No narcotics. I told them I only want ibuprofen." He watched her pick at the blanket for a few seconds before she met his eyes. "Did Gia make it to Florida okay?"

"When Max let her know what happened, she insisted Sam's guys bring her back."

"You don't have to stay. Gia is probably worried sick about you. Poor thing meets you one day after 34 years and almost loses you the next. I'm sure she'll be glad to see me go." She forced a lopsided smile.

Bash pulled his chair closer to the bed and tightened his grip on her hand. "That's not true. Gia and Max came by to see you while you were asleep. The nurse forced them out. They will be back in the morning after you've had some uninterrupted sleep."

"But they let you stay?" she whispered.

"I threatened to write a terrible review and post it on my social media accounts with over 3 million followers."

Morgan chuckled, then frowned, rubbing her face. "Don't make me laugh." Her eyes flew to the window. "What time is it? It's dark outside."

Bash pulled out his phone. "8:38 p.m. You missed supper. If you're hungry, they can get you something. It's going to have to be liquid for a couple of days or until you feel you can move your jaw. You have to stay hydrated."

He handed her a glass of water with a straw. "I hope it's still cold."

She took a sip. "It's fine."

When she put it down on the tray, she took his hand in both of hers, her expression serious. "Can we talk?"

Bash felt a tightening in his chest. A worry about what she might say, but before she could respond, there was a soft knock at the door.

"Come in," she called.

Agent Perez stepped in the door and closed it gently behind him. His black suit was wrinkled with grass stains on his torn pants. He looked like he had lost at a fight club. He nodded toward Bash.

"I'm sorry it's so late, but I took a chance you were up. Our investigation has moved rapidly. I wanted to share some news. I thought it would give you both peace of mind."

"What happened?" Morgan asked, sitting up straighter against the pillows.

The agent spoke to Bash. "I've already shared this with Max Fontana."

Bash and Morgan gaped at each other.

The exchange wasn't lost on the agent. "Yeah. I know who he is. It might have been nice if someone had told me earlier."

"Would it have changed anything? Added more security to your team?" Bash asked.

"Doubtful," the agent answered honestly.

"What did you want to share with us," Morgan asked.

He blew out a breath and began. "Once we had the crime scene techs from Portland, we had a clearer picture of what happened today. The driver of the black sedan you found was Bart Spano, right-hand man to Enzo Fontana. His cell was in his pants pocket. No passcode. Texts from Enzo Fontana ordering him to take the ledger and get rid of the DF members. There was an address to Ms. Martin's home. Or should I say the former Gia Fontana? He probably learned about the ledger from Kline. It appears they didn't trust each other. Seems Kline got the best of him. We are still working on how they got Ms. Martin's address.

"Our office in New York picked up Enzo Fontana this

afternoon before he left the country. They weren't happy because Enzo Fontana was already under a federal investigation. Apparently, Max Fontana contacted their office about two weeks after he took over the position of CEO and reported inconsistencies in the accounting in a couple of divisions. The New York office was close to an arrest when all of this happened. They arrested Leone Fontana today, as well. His first words were, 'I want a plea deal. Didn't have shit to do with murder.' As we speak, a swarm of FBI agents are descending on Fontana Properties & Development. According to the agents interrogating Leone Fontana, he wanted no part of the murder plot against Max and his son. Which is very interesting, Mr. Bartoli. No one told me Maximillian Fontana was your father either." His eyes bore into Bash.

"Before you get all bent out of shape or try to make a conspiracy out of this, I only learned Max was my father a few days ago. I was hiding from the man, refusing to meet with him solely based on his reputation. It's a long story and totally irrelevant to your case. We ended up connecting and realizing we were all in danger. We were waiting for Morgan to get a deal with the FBI to transfer the ledger over to your guys. Then we were going to figure out how to get help with the Enzo problem."

"I believe your Enzo problem has been handled. He has been trying to set up Max Fontana for embezzlement. He held secret meetings with board members to have Max quietly removed on the pretense that if an embezzlement scandal went public, the company would be ruined. Enzo knew a formal investigation would uncover his illegal handiwork. Once Enzo found out Max's son was alive and would be the new heir to the controlling shares, Enzo changed his elimination strategy to murder."

"Is Max's wife involved?" Bash asked.

"Leone admitted Enzo was having an affair with her. She was passing Enzo any information she could find in Max's home office. There is a lot of work to do before we can tie her to anything. Max may not have a company to go back to, but he doesn't seem to be concerned. That man is not who I expected. If it weren't for Max Fontana and Sam Barrett, I'd probably be on my way to the morgue. No way I could have handled those four men by myself."

The agent cleared his throat, his eyes flicking between Bash and Morgan's. "I'm sorry. You guys tried to warn me I was unprepared, but as I said before, my instructions from my supervisors were a simple signed agreement. They were unwilling to invest resources in something that could be a 25-year-old journal of an old man's ramblings. When I asked my boss who my backup was, he literally pointed to Agent Scott, a non-field agent who was sitting outside his office, and said, 'Take Agent Scott. She needs to get out more.' With three dead bodies, a kidnapped agent, multiple civilian and federal employee injuries, an attack on a federal building, and ties to an outlaw motorcycle gang—shit is rolling uphill. Luckily, there were only minor injuries to a few postal workers and civilians."

"They don't suspect Max, do they?" Bash asked.

The agent pursed his lips. "Max Fontana was investigated the day he met with our agents months ago. Before he was CEO, he was the VP of Legal. At his suggestion, an agent took a temporary undercover position in his office. Everything Max and his staff touched came up clean."

Bash and Morgan exchanged looks. He hoped the threats from Max's family were gone.

"What about the Dragon Fire MC club? Is Asa Kline still alive?" Bash asked.

"Kline lost a lot of blood and has a collapsed lung. Too soon to tell if he's going to make it. If he does, he'll be back in prison. Then, stand trial on numerous charges. One of his gang members is dead, and two others are critically wounded. The driver of the van should make it, but we haven't identified him yet. Says his name in Brutus. We're running prints."

"Is the DF Club still coming after Morgan?" Bash asked.

"Brutus said the four of them were on their own. Of course, he would say that. We have people watching the Dragon Fire in California. When this all hits the papers, they will realize the FBI has their men in custody. We're hoping they will turn a blind eye. Morgan's name will never be associated with it."

"So, it's finished. I can go back to my life," Morgan said in a small voice.

He nodded. "Except for testifying when these guys go to trial, you should be good. Maybe we'll get lucky, and they plead out. Get some rest. Mend. Life should go back to normal."

Her life will never go back to normal, but I'm going to do my best to give her a better one.

Agent Perez seemed to have gone through a transformation. The all-business, impersonal, and dismissive man they met that morning now seemed empathetic, haggard, and approachable.

"How is Agent Scott?" Morgan asked.

"She was airlifted to Portland. A severe concussion. Stitches in the back of her head, but she should be fine. I wouldn't doubt if she left the bureau."

"I'm glad she's okay," Morgan said. "I can't help but feel responsible."

"This is squarely on us, Ms. Skylar. You did everything you possibly could."

Agent Perez stuck his hand out to Bash. He took it in a firm handshake. "Thanks, Mr. Bartoli. If you hadn't led us to Kline, who knows how many other people would have died. You might not feel the need now, but I recommend you see a therapist. Shooting someone is mentally a big deal. Especially for someone not in law enforcement." He turned to Morgan. "You too, Ms. Skylar. The forensic team hasn't completed their analysis yet, but from a preliminary review, we believe Mr. Bartoli's bullet hit Mr. Kline. Judging from the height of the impact, Kline was already falling backward from your shot that hit the tree. Don't know if that is a relief or not, but I thought you might want to know." He held his hand out, and Morgan took it. Then he handed her a card.

"You are a brave and honest young woman. A lot of people would have kept that ledger. Tried to use it to their benefit. It's in the hands of the analysts now, but I got a brief glance through it.

It's a whole bag of worms. Don't worry. None of your names will ever come up in association with the ledger. It was the property of Clark Wayne Kline, not Eli Skylar. You take care and call me if I can ever do anything for you."

When Bash pulled Morgan into his arms, she broke down in his arms. "It'll be okay, baby. You're not alone."

When she finally pulled away, her eyes were red and swollen. He gently wiped her face with a tissue and kissed her forehead.

"Have you talked to Gray?"

"I have. We've worked things out. He will always be my brother. I told him I'm taking a more active role in the business decisions. He's fine with that. I'm the one who pulled away and let my team run things. I took advantage of them. They just got used to it. He's setting up a meeting with the team when I get home. He can't wait to meet you. You'll love him."

"I know I will. I'm so glad you worked things out. He's too important to you to let things fester."

Bash nodded.

She sighed. "I need to go home, Bash."

"Come home with me."

"I can't. I've brought enough turmoil into your life. You need to spend time with your new family. There's going to be an adjustment integrating them into your life. That's what's important. Not me and my problems."

Bash stared at her like she had three eyes. Then he rested his hand against her uninjured cheek. "You are important to me too, Morgan. More so than any woman I've ever known who wasn't related to me. We've been through hell and back. We've laughed. We've cried. Argued. We've had each other's back every step of the way. And we've had fun too. You gave me a Harley." The last part elicited an eye roll. "That's a big step in a relationship, don't you think?

She chuckled. "A Harley isn't exactly a promise ring."

He quirked a brow. "It could be. I'm not letting you go. Not without a fight."

Her voice became small and unsure. He hated that he had somehow made her feel like that. "I'm not your type, Bash. You need classy, beautiful, sophisticated, cultured. I'm a redneck from North Georgia with tons of baggage. You're feeling grateful. You have no obligation to me. Really. I'll be fine."

"So, you have no other feelings for me other than gratitude?" he asked, his face falling. The words felt like acid in his stomach.

"I didn't say that," she spoke softly.

"Yes, Morgan. You did." He couldn't hide the hurt from his voice.

"I just don't want to get hurt. My heart couldn't take another disappointment. I wouldn't survive." Tears sprung to her eyes.

"Then you do have real feelings for me?"

She nodded.

"Are you attracted to me?"

She slowly nodded again.

"Considering I feel the same about you, I think we owe it to ourselves to give our relationship a shot. I want you in my life. I want you in Chicago. You can stay in my guest house for as long as you want. We can find you a teaching position. Or open a gun range." They both laughed. "You can teach people how to shoot." Another eye roll. "No matter what happens in the long term, Morgan, I will always want you to be a part of my life. But I'm betting on the long term."

"Don't make me smile. It hurts."

"Sorry, baby. I'll try to be grumpy," he said, kissing her hands. "It's settled. We'll leave for Georgia tomorrow. Get your apartment and job squared away. Pack your stuff. Then we're off to Chicago."

"Sounds good," she said weakly.

"It's not going to be as easy as it sounds. I'm aware. A lot of stuff has happened to both of us, and I'm not trying to make light of any of it. But Morgan, I've got to tell you … I can't imagine getting through it without you. You made it all worth it."

"You did, too," she said through watery eyes.

CHAPTER FORTY-NINE

While Max settled into the backseat, he sighed at the sound of the cabby tossing his luggage unceremoniously in the trunk. The flight from New York to Chicago had been smooth. It gave him time to reflect on the whirlwind of the past two months when everything imploded in Maine. His anticipation built the closer he got to Sebastian's home on Lake Michigan just north of Chicago. They had spoken by phone or texted almost every day. Due to the legal turmoil in his company, they had not been able to get together during the Christmas holidays.

A lot had changed in a relatively short period of time. His family company sustained major financial hits from the embezzlement scandal. The FBI had no trouble following the withdrawals back to a hacker employed by Enzo. Leone had been a willing but hands-off partner. Due to his cooperation, he was granted one-million-dollar bail and a lighter sentence to be served in a minimum-security federal prison. Enzo was charged with a multitude of offenses ranging from extortion to murder for hire. No bail was granted, and he was facing a long prison term.

Max felt no joy from the justice Enzo would receive, only relief. He had never wanted any part of the company and had no qualms about letting it go. The only obligation he felt was to the thousands of hard-working employees who deserved to keep their livelihood with a better leadership team. Max was pleased when the Board of Directors found a reputable company to buy his controlling interest in Fontana Properties & Development.

Fatima had forged Max's name on numerous incriminating documents. Wanting his wife out of his life as expeditiously as possible, Max had Stephen Gallagher negotiate a deal for her with the FBI. She would cooperate fully in exchange for two years of probation. Max's part of the arrangement guaranteed a speedy, uncontested divorce to be finalized within the next six months.

Sebastian and Morgan had flown to Atlanta after she was released from the hospital. After packing up her apartment, she met with her school principal and resigned from her position. With the inheritance from her grandfather, she had time to decide the next steps in her career.

To maintain her independence, Morgan had moved into Sebastian's guest house. From what Max had gathered from their conversations, things were going better than either of them had anticipated. The prior week, Morgan had moved into Sebastian's room. She had also taken a teaching position with the local school district to cover for a teacher on a four-month medical leave. Their love story was an unlikely one, but Max had a gut feeling it would be their forever.

This visit had a dual purpose. Most importantly to spend time with Sebastian and Morgan, but also to look for a home close to his son. Stephen Gallagher, who wanted to move his family out of New York, agreed to partner with Max on a property development business in Chicago. Max could be as involved or as hands-off as he wanted to be. At this point in his life, family was everything.

As soon as the taxi stopped in front of the beautiful, ultra-modern home of tinted glass, dark wood, and steel, Max jumped out of the car to retrieve his luggage. Sebastian and Morgan were at a book signing and wouldn't be home for another hour. Sebastian had given him the code to the front door, insisting he make himself at home. They were bringing home take-out for dinner. Since Max was staying at the guest house, he decided he had time to get settled and unpacked. He figured the codes were the same to both houses.

The guest house was supposed to be behind and to the left

of the main house. The sun was setting, so Max followed the solar lighting along the stone path leading around the house. Weaving through a mostly dormant garden with hedges and flowerless rosebushes, Max came to a lovely, white Cape Cod bungalow. It was a sharp contrast to the ultra-modern main house.

The porch light was burning, and a few lights were on inside the house. The code didn't work, but when he turned the handle, the door opened. Sebastian must have anticipated he might go there first. Pulling his luggage through the doorway, he took in the interior. The spacious room was decorated in white. White leather sofa, white chairs, white walls, white blinds, blond wood. Ensile Adams prints lined the walls. He noticed a portrait over the white stone fireplace that literally took his breath away. It was her. The woman his heart had never let go. His Izzy.

Tears sprung to his eyes. He had been so busy the past couple of months he hadn't had time to grieve her death. Hadn't even asked Sebastian for details. It had all been too much. Focusing on Sebastian had kept him sane. Kept the regrets at bay. Now, they washed over him like a tsunami, squeezing the oxygen from his lungs. It suddenly felt unbearable.

"Maxie," whispered a soft feminine voice. It was familiar… but it couldn't be. It was wishful thinking, he knew. He was remembering her voice as if he had heard it yesterday. If he could turn back the clock, she wouldn't have been afraid. Didn't run. Trusted him.

"Oh, Izzy," he breathed in a strangled breath. Felt the tears threatening. "I'm so damn sorry."

"It wasn't your fault, Maxie," came a faint reply.

Max froze. Held his breath. It sounded real, but also like he was in a dream. He couldn't move. Terrified that if he did, her voice would disappear.

"I'm the one who should apologize. I should never have given in to my fear. I should have trusted you to protect us. I should have fought t…," her voice broke into a sob.

The voice came from behind him. He spun around and clutched his chest. Izzy stood before him, leaning against a door frame. She wore a soft, dove gray over-the-shoulder sweater and a muted pale gray and pink floral long skirt. Her honey-blond hair, lightly streaked with white strands, fell a couple of inches above her shoulders. Her hazel eyes were filled with tears. Her fair skin was as smooth and flawless as he remembered. She appeared ethereal. The years had not damped her radiance. He could barely force words from his mouth.

"Izzy? How can this be?" he asked shakily. *Am I hallucinating?*

CHAPTER FIFTY

A loud bang drew their attention to the front door slamming against the doorstop. Sebastian stood in the doorway with panic on his face.

"Oh, God, Dad. I was going to explain this before you saw her. I swear…" he stopped and peered back and forth between his mom and dad. His face strained with guilt. "Christ. I screwed up, Mom. I never meant for this to happen like this."

Max instantly knew. Sebastian had lied. He wasn't hallucinating. Izzy wasn't dead. The realization tore him apart from the inside out. The pain of betrayal was a reminder of what he had experienced 35 years ago. He couldn't get his head around it. He thought they were in a good place. "Why Sebastian? Why would you lie to me?" Max asked, unable to mask the pain in his voice.

Sebastian nervously ran his hand through his hair. His face contorted with indecision. "Dad…I didn't know you, okay? For all I knew, you were the mobster who sent two goons to kill me or kidnap me or whatever the hell was going on. When you told me you were my father, and you had been looking for my mother for years, I didn't know if I could trust you. If you wanted revenge on Mom. Or me. All I knew was that if what you said was all true, why had Mom felt the need to run away from you. She had to have had a good reason, or she never would have left. When you asked about her, my first instinct was to protect her until I knew more about you. Figure out if what you told me was the truth. I needed to talk to her, but she and Gray's mother were on a cruise in South America. The last thing I wanted to do was screw that up for her. She was safe where she was. I didn't want to worry her or put her in danger." He rubbed his hands over his face. "Don't you understand? I didn't know what to believe!" his cried, throwing his hands out in a pleading gesture.

Max shook his head. "I can understand your initial reaction. I would have done the same thing for my mamma, but it's been two months, Sebastian. You've had *two* months to tell me. Why didn't you?"

Sebastian's face fell. All color gone. He glanced at Izzy, holding her eyes, speaking in a language only the two of them could understand. A language they had had years to create without Max.

"I know I should h…" he started but didn't finish.

"It was me, Maxie," Izzy said, a forced calm in her voice. "I asked him to wait."

Max was not sure if that made him feel better or worse. "How long have you known…about me?"

"Since a few days after Bash got back from Georgia."

Max didn't know what to think. Maybe he had read the whole situation with Sebastian wrong. He never intended to pressure his son into a relationship. All the plans he made were merely an illusion of a family he was trying to push on Sebastian. One he was obviously not ready to accept. Max needed to leave before he broke down and made a fool of himself. He broke eye contact with Izzy, walked to the door, and began to gather his luggage.

"What are you doing?" Sebastian choked. His feelings were raw. "You're just going to leave? You've barely come back into my life, and now you're going to leave the first time things get uncomfortable? I'm sorry. I should have told you. I was caught in the fuckin' middle!" His hand motioned between Izzy and him.

Max put his hand on his son's shoulder. He didn't know what to do. "The last thing I want to do is cause you or your mother more discomfort. I've obviously pushed too hard for us to be a family. I can go back to New York, and we can take it slow. But I love you, Sebastian, and I will never leave you again. Never."

Max felt a hand on his arm.

"Don't go, Maxie. Please. Let me explain," Izzy implored. "I...I... was scared. Scared you hated me. Scared to face you after all these years. Embarrassed to find out Sebastian knew the truth about what I had done. He learned that I was a coward who kept him from his father. Then, after these years of not knowing your son, you fought for him. You protected him from your family. Like you would have done 35 years ago. I was so ashamed, Maxie."

Tears began to steadily stream down her cheeks. "It was all proof that I had made the biggest mistake of my life. But I was so terrified of your father. I...I felt powerless. He threatened to take Sebastian away from me and never let me see him again if I got out of line. On our wedding day, Max! I panicked. I knew our child would always be a threat that he would hold over me. Over us. I couldn't let Sebastian be a pawn, and I couldn't risk losing him. It was a fight or flight moment, and I had no bargaining power. You would always be under your dad's thumb if I stayed. I couldn't let us live like that. If I left, maybe you could break free. Once some time passed, we could be together again. Maybe when you graduated from law school.

"Then you were married in the wedding of the year, according to the New York Times. It killed me because it should have been us. Sebastian and me. And I was the reason for that. It was my fault. When you got divorced, I felt it was too late. You had moved on. Then you remarried, and life seemed to be good for you." She stopped to take a trembling breath and wipe her eyes. "I have lived with so many regrets. Second-guessing every decision that I've ever made. Knowing you would never forgive me for taking your son away from you," her voice trailed.

Max's emotions were at war within him. Hurt. Guilt. Love. Regret. But he couldn't bear to lose them again. "That's just it, Izzy. I never moved on. I had P.I.s searching for you for years, all the while praying they would find you before my father did. He was humiliated. His son had been left at the altar. He wasn't going to let it go unpunished. When I graduated from law school, he told me he had indulged me long enough. I had to stop searching for you and settle down with a nice girl. I refused. If I didn't marry soon, when he found you, he would end you."

Izzy's eyes went wide.

"He threatened to kill her?" Sebastian's voice was strained.

"My father was ruthless. I had no doubt. He promised he would stop looking if I moved on. I found out years later that was a lie too. He never stopped looking for you, but at the time, the threat was enough to push me into dating. Hoping he would forget about you. Rose was a concession for my father. A guarantee of your safety, or so I thought. Rose is a wonderful woman, but I never loved her. When she realized she couldn't replace you in my heart, she divorced me. She thought she deserved better. I agreed. Frankie is the best thing that came out of the marriage. Fatima was an arrangement. Again, at my father's insistence. Thankfully, she will be out of my life soon. So no, Izzy. I never emotionally moved on.

"I was devastated. I couldn't believe you would do that to us, but I knew you wouldn't have left without a good reason. Before my father died, he told me that threatening to take our baby away from you at the wedding had been a huge mistake. He should have waited until after the baby was born. Then, he would have had more control. He also admitted he had never stopped looking for you. If he hadn't already been given a medical death sentence, I might have killed him."

"I couldn't move on either, Maxie. No one measured up. I wasn't going to bring anyone into Sebastian's life unless I was sure about them."

For a few minutes, no one spoke.

Sebastian put his hand on his dad's back. "I was going to tell you about Mom tonight, Dad. That's the reason I asked you to wait for us in the main house. I knew she was here. Waiting to meet with you. I had no idea you would come over here." He took a deep breath and swallowed hard. "You guys need to talk.

I'll give you some space, but Dad, please promise me you won't leave. If you change your mind about moving here and being a family, you will crush Morgan…and me."

Max hugged his son. "I would only leave if I was making you or your mother unhappy, but you are correct. Izzy and I need to talk."

CHAPTER FIFTY-ONE

"Maybe we should sit down," Max said, motioning Izzy to the sofa. "Do you live in Chicago?"

She sat next to him. The tension hung heavily between them. "When I retired a couple of years ago, Bash bought me a condo near his in downtown Chicago. During the summer, I stay in the guest house to give him more privacy."

Max couldn't help staring at her. All he could see was the beautiful young woman he had fallen in love with. "You haven't changed," he said, reaching for her hands.

"You are such a liar. It is only recently that I went back to my natural hair color. I have spent the past thirty-five years with raven hair. After your father died, I hate to say it, but I finally felt safe enough to be myself."

His eyebrows raised. "It kills me that you had to live like that."

She nodded, staring at her hands. When she looked up at him, she burst into tears and fell into his arms. He held her tightly against his chest, smoothing her hair, her tears soaking his shirt. As if no time had passed, he didn't want to let her go.

When her sobs subsided, he said, "You have raised a remarkable man, Izzy. He's so accomplished. Intelligent. Witty. Loyal to a fault."

She pulled away from his arms and sat up straight, wiping her eyes. "He is, isn't he? I'll gladly take some credit for that," she said with an impish grin.

He laughed, and she joined in. Then they talked—for

hours. Not moving from the couch, they opened their hearts to each other. Max felt as though his heart was literally glowing inside his chest. He felt lighter than he had in years.

"Is there anyone in your life?" Max asked, holding his breath.

"There is no one. I never stopped loving you, Maxie," she said, a fresh tear in the corner of her eye. "I'm not foolish enough to think we can just magically pick up where we left off, but I don't want to see you disappear from my life."

He smiled and kissed her hand, a calm washing over him. "I want you in my life, too, Izzy. So badly. I'm afraid if I stop touching you, you'll disappear, or I'll wake up from a really great dream."

She gave him a tender smile despite the fresh tears. "If I'm dreaming, I don't want to wake up."

He reached up and gently wiped a tear from her chin and cleared his throat, clogged with emotion.

"Maybe we can plan a wedding together. Morgan is a treasure. She's so good for Bash. Pushes him out of his comfort zone. When they are together, he can't stop touching her. He hasn't been this inspired about anything since he graduated from college and sold his first book. Did you know he has almost finished his next one?"

"I did. From what he has described, it sounds a lot like a variation of his adventures with Morgan. He really loves her, doesn't he?" He couldn't stop marveling at her penetrating hazel eyes that still took his breath away.

Cupping his face in her hands, she whispered, "And she loves him just as much, if not much more."

The double meaning of her words filled him with hope.

Joy York grew up in Alabama but has spent much of her adult life in the Midwest, currently living with her husband, Terry, in Indiana with their golden doodle, Bailey. Inspired by a family legacy of oral storytelling, she began creating stories and adventures for her son when he was growing up. With encouragement from family and friends, she began to write them down. Her first book, *The Bloody Shoe Affair: A daring and thrilling adventure with the jailer's daughter*, a YA mystery set in the rural south in 1968, was published in 2015. The sequel (also a standalone), *The Jailer's Daughter*, is currently being edited. *Genuine Deceit: A Suspense Novel*, her second novel, was published on Amazon in May 2021. *Protective Instinct*, a mystery/suspense, is coming soon. For more information, visit https://www.joyyork.com. Twitter @joyyorkauthor Facebook: Joy York Author Instagram: @JoyYorkBooks

www.ingramcontent.com/pod-product-compliance
Lightning Source LLC
Chambersburg PA
CBHW021520240626
47154CB00002B/709